D0804285

The Union of
the North
and the South

by
Ann Mock

This book is a work of fiction. Names, characters, places, and incidents are either the product of the author's imagination or are used fictitiously. Any resemblance to actual persons, living or dead, business establishments, events, or locales is entirely coincidental.

Copyright © 2014 Ann Mock
All rights reserved.

ISBN: 1495249263
ISBN 13: 9781495249266
Library of Congress Control Number: 2014901300
CreateSpace Independent Publishing Platform
North Charleston, South Carolina

F MOC

1768-8279 11/10/2014 WBL

Mock. Ann

The Union of the North and
the South.   <cjg>

LeRoy Collins Leon County
Public Library System
200 West Park Avenue
Tallahassee, FL 32301

To my wonderful husband, Dave~
His encouragement and love made this book possible.
He has allowed my dreams to come true.

*Be kind to one another, tenderhearted, forgiving
one another, as God in Christ forgave you.*

Ephesians 4:32

Contents

Acknowledgments

I couldn't have written this novel without my husband, Dave, who was by my side editing, encouraging, and using his computer expertise as I wrote my book.

I would also like to acknowledge my good friend and author, Ann Port, for inspiring me to write this book, reading my manuscript, and offering constructive suggestions. In addition I thank my longtime friend, Ginger Cook, who provided valuable insights and gave me much-needed support along the way.

The love and encouragement of my amazing family is much appreciated as well. I would like to recognize my children, Sonia, Kim, Paul, and Scott; my sons-in-law, Darren and Tim; my daughter-in-law, Stacy; and all my grandchildren, Elizabeth, Ian, Gavin, Josephine, Luke, Max, and Nate.

The enthusiasm and insights of hostesses and guides who led tours through the beautiful Southern landmarks that inspired me to write this novel also contributed to this project in many ways. Their knowledge and expertise allow our American history to be preserved for future generations.

Last but not least, my trip on a steamboat was truly inspirational. I had the opportunity to see the Mississippi River from the front porch of the riverboat where I was able to relax while visiting many picturesque towns along the Mississippi, including Memphis, Natchez, Vicksburg, Helena-West Helena, St. Francisville, Baton Rouge, and New Orleans.

Chapter One

Memories from the Past

Vicksburg, Mississippi
1875

Fascinated, Jenny sat on the grassy bank beside the stream, watching a proud mother duck lead her ducklings down the short waterfall. Suddenly she cried out in her childish voice, “Look, Sissy. One of the baby ducks is still way behind. It’ll be left!”

Jenny’s eyes welled up on the verge of tears as Laura softly spoke. “Look, the other ducks have slowed down. Now reach out and get the baby duck that’s being left behind.”

After gently lifting the soft yellow duck in her small chubby hands, Jenny placed the duckling by its mother as it pecked at her hand. As she watched the baby duck join its mother and the other ducklings, she reached over and squeezed Laura’s neck. “I love you, Sissy!”

Laura’s heart cried out deep inside her, for she wished so much that Jenny could acknowledge her for who she was. She longed to hear the words "I love you, Mama" on her child's lips.

Abruptly standing up, Laura brushed the grass off of her long blue dress. As she gazed down, she saw the blond curls that fell down Jenny's back. Jenny's sapphire-blue eyes looked up at Laura. Jenny was a re-creation of Gerald in every way. It was as though he had been reborn in the lively child. The pain of her husband's death still made her feel lost, even though he had passed away five years ago. Five years was a long time for a love to fade, but Laura's love for Gerald had only grown.

Laura loved to relive the happy memories, as she dreamily thought back to her childhood, when she was no bigger than Jenny and ran with Gerald through fields covered with pink, purple, and white wildflowers. He had been two years older, but was thoughtful and kind to her. They had been constant companions since they'd first met in the small white chapel near Oak Grove, her ancestral home. Nanny, Gerald's childhood nurse, brought him to church, since his parents didn't feel they needed to go and were always too busy to attend.

After the church services, Laura and Gerald occasionally explored the woods together. He often helped her step over dead branches that had fallen on the secret path leading to an abandoned cottage that was located in the far southeast corner of his father's estate. When they arrived she would pretend to be the cottage's mistress and sweep the wooden floor with the small broom Gerald had created from a thicket of tall grass by the door. Laura remembered how he pretended to smoke a pipe while he sat in a rickety rocking chair by the hearth. He gently pulled thorns out of Laura's tangled hair, which was always left to fall free in loose curls down her back.

❦

Realizing they were going to stay by the stream longer, Laura sat down by Jenny as she sadly thought back to the time when she was ten years old and the War Between the States had started, bringing devastation to the South and all its inhabitants. Her family didn't believe in slavery and therefore didn't own any slaves. She was glad that slavery no longer existed in the South and wished the conflict could have been avoided and the slaves set free without the horrors of war. The loss of lives and property that the war had brought to Mississippi saddened her. Gerald hadn't been old enough to fight during the war, but had enrolled in a military school. By the time he had graduated, the war was over.

The war was very personal for Laura since she lived near Vicksburg, Mississippi. "Vicksburg is the key. The war can never be brought to a close until that key is in our pocket," President Lincoln had once said. Located on a high bluff overlooking a bend in the Mississippi River, Vicksburg was well protected. The city and its people had fought long and hard. Still the Union Army was able to capture the city in 1863.

Laura remembered when General Grant and his men had used her home, Oak Grove, as a hospital for sick and wounded soldiers before moving farther south. He had even slept in her parents' four-poster bed. His men had treated her and her family kindly and never damaged any of their belongings.

Fortunately, the Union soldiers never discovered the secret room behind a bookcase in the study. Because of the gold Laura's father had hidden there, he was able to recover after the war and restart his bank.

❧

Laura remembered the day Gerald returned home. He had grown up and was no longer interested in their childhood games. He only spoke to her briefly when they happened to meet on Sundays. His family's plantation had survived, but their means of livelihood had been destroyed as the armies of both the Union and Confederacy had conscripted their livestock, including their prizewinning racehorses. His father also had lost his judgeship, which further reduced the family's fortunes. After the war Gerald was lucky because he was able to get a job on a barge that hauled freight for wealthy Northerners who had moved to Vicksburg.

Saundra Boulogne and her family had also returned to Vicksburg after the war. She had grown up in Vicksburg with Laura and Gerald, but when her father realized the South wasn't going to win, Mr. Boulogne went north and sold secrets to the Union Army. After the war Saundra's father had received an appointment to take control of the local government until elections could be held. Saundra and her father built a large mansion that overlooked the river on the same site of their former home. They named their plantation Camellia Hall, after their original home, which had been burned down during the war. At their new home, Saundra entertained in a fashion unseen since the war had begun. She even invited many of the prominent local families to attend the festivities. At first the leading residents of Vicksburg refused to go, but with time they reluctantly attended, sadly acknowledging the power the Boulognes now had over their lives.

Laura sighed as she thought back to the first time she had heard rumors that Gerald was particularly interested in Saundra. With her fiery red hair and green eyes, the prominent Boulogne heir seemed, in fact, to have all of Warren County's eligible young men interested in her—that is, everyone except Gerald. Saundra always wanted what she couldn't have, and she longed only for him. Laura later learned that Saundra herself had started the rumors of Gerald's infatuation with her. As it was, the rumors died quickly, because he had never shown any interest in Saundra. Instead, Laura, whose light-brown hair was highlighted with specks of gold, increasingly intrigued him. Gerald liked the long tresses that fell loosely down her back. Her eyes were always twinkling, reflecting her love of life. Soon Gerald had eyes only for Laura and her for him. Inevitably they fell in love.

Gerald's father had different aspirations for his son. The judge had suffered extensive financial losses with the war. Now he wanted his son to marry Saundra because he believed a marriage into the prominent Boulogne family would allow him to be reappointed as a judge in the new government and thereby rebuild his wealth.

The judge was understandably displeased with what he had heard from his neighbors, who told him of Gerald's fondness for Laura and of their constant companionship; in fact he was furious. Gerald later would tell Laura how awful his father had made him feel as he demanded that he marry Saundra. His father said their entire financial future depended on this marriage. The two men argued heatedly for months about the matter before Gerald made his own decision despite his father's feelings.

One day Gerald unexpectedly showed up at Oak Grove. Laura clearly remembered running down the long, curving stairs to find him, fuming and upset, in the entryway. "Gerald, what's happening?" Laura wondered.

"I've been ordered to stop seeing you. So I've decided we'll marry right now!" he stated, as he reached out his hand to hers.

She was stunned. She lovingly placed her delicate hand in his. Laura loved Gerald and hoped to marry him one day, but she had never dreamed of marrying in haste behind his father's back.

"Oh, Gerald, I love you too!" Gazing into blue eyes filled with his love and determination, she added, "We'll go now, if that's what you wish."

Still reliving her memories, Laura thought back to the way Gerald had gently pulled her down to the landing by him. He lifted her chin and looked into sparkling eyes that seemed to radiate with the happiness they would find together. After he gently kissed her, he told her to run upstairs and get her possessions. They'd go to the chapel they'd attended for so many years. He had arranged for their minister to marry them that very afternoon.

Laura's mother had known of the romance and of Laura's infatuation with Gerald, but even she didn't know the depth of her daughter's feelings. She now realized Laura was a woman who could make her own decisions. But she was still taken aback when Laura burst into her room, saying, "Mama, please help me pack my things. I'm going to marry Gerald!"

"But you're so young, and Gerald's parents don't—"

"I know, Mama, but it's not their life. It's ours."

Laura's mother knew that her husband, who was due home any minute, would be upset. But he was a kind man and loved Laura as much as a father could, so he would ultimately understand and support his daughter's decision.

The couple raced to the chapel. After saying their vows, Gerald took his new bride to the cottage where they had played when they were children. He told her how he had saved his money and purchased the cottage from his father. Laura was beside herself because now it was their very own home where they would start their new life together.

"Oh, Gerald it looks so charming!" she told him. "You really have done wonders cleaning and making needed repairs."

Gerald grinned. "I was going to surprise you with this later in the week. I've been working evenings cleaning the inside and patching the roof. Billy, the gardener we used to have, even came out yesterday to tidy up the yard as a favor to me. He removed some of the beggarweeds that used to catch in your hair." Gerald reached up to Laura and lifted her down from her horse. He then picked her up and carried her over the threshold into the cozy cottage.

As he placed her gently on the floor, Laura said ecstatically, "The rocker you used to sit in is fixed. Look! My broom is still here! It's right where we left it."

Gerald chuckled as a smile spread over his features. "I hope this will be suitable for the honeymoon, because it took all of my savings to buy the cottage and fix it up."

Laura hugged his neck and said, "I know of no place I'd rather be."

❧

Jenny, still busy watching the ducks, allowed Laura to recall the happy days of her marriage. As if they were in a dream, the months passed swiftly for Laura and Gerald. Then one night they heard someone pound on the cottage door. A booming voice cried, "Is anyone there? Please let me in. There's been an accident, and I need help!"

Gerald threw open the door to find a tall, frantic man he immediately recognized as Tommy Burns, a former slave and now a stable hand for the Boulogne family.

Tommy spoke hurriedly. "My daughter, Aimee, was thrown from her horse. She's clinging to a branch in the ravine. Please help me pull her up. Do you have a rope I can borrow?"

Gerald grabbed a rope and rushed to his horse, yelling over his shoulder, "Laura, please wait here and prepare a place to lay the child in case she's hurt."

Laura waited for what seemed an eternity until she heard a voice outside the cottage. She flung open the door. Aimee's father entered the cottage carrying his sleeping child.

"Where's Gerald?" Laura asked in a mere whisper so as not to awaken the child.

A pained expression filled Tommy's face as he began, "Your husband has had a serious accident."

The words drew a gasp from Laura as she disbelievingly asked him what had happened.

Tommy explained, "Your husband threw the rope over the cliff, and I held the rope as he lowered himself down the hillside. Gradually he made his way to the small ledge that supported Aimee as she clung there. She leaned forward as he stretched out his arms to her and with his help climbed to safety. After I grabbed her, I threw the rope to your husband and started to pull him up when I heard a tearing sound. The rope broke, and your husband fell into the ravine. I'm going to go for help."

Laura remembered being so stricken she couldn't initially speak. After a few moments, she had, however, recovered enough to tell Tommy where to go to find help. After he rushed off, she wrapped the small girl in a wool blanket and placed her near the warmth of the blazing fire. Laura was glad she had something to do—taking care of Aimee. As she gazed down at the child's peaceful, sleeping face, Laura whispered to herself, "I want us to have a child so much. Oh, please, God, let him be safe."

On that fateful evening, Laura waited anxiously until a gentle tapping on the door startled her. She remembered how her father hesitantly entered the room and knelt beside her, saying sorrowfully, "I'm so sorry, Laura. We found Gerald, but we were too late to save him."

Chapter Two

The Blessings of Jenny

❧

" $\mathscr{S}$ issy, Sissy, come on. The ducks have all gone, and I want to go home!" Jenny insisted as she tugged on Laura's hand, startling her out of her dreamlike state.

Laura had been lost in her thoughts too long and knew she must get back home to her parents, who had provided her with so much love and support since Gerald's death. She felt she had been thinking too much about the past and had to think of the future. Laura was, however, reluctant to surrender a past that held fond memories of a husband who had been so dear to her.

Jenny chased after yellow butterflies that filled the forest as Laura slowly followed her. Together they rounded the bend in the path that led back to their antebellum home. Oak Grove was a stately house painted white, with black shutters framing windows that looked out onto a majestic lawn. A large veranda swept around the first and second floors, softening the square lines of the home. Six massive white pillars at the front and five matching pillars along each side gave Oak Grove an air of grandeur. On the second floor, two small doors opened onto a large balcony. This was Laura's favorite spot. From here she could see the Mississippi gently flow south toward New Orleans and the rest of the world. She'd often stood on this very spot, watching for signs of Gerald's horse galloping up the path that led to her home. She may not have him now, but at least she had Jenny and her memories. Laura was so thankful her home had been spared by the war.

"Mama, Mama, we saw some baby ducks," Jenny laughingly said as she raced toward Laura's mother, who stood in the doorway.

"Tell me all about it after you've eaten," Laura's mother said as she took Jenny's hand and led her into the dining room. After Laura's mother got Jenny some food, she found Laura and asked, "How was your walk with Jenny?"

"We had a great time. Jenny loved the ducks. Is Father playing chess with Dr. Ellerby?"

Laura's mother said, "Yes. He's having a great time since he's winning again. Dr. Ellerby is a great sport to come back week after week and get beaten."

"They are such good friends. Let me know if you need any help with Jenny." Laura excused herself and hurried up the stairs to her room. She went onto the balcony and let her thoughts once more return to the events that had created the situation in which Jenny didn't know she was her mother.

After Gerald's accident, Laura's parents took her back to their home. The tears she had held back suddenly broke through as her mother helped her into her large four-poster bed. Her mother whispered, "Rest now, Laura. You'll feel better soon. You're young, and your grief will end with time. Just turn yourself over to the Lord, and He will help you through."

Instead of accepting God's will, Laura was angry at Him for taking her new husband from her. She kept asking herself, *What have I done to deserve this?*

Laura had rested fitfully during the night and awoke tired but able to face her family. As she came down the curving staircase, her mother led her into the dining room. Laura glanced up at her mother, Ruth, who immediately noticed that the usual gleam in her daughter's eyes was missing. In its place was a lost and hopeless stare.

The next month was like a nightmare to Laura. Food had no taste. Flowers had no color. Birds were silent. Sleep? Who could sleep? And then there was Gerald's father. As soon as he received word of his son's death, he sent a terse message to Laura:

Dear Miss Malcolm,

This is to advise you that your marriage to my son, Gerald Taylor Jr., has been annulled. Therefore you have no legal claim to his property. He should have never disobeyed me and married you as he did. My family and I will be leaving Vicksburg, since the memories of our only son still linger in our home.

Sincerely,
Judge Gerald Taylor Sr.

Laura trembled with fury as she crumpled the message and hurled it to the floor. "How could he dare deny my existence as his son's wife?" she raged. "No, he can't be that cruel!"

Her mother entered her bedroom and rushed to her side. "What's happened?"

"Judge Taylor has annulled my marriage!" cried Laura. Her mother tried quietly to comfort her as Laura stated, "I'll never remove the ring Gerald gave me. His father can't take my ring or my love for Gerald."

⊷≋⊶

Laura remained on the balcony rocking slowly. A shadow fell over her as the sun went behind a cloud, echoing the gloom Laura felt when she thought back to the time after Gerald had passed away. Laura's parents decided to have a small party to help cheer her. She appreciated the gesture and knew she had to put the past behind her. Edward, Laura's father, came toward her, smiling with open arms. He had built Oak Grove on the land his grandfather had bought in the early 1800s. A good deal older than Ruth, he had worked very hard in banking and lumber until he could afford to take a wife. In 1847 Edward met Ruth and waited patiently until she matured so he could make her his bride. They married when Ruth was sixteen and he was twenty-eight. Soon after they married, they had their only child, Laura. They were never able to have any more children, but their daughter filled their lives. Edward retained his charming and self-assured manner that had first attracted his stunning wife so many years before. He gently took Laura's hand and escorted her into the large parlor that was now filled with their neighbors. Laura squared her shoulders as she confidently entered the room. Everyone had heard of the judge's cruel actions and had sided completely with Laura and her family—that is, everyone except Saundra Boulogne, who looked maliciously toward Laura as she walked into the party.

Despite Saundra's obvious hostility, Laura greeted her. "Good afternoon, Saundra. How are Aimee and her father?"

Saundra smirked. "Oh, they're fine. It's too bad what happened that night, but I guess it was for the best since you would've lost Gerald one way or the other. You were never what Mr. Taylor wanted for his son. It's a shame you weren't good enough in the judge's eyes, but I'm sure you'll find someone you are good enough for."

Taken aback by the direct attack, Laura replied, "No one can ever take away the love Gerald and I had."

Saundra pretended not to hear and abruptly turned to flirt with a handsome man beside her. Laura tried to appear happy, but her heart was not in it.

Several weeks passed, and a new spark became apparent in Laura's eyes that had not been there for a while, for she knew a new life was growing inside her.

One day Ruth remarked, "Laura, I'm so glad you're feeling better."

Laura couldn't keep her secret any longer. She burst out, "Oh, Mother, I'm going to have Gerald's baby!"

Ruth was surprised but also glad for Laura. Looking concerned, though, she said, "But what about the Taylors? How will they take this news?"

"I've thought about this these past few days and know what I must do. Gerald's father must never know of this child. He gave up that right when he annulled our marriage. He would only want our baby to take the place of his son. My child shall never know of his cruelty, nor shall Judge Taylor ever know of his grandchild's existence."

Laura started pacing up and down the floor. Her brow was wrinkled as she considered what to do about the Taylors. She thought for a moment longer and then said, "Would you and Father meet me in the study? I desperately need both of you to help me solve this dilemma."

Ruth called for her husband and asked him to join her in the study. Once they were both there, Laura's mother shared, "Edward, I have great news. Laura just told me she's going to have Gerald's baby. She'll be here in a minute to talk with us about how we can keep the news of the child away from the Taylors. You know how heartless they've been to her, and Laura is worried about their taking her baby."

A few minutes later, Laura entered the study to find her parents discussing her situation. As she approached them, she said, "I need your help. I don't know what to do. Can you think of any way we can hide my baby from the Taylors?"

Edward said gently, "I'm so happy for you! Your child will be very special to all of us. I've thought this matter over. If you feel it's important to keep your baby from Judge Taylor, there's only one way I know to accomplish it." He paused before continuing, "Laura, you must let your mother pretend that she's having the baby and that you're the baby's sister."

Laura was shocked but intrigued. She hadn't thought of this unusual solution, but she knew in her heart this might work since her mother was only in her mid-thirties, and everyone knew her parents had hoped for more than one child.

"Laura," Ruth spoke gently, "We could go into confinement together, and no one would ever know."

Sadly Laura agreed because she knew this might be her only option. Yet her heart ached for the joy of motherhood she would be denied. She hugged her parents and thanked them for their idea to keep her baby a secret. She felt sure the plan would work as long as no one ever let the secret out. Laura shuddered, thinking how quickly Gerald's father would try to take her child if he ever discovered the truth.

A trusted seamstress was engaged to create dresses for Laura and her mother. Fortunately Laura was small and dainty. The dresses accentuated her grace and petite size while completely hiding the child she was carrying. To be extra careful, she and Ruth remained close to their rooms and never received callers. They didn't even attend church. These days Laura didn't care about church anyway; she was still angry with God.

Ruth and her daughter spent the months reading and making quilts. Their favorite entertainment, however, was sewing clothes for the baby. One afternoon Laura watched her mother sew tiny stitches onto the baby's gown. Laura asked, "What name should the baby call you?"

"I guess the baby should call me 'Mama,'" Ruth suggested. "Is that all right with you?"

Laura sighed. "Yes, that's fine. I wonder if the baby will be a boy or a girl." The thought of a beautiful little baby always snapped Laura out of her self-pity, for she knew her mother would always share the baby with her.

Ruth pondered that question then said, "Whatever you have I know the baby will get lots of love."

Continuing to rock on the balcony, Laura recalled how the months passed busily while they prepared for the baby that would soon arrive. No one was permitted into Laura and Ruth's rooms except the doctor and Laura's father. Being a family friend, Dr. Ellerby understood Laura's concern about the Taylors and agreed to keep the family secret.

On the doctor's last visit, he advised, "Laura, the baby should come any day now. I feel the delivery should be very easy because you're young and healthy."

She hurried to tell her mother the exciting news. "Oh, Mama, our wait is almost over. Doctor Ellerby said the baby should come very soon."

Early one morning, as the sun was just coming up, Laura felt her first sharp pains. The doctor was summoned immediately. He told her to lie in her bed and wait.

Ruth nervously fussed around Laura, propping pillows and asking, "Do you want the drapes pulled? Would you like me to place a cool cloth on your forehead?"

Since the doctor had said the baby would probably not arrive for several hours, Laura asked for a book to read to take her mind off the contractions. The afternoon passed with minor pains, but as the evening approached, the contractions became strong enough to require all of Laura's attention.

Her mother coaxed her to take deep breaths and relax. "You're coming along nicely, Laura. It won't be long now," Ruth reassured her. She gently rubbed her daughter's forehead for what Laura felt was an eternity. Laura worked with her body to help her child into the world. Finally she heard Dr. Ellerby exclaim, "It's a girl!"

He held up the wrinkled, crying baby and laid her in Laura's arms.

"Oh, how I wish Gerald were here to see our beautiful child," Laura whispered in awe, with tears of happiness in her eyes. Some of her anger against God eased as she saw what a miraculous gift He had given her. Laura thought back to the expression of which she was once so fond: "When God shuts a door, He opens a window."

❧

The child was christened "Jennifer" in the small chapel in the woods, but everyone called her "Jenny." The first year was heaven for Laura and Jenny, for the relationship of mother and child was temporarily allowed to be as nature intended. Laura spent hours singing to Jenny, nursing her, and rocking her to sleep. She knew a bond was growing, even if she would never be able to tell the world that this was her daughter.

Her parents loved the baby as their own. One day Ruth said, "We must have a party for Jenny's first birthday and invite all the neighbors."

Laura's face turned ashen gray as she said, "Mother, very few people have ever seen Jenny, and when they do, someone might guess the truth."

Her mother frowned. "That's true, for Jenny, with her blond curls and blue eyes, does resemble Gerald."

Edward wisely spoke up. "We can't hide Jenny from the rest of the world forever. The sooner we pretend everything is as we say, the easier it'll be."

Laura agreed, but a small fear still remained in the depths of her heart. She knew it would destroy her if Gerald's father ever took Jenny from her.

The party was set for the following week. The entire house was busy with the preparations. Laura could even sense the excitement in Jenny as she babbled away, alternately crawling and stopping to pull herself up onto furnishings. She was a perfect baby and rarely cried. She was always smiling and also had the same twinkle in her eye that Gerald had loved in Laura.

The day before the party, Ruth approached her daughter about who should carry Jenny into the room. Until this time Jenny and Laura had been inseparable, but Laura realized this would not do. "Mother, you should carry her in," she replied. "You should take Jenny this afternoon so she'll become accustomed to the idea."

Laura quickly left the room before her tears fell when she saw Jenny reaching out her arms to Ruth and heard her babbling, "Mama."

The next morning Saundra was the first guest to arrive at the party. Laura greeted her stiffly, leading her into the room that was brightly decorated with ribbons and presents. A large pink cake with one candle in the middle dominated the center of the room.

"How charming," Saundra said. "You certainly went to a great deal of expense. I didn't realize you could afford such a nice party!"

Laura replied proudly, "The war has been over for several years now, Saundra, and Father's banking and lumber businesses have picked up nicely since then." She added, "Plus my parents have wanted this child for a long time." Noticing that new guests had arrived, she excused herself to greet them.

As Ruth entered the room carrying Jenny, all eyes fell on the darling toddler. Laura held her breath, fearing someone would say something. Instead she only heard the guests comment, "What a charming child!"

Laura's body trembled with relief as she went to help with the refreshments. As she turned to go outside to the kitchen, she came face-to-face with Saundra, who said nothing. Deep in the depths of her green oval eyes, however, Laura saw a revealing gleam she pretended not to notice. Laura asked, "May I pass?"

"Surely," Saundra replied cattily.

The party was a huge success. Laura tried to forget Saundra's haunting look; the fear, however, was always in the back of her mind that Saundra had guessed the truth.

⁂

As Laura stood after sitting in the rocking chair, she continued to daydream about the wonderful years during which Jenny grew into a delightful child. Time passed swiftly as love and security filled the household. Laura's father showered his granddaughter with gifts. Jenny's favorite present was the gray pony her "papa" gave her on her third birthday. By the time she was four, she had become quite an accomplished rider. She rode her pony all around the pastures of Oak Grove. It was a happy time for all, even though Laura wished she could be more than just "Sissy" to Jenny.

Laura, Jenny, and her parents returned to the chapel she and Gerald had attended a few years before. Laura felt closer to God now and was so glad He had brought her Jenny. Now her only wish was that He help her forgive Gerald's parents for what they had done to her so she could find peace in her life and honor God.

Chapter Three

A Life-Changing Decision

❦

s Laura stood on her balcony watching a paddle-wheeler steam down the Mississippi, she was snapped out of her reverie and back to the present when she heard a loud scream coming from her father's room. Laura raced from the balcony into her father's bedroom. There, by his bed, she saw Dr. Ellerby consoling her mother's sobbing frame. Ruth looked up as Laura entered the room. "Oh, Laura, your father…" The words died on her lips as Laura helped her mother up and assisted her from her husband's room into her bedroom.

The doctor motioned to Laura as she returned from her mother's room.

"What's wrong with Father?" Laura asked.

"He was feeling fine while we were playing chess and then he passed out. He must have had a heart attack. I'm so sorry. I doubt he will live through the night. But he's coherent and insists that he talk to you."

Laura quietly entered the room and knelt by her father. She pressed her hand into his shaking hand and whispered, "Father, I'm here."

Edward's eyes opened, and he said, "Laura, I have something I must tell you." She saw shadows of pain in his gray eyes as he spoke with difficulty. "I've done a terrible thing."

Laura patted his shoulder and urged him not to worry himself. "Whatever it is, the most important thing is for you to get well."

"Wait, Laura. I must tell you, for it concerns you all." Laura sat on the edge of his bed and waited as he took a shallow breath and confessed, "I've lost everything...our lands, house, and securities."

Laura was stunned but tried to hide her reaction to spare her father. "What do you mean? I thought you'd done fine after the war with the gold you hid in the study."

"Yes, we could've managed on that money, but after Judge Taylor rejected you, I borrowed more money from an old friend of mine, James Hampton, to try to build up our circumstances. I felt Gerald's father would no longer be able to reject you if he knew we were very wealthy. Then you could openly be Jenny's mother and be happy again."

"Oh, Father, I've always been happy because you and Mother have given Jenny and me so much love," Laura consoled him as she hugged his sunken frame.

Patting Laura's hand, Edward said, "Please, let me finish. My investments went bad, and I borrowed more and more money, hoping to recover my losses. I lost everything, even the money I borrowed from James Hampton. Now we no longer have anything and must depend on James's decency. I haven't heard from my friend in quite a while. I hope he's doing well. He told me not to worry and wanted to give me time to decide what to do." Utter failure and dismay filled his eyes as he looked to Laura. "You must take care of the family and try to forgive me."

The doctor entered the room as Laura whispered in her father's ear, "There's nothing to forgive. Please get well now, Father." Doctor Ellerby told her she should leave. Laura tiptoed out of the room as her father's tired eyes closed for the last time.

The next morning the doctor told Laura what she feared—that her father had passed away during the night. He added, "Your mother is in a state of shock after hearing about your father and must be kept very quiet. She needs rest and should not be disturbed."

"I'll keep her quiet but I must talk with her about a few matters Father discussed with me before he died."

"Laura, your mother is very sick." Dr. Ellerby paused, then added gently, "You'll have to solve these matters without her help."

Laura left the parlor not knowing to whom she could turn. She ran upstairs to help comfort her mother. As she entered the room, she realized the doctor's words were true. Ruth raised her face to look up at Laura; her cheeks were red from her continued crying. "Mother, you must go to bed and rest," Laura said. She helped Ruth into her cotton nightgown and pulled a quilt up over her shoulders. When she kissed her mother's cheek, she noticed her swollen eyes closing, so she quietly left the room.

Jenny almost collided into her as she came down the hall from outside. "Sissy, Sissy, what's the matter? I was out riding Scamp. When I got back, everyone was crying. Is Papa better? Where's Mama? Dr. Ellerby saw me coming down the hall and said it would be best if I found you."

Laura bent down and took Jenny's hand, walking with her through the hall and onto the balcony. The breeze blew Laura's hair gently as Jenny climbed into a big rocker with Laura so she could snuggle in her lap. Rocking slowly Laura said, "Jenny, Papa died last night. He was a very sick man."

Jenny said, "But I don't want him to die." She clung to Laura's neck as Laura stroked her blond curls.

"Mama will need our help, for she loved Papa very much."

Jenny's round eyes were full of tears as she looked up at Laura and asked, "Can I see Mama?"

"Maybe in a little while, Jenny," replied Laura. "She is very sad so we must try to comfort her and remind her that Papa is waiting in heaven and will see us all again one day."

Jenny wiped her eyes as she slid out of Laura's lap. "I'll be brave, Sissy. I have to go and feed Scamp because I'm going to have to care for him all by myself now."

Nodding, Laura realized her little girl was growing up. "Oh, Jenny, Papa would be so proud of you. If you need any help, let me know."

"I will, Sissy," Jenny whispered as she tiptoed down the stairs, quietly shutting the front door so as not to disturb Mama.

After a moment Laura stood and turned to look out over the front lawn of Oak Grove. The sorrow that filled her heart over the loss of her father deepened as she took in the regal oaks stretching their long branches in the breeze around the front porch. The Spanish moss blew gently in the wind as some of the majestic branches of the great live oaks lightly rested on the ground below. The beauty of her ancestral land was breathtaking. Now it belonged to a man she didn't even know. Her mind was in turmoil. What would they do? Where would they go? These questions weighed heavily on her mind as she turned to go inside.

A few weeks later, as Laura entered the hall, she heard a knock on the front door. A delivery boy handed her a letter addressed to Mrs. Edward Malcolm. Laura knew her mother was in no condition to handle whatever message lay within the envelope. So she opened the letter, which was written in a bold, masculine script.

Dear Madam,

I received word last night of your husband's death. I feel deeply saddened by this news. Your husband was a good friend of my father's. My father also passed away several months ago, so I will come in person from New York to discuss some business they had between them. Please inform me of a time that would be convenient.

Your servant,
Bradford Hampton

A Northerner, Laura thought. The Malcolms had made it through a war, and now a former enemy would take their things after all! Laura dreaded the moment when she would have to come face-to-face with this man, but she knew she must do it as soon as possible.

She hastily scribbled a message, saying a month from now would be satisfactory, and explained that she, and not her mother, would handle any business between them. Laura was hoping that a month would give her mother a little more time to recover.

❧

Bradford was surprised at the promptness of Laura's response. Before he opened her letter, his gaze rested on the small oval painting of his loving mother. She had died when he was only two. All he could remember of his childhood was the strict upbringing by his father, James. In his grief over the loss of his wife, James had turned his complete attention to making money and had enjoyed every detail in his business dealings. He had taught his son to make good in every financial transaction and never to let emotions interfere with business. This training had led Bradford to become a very wealthy and powerful man in his own right. He had amassed countless wealth and was kept extremely busy overseeing his vast holdings.

Before Bradford's father died, he handed him a small, worn Bible. As his ailing father passed it to him, he desperately whispered, "Please take good care of your mother's Bible. She loved it so."

The Bible was one of the few possessions Bradford had from his caring mother, because his grief-stricken father had gotten rid of most of her possessions. Inside the front cover of the Bible, his mother had written in her graceful script, "Forgiveness is the key to being truly happy." Bradford hoped that one day he could forgive his father for his relentless pursuit of wealth regardless of its personal toll on him, his father, and those with whom he had done business.

Many months later while going through his father's records, Bradford discovered that his father, when dealing with his old friend, Edward Malcolm, had broken his one rule of never letting sentiment get in the way of a business arrangement. His father had loaned money that he knew his friend would never be able to repay. The plantation was worth something, but it probably wouldn't make up for the Malcolms' extensive financial losses. Bradford's cold upbringing had not allowed him many friends, so he failed to understand how his father had given away so much money to anyone—even a friend. Since Bradford had many pressing matters, he knew he should send one of his representatives to dispose of the Malcolm's estate. The sale of Oak Grove should be easy because it was reportedly in fine condition. The proceeds should help cover some of the Malcolm's debt. But curiosity stirred him. Bradford personally wanted to see what had caused his father to break the one rule he had taught his son since childhood. After reading Laura's short message, he smiled, thinking he would have no trouble getting to the bottom of this mystery before returning to his other affairs.

Laura was kept so busy tending to her mother, supervising the running of the plantation, and trying to entertain Jenny that she had little time to prepare for her meeting with Mr. Hampton. She hadn't thought of what she would say and had even avoided thinking about the most pressing issue of where they would live. The whole matter seemed totally hopeless, but her pride would not let her admit failure. As the day of her appointment approached, she decided to devote that morning to determining her course of action.

The sun rose to find Laura already up and about. She dressed with immaculate care, putting on one of her nicest gowns with long silk sleeves. Its curved neckline was very flattering, complementing the creamy white of her flawless skin. The waist fit snugly around her slender figure, and the skirt fell in long folds, accentuating her gracefulness as she walked. She told everyone she was not to be disturbed that morning, for she had a very important matter to which she must attend. She had always felt free on the balcony, so she went there to think. She stood gazing through trees gently swaying in the breeze as she looked toward the Mississippi. Her eyes narrowed as she spotted an elegantly dressed man riding up to the house. All of a sudden her hands turned white as she gripped the railing. Holding her head high, she left the balcony and went into the hallway, descending the curved stairway to greet the stranger who now owned her family estate.

As Bradford approached the plantation, he caught sight of a lady standing on the balcony, the wind blowing her long golden-brown hair toward the plantation house. He had never dreamed he would discover such a lovely lady way out here in the country. Many gorgeous women desired his company, but they always bored him with their pointless chatter and artificial ways. Slowly he got off his horse and surveyed the grounds. As he approached the house, he acknowledged Oak Grove was in far better shape than he had imagined. Bradford now realized that selling this antebellum home and its grounds would easily bring enough money to clear most, if not all, of the Malcolms' debts.

Bradford entered the beautiful foyer. Large gold-leaf mirrors towered over each side of the stairwell. He was impressed—very impressed. He looked up as Laura descended a grand staircase that would be found only in the very best mansions in the North.

"We weren't expecting you until later this afternoon," Laura said.

Bradford reached up and took her hand as she stepped onto the last step before the landing. Bending over her delicate hand, he held it firmly in his, as he said, "My apologies, madam, but I arrived faster than I'd expected."

Laura was taken aback, for she hadn't expected him to be so young or so handsome. His black hair was combed smoothly back. Dark eyebrows arched high over light-blue eyes as he gazed into her eyes. Suddenly, remembering the purpose of his call, Laura immediately removed her hand from his. "I take it you are Mr. Hampton?" she stated coolly.

Surprised by this abrupt mood change, he replied, "Yes, I am. Being here has brought back fond memories of the time I was stationed near here. I was on a ship that patrolled the Mississippi during the last year of the war."

"Yes," Laura flared. "We have a souvenir of the Union ships that blasted their cannons at the house." Fingering a small black cannonball lodged in the thick wall of the entryway, she said, "Mama was proud of it and allowed no one to remove it. Our home served as a hospital for Union soldiers. General Grant slept in my parents' bed after Vicksburg surrendered, so Oak Grove was spared."

Bradford stood by her as he touched the smooth ball. "You were lucky no one was hurt."

"Yes, even Father's business survived. We were very fortunate. Until now!"

He looked down at her small chin, held up proudly as they stood together. "The war ended over ten years ago. But I see some of us are still fighting it. Now please call me 'Bradford.' You must be Mrs. Malcolm's daughter?"

"Yes, please come in and sit down," Laura said, remembering her manners. Directing him into the study, she pointed to a brown leather chair near a fireplace of white Italian marble. Sinking into a chair opposite him, she suggested, "Please call me 'Laura.' I'll speak for my mother, Ruth. Since my father's death, I've been taking care of her affairs because she hasn't been well."

"I'm very sorry to hear that," Bradford said with sincere sorrow in his voice. Then he assumed an abrupt, businesslike manner. "I've briefly reviewed our fathers' affairs with my lawyer. Your plantation is now mine."

Laura stood up, shocked by his cold attitude and gruff manner. Speaking loudly, she said, "Yes, it is. We'll leave immediately. We wouldn't want to trespass on your property any longer than absolutely necessary." Her small foot stomped the floor in anger as she turned toward the door.

Bradford firmly gripped her shoulder and stopped her. "Wait, please. There's more you need to know." His hand dropped from her shoulder as she turned around. "Please sit down so we can continue."

Puzzled, Laura sank into the chair and turned to find him staring at her. "You shouldn't be so hasty, for as I understand it, you have no relatives you can go to."

Laura nodded, but now, provoked by his cold attitude, her violet eyes blazed with anger. "Don't bother to concern yourself with that. We'll do something!"

"Well, I don't believe that will be necessary, because your father didn't leave you totally poverty stricken," Bradford interjected, a small smile pulling up the corners of his mouth.

Laura's anger turned to curiosity as she leaned forward on the edge of her seat, waiting to hear what he had to say. She had assumed her father had left them penniless, and this news was indeed a blessing. Now, maybe, they could stay and start a new life.

Bradford continued with a warmer tone. "I understand you own a small cottage only a couple of miles from Oak Grove."

Laura questioned, "But I thought..." Suddenly she realized what must have happened and stopped before finishing her sentence.

His eyebrows arched with a puzzled expression as he spoke. "I could be mistaken, but my lawyer said your name has been on the deed to a cottage for about five years." He continued in his businesslike manner, "At that time your father set aside a small trust in your name in case anything happened to him. It won't be what you're accustomed to, but it should be adequate, if the cottage is in good condition."

Laura's eyes stung as tears threatened to pour down her face. She had never dreamed that all this time the cottage where she and Gerald had lived for such a short time was hers. She thought Judge Taylor had taken everything from her. She hadn't been to see it since Gerald's accident, but the cottage had often been in her thoughts.

Bradford longed to know what mystery lay behind the sorrowful expression that now filled Laura's pensive look.

Laura was aware of his questioning gaze. Quickly trying to hide her emotions, she muttered, "Oh, yes, it slipped my mind. Everything has been in such turmoil since Father's death. The cottage should be perfect for my mother, my sister, and me."

Bradford suspected there was more behind this and longed to find out. Suddenly they heard rapid footsteps bounding down the stairs, and the door to the study flew open.

"Sissy, where have you been? I want to show you the new tricks Scamp learned," Jenny said as she ran to Laura's side.

Laura smiled as she pulled Jenny close and told her in a solemn voice, "First you must apologize to Mr. Hampton for interrupting him."

Jenny turned, looking at him with her big blue eyes, and apologized. "Oh, I am so sorry." Breathlessly she politely curtseyed and added with a winning smile, "You may come with Sissy too and watch Scamp's new trick."

Jenny reached over and took his hand, pulling him out of the wingback chair. Then she took Laura's hand, and together they walked outside. Laura looked at him with apprehension but was reassured by Bradford's warm smile at Jenny. Laura relaxed as they walked the short distance to the corral.

Jenny ran ahead and jumped on Scamp. "Everyone watch!" she yelled as she spurred Scamp into motion. The pony raced toward a small pile of logs. He cleared them gracefully and with little effort. Jenny then circled around the field and rode up to Laura and Bradford.

"See? Wasn't that magnificent?" Jenny declared as she sat proudly in her saddle.

"That *was* magnificent!" replied Bradford. "You'll soon be ready for a larger horse, and then you can jump even higher. In the meantime you need to teach Scamp how to do some other tricks, like prancing. All the great show horses can do that."

Intrigued, Jenny started to ask lots of questions about horse shows when Laura interrupted, "Now run along and get ready for lunch. Mr. Hampton is a busy man. I'm sure he has lots of things he must see to."

Jenny reluctantly rode Scamp to the stables. After she left, Bradford noted, "She's such a charming child!"

As Laura beamed at him, he was immediately aware of her sparkling eyes fringed with long dark-brown lashes. Then, as if she had just remembered why he was there, her eyes clouded up, and she stared ahead.

Bradford broke the silence as they walked toward his horse. "I'd like to see this cottage for myself. Would tomorrow morning around ten be a good time for us to ride out and take a look?"

"It won't be necessary for you to go for it's only a couple of miles away, and I can see to it quite well by myself," she answered, lifting her chin with pride.

"We have other matters to discuss, and anyway, I'd like to see what condition the grounds are in around the plantation."

Laura proudly retorted, "The grounds are in perfect condition!"

"I'm sure they are," Bradford replied, chuckling to himself as he climbed onto his horse and rode off in the direction of Vicksburg.

Laura quickly turned and entered the foyer. She knew her family would have to prepare to leave immediately for her cottage regardless of its condition. She would not accept charity from anyone, especially Mr. Bradford Hampton.

She slowly climbed the stairs as she thought about all the packing they would have to do. Her mother still despaired over her husband's death, and now she had to face the loss of her home too. Laura had put off telling her mother about the loss of Oak Grove as long as she could. Fortunately Ruth no longer required constant attention and took the news much better than Laura expected. Laura reasoned that preparing to move would keep her mother busy and hopefully help her deal with her mourning.

On that thought she entered her mother's room. Ruth asked how the meeting with Mr. Hampton had gone. After Laura filled her in on what they had discussed, Ruth agreed that they had to leave, but thought they should not be overly hasty. She felt it was important to wait until they knew the cottage was in suitable condition for Jenny.

Laura firmly reminded her mother that they wouldn't accept charity. After she left the room, Ruth began to pack, thankful that at least they had somewhere to live.

Laura was glad her mother seemed resigned to what must be done because she knew this would be harder on her than anyone else. Oak Grove had been her home since she had married. All the memories of her long, loving marriage were held here in this home.

Balling up her hand, Laura thought of Mr. Hampton's cold attitude about the whole affair. How dare he be so arrogant about their losing everything? With that thought she remembered she had failed to ask him whether she could claim any of the household items. She hoped that tomorrow, when they went over the house and discussed its furnishings, he would be generous enough to allow her to have some of her family's possessions.

Dread suddenly filled her as she realized tomorrow would mean returning to the cottage where she and Gerald had been so happy. Knowing she should be thankful because she had a place to take her mother and child, she quickly descended the stairs as if to shake off her gloom and sense of foreboding.

Chapter Four

A Surprise at the Cottage

～※～

ike fingers playing a harp, long rays of sun rippled on Laura's bed. Chirping birds and a distant calf bellowing for its mother made Laura aware that she must have slept later than she had planned. Flinging back her patchwork quilt, she quickly jumped out of bed and prepared to bathe. The warm water seemed to ease all the tension that had been gnawing at her. Now, relaxed and cool, she slipped into a linen dress and a light jacket made of lace. Since the day was apparently going to be very hot, she wanted to be as cool as possible.

As she entered the breakfast room, she saw that her mother and Jenny had just finished their meal.

"I hope you had a good night's rest," Laura's mother remarked.

"Yes," Laura replied cheerfully. "Sleep did wonders for my spirit." She sat down and nibbled at the cheese omelet her mother knew was her favorite.

Jenny slid out of her chair and came over to give her a hug. "Are we leaving our house?" she asked with a note of distress in her voice.

"We'll only be going a short distance away to a cottage. I know you'll like it," Laura replied, returning the hug and patting Jenny on the back. "Mr. Hampton is taking me over this morning so we can see how soon we'll be able to move in."

"May I go too?" Jenny asked eagerly.

"Not this time, Jenny," Ruth replied. "I need you to help me pack your clothes and toys. I might forget something important, like your new dress or some of your china dolls."

Laura gave her mother a knowing grin and heaved a sigh of relief, for she had succeeded in distracting Jenny. When the bells of the old grandfather clock started to chime, Laura silently counted to ten. She got up from the table as she heard the hooves of a horse pounding down the path to the house. Seconds after Bradford knocked, Laura greeted him cordially while trying to avoid eyes that seemed to see right through her.

"Shall we go?" Bradford asked as he led her out to the horses.

They mounted their horses and rode in the direction of the cottage. Laura knew the day was going to be incurably hot as the sun struck their backs. She was thankful for her earlier choice of gowns as they passed beyond the oaks. The gown's light fabric kept her cool in the stifling heat.

They entered a short stretch of woods, dark and shaded under large oak trees draped with Spanish moss. The birds chirped happily. Nearby a wood-pecker pounded on a small branch high above their heads.

Bradford turned in his saddle, shattering the peaceful moment by saying abruptly, "Tell me why this cottage is in your name, yet you seemed unaware of it."

"I don't see how that should concern you," Laura replied coolly. As she spoke these words, she and Bradford left the shelter of the trees and were again in the dazzling sun.

Bradford glanced down, noticing the light bouncing off the small gold ring Laura wore on her wedding finger. Confused, he said, "I wasn't aware that you're married."

"I'm a widow. My husband was killed five years ago, shortly after our wedding." Tears threatened to spill out as she tried to look ahead into the blinding sunlight.

"That answers a lot of my questions," he commented insightfully. "I guess you and he once lived in the cottage we're going to visit."

"Yes," Laura said, trying not to be upset at his discovery. "Gerald and I were very happy there during our short time together."

Bradford saw a tear roll down Laura's cheek. "May I inquire as to the cause of his death?"

"Gerald died saving a little girl who had fallen into a ravine. I haven't been back to the cottage since that night," she explained with a catch in her voice.

"I'm sorry," he said quietly. "The grounds of this plantation are in fine shape," he reported, trying to change the subject and snap Laura out of her melancholy.

Remembering their conversation of the previous day, Laura forgot her sadness. "I should hope so! My father wasn't expecting to have some Northerner take them over."

Giving her horse a slight kick, she pulled ahead and raced into another thicket of trees. Bradford's horse chased after her as they flew into the woods. Laura rode sidesaddle with grace and ease as she maneuvered her horse over rocks and branches that had fallen across the path. Before she knew it, she was in the clearing that led to the cottage.

There the cottage stood, looking just like a drawing in a fairy tale. One of Gerald's uncles had built the cottage years before, designing it after the country farmhouse he had known as a boy in England. It was larger than most of the cottages in the area, with three bedrooms upstairs and one downstairs. With a pitched roof, bay window, and decorative half-timbering, it was as charming as she remembered it.

Bradford halted his horse beside Laura's and reached up to help her dismount. As soon as his strong hands lowered her to the ground, she immediately walked up the path. He asked, "What's the hurry?"

Laura replied tartly, "I'd like to get this over with so I can get on with our packing. We don't want to impose on you any more than necessary." She swung her long wavy hair over her shoulder and headed up the flagstone path to the cottage door. "It looks as though someone has been living here," she noted, knocking on the arched wooden door.

Nanny, Gerald's childhood nurse, immediately opened the door. She had come as an indentured servant to the Taylors from Ireland in order to escape the potato famine. She had raised Gerald from infancy and in many ways had been like his second mother.

"Why, 'tis Miss Laura. What brings you here?" Nanny inquired in her delightful Irish brogue. As she wrapped her motherly arms around Laura's slender shoulders, she glanced up and saw Bradford tying up their horses. "Who's the handsome gentleman accompanying you?" she asked, eyeing him speculatively.

Pink color rushed to Laura's cheeks as she said, "The gentleman is Mr. Bradford Hampton, the new owner of Oak Grove."

Startled, Nanny looked mystified as she invited, "Come in, both of you, and tell me what's going on. I can tell I've been hiding in these woods for far too long."

Laura laughed as Nanny ushered her into the cool comfort of the sitting room. Laura sat in the bay window on a little bench with soft cushions of pale blue velvet. From here she could glance at the roses just outside the window.

She turned to study the rest of the delightful room. The paneling had retained the rich, golden hue Laura remembered so well. The room now had a cheery look, though. She was quick to see why. The dull-brown plank floor had been covered with a light-blue rug, and several of the stuffed chairs had been reupholstered with colorful fabrics decorated with large embroidered flowers. As she looked to her left, she saw the kitchen had a new cast iron stove.

Lemon-yellow curtains framed the windows. Laura was eager to see what had been done to the rest of the cottage, especially the small bedrooms upstairs, but knew that too many questions had to be answered first. After Laura told Nanny how the Malcolms had lost their plantation, she said, "We're going to come here to live with you." She continued, "Nanny, why didn't anyone tell me you were here?"

Nanny settled down in one of the brightly upholstered chairs across from Bradford, who had just entered the cottage. "I'm so happy you're going to live with me! It will be nice to have your family in the house." Nanny continued, "Well, after the war the Taylors lost all their money and couldn't afford to keep me on since I'd already served my time as an indentured servant. After Gerald passed on, his parents sadly decided to leave Vicksburg. Your father asked me if I'd like to stay here and keep up the cottage. He gave me some money to fix up the place and make it a little more cheerful. I've really enjoyed trying my hand at that," she added with a chuckle.

"You've certainly been successful." Laura beamed as she took in the lovely room. A tear formed in her eyes as she thought of how generous her father had been to give Nanny a place to live and at the same time preserve the cottage that had been Gerald's and her home.

Puzzled by all this, Bradford interrupted, "If Laura wasn't going to live here, why did her father go to this trouble?"

Nanny continued, "He was unsure what Laura wanted because she was a grown, married woman. He knew Gerald had left the cottage to her, and he wanted her to have a place to live if she seemed unhappy under his roof, especially when…" Nanny was unable to complete her statement as she saw Laura vigorously shake her head at her.

Laura jumped up. She didn't know whether Nanny knew the truth about Jenny, but she certainly didn't want Bradford to learn her secret. She quickly blurted to Nanny, "We're all getting ready to move in with you. There's no need to wait any longer. I'm sure Mr. Hampton has much to do at Oak Grove, and we've got to get packed." She quickly ran over and embraced Nanny.

With a smile on her face, Nanny waved good-bye to Laura and Bradford as they walked down the flagstone path to their horses.

Following Laura out, Bradford wore a perplexed look as he mulled over what had just happened. He was determined to find out what lay behind Laura's abrupt decision to leave the cottage. As they approached the woods on their way back to Oak Grove, he pointed to a huge oak. "Let's rest under that tree over there."

They pulled up their horses, and he helped Laura dismount. Then he asked, "What didn't you let Nanny finish telling me back at the cottage?"

Fidgeting with her lace jacket, Laura looked away, trying to think up a good answer. "Oh, I was afraid she'd go on and on about the family and bore you to death, so I decided to leave. Also, we do have lots of packing to do."

He gently took her by the shoulders and turned her around to face him. Smiling into her eyes, he speculated, "I know that isn't the reason." Suddenly, before Laura knew what was happening, his lips were on hers. The warmth of his kiss was intoxicating. At first his lips gently brushed hers, and then they gradually increased their pressure. Laura was shocked at the rush of her feelings. As though she were drowning, she fought to regain control of the situation. She pushed hard on his chest with her hands, and he abruptly let her go.

His blue eyes flared as he said, "I guess no one will ever be able to compete with Gerald."

"Why are you bringing up Gerald?" she challenged. "You had no right to kiss me like that. We must return to Oak Grove immediately." Still weak and stunned from the effect of his kiss, she added, "No one can ever compete with Gerald, for I'll always care only for him."

With that she mounted her horse. Turning in the saddle, she tried to change the subject. "I'd like to discuss which items you would like left at the plantation so I can get on with my packing."

"Take whatever you wish. I'll not have need of anything," he replied with a scornful smirk pulling up the corners of his mouth.

After returning to Oak Grove, Laura saw Jenny, who was full of questions, run up to greet them. The one that was foremost in her mind she asked immediately. "Is there a place for Scamp at the cottage?"

Laura laughed. "I don't know, Jenny, but we'll make a place for your pony. The cottage is perfect. We should be able to move in as soon as we're packed."

Bradford looked directly at Laura as he spoke. "Scamp will need a well-run stable, so your sister can keep him here for the time being. I'll look after him personally."

"Oh, would you?" Jenny asked, running up to him and giving him a thankful hug.

Shrugging, Laura said, "I didn't get the impression that you'd be staying here, since you're such a busy man."

Patting his horse's neck, Bradford returned, "My business can wait. I'd like to get in a little hunting and fishing while I'm down South."

"Oh," a surprised Laura remarked, turning back to the house and leaving Jenny and Bradford to talk about horses. Still remembering the hot pressure of his lips, she briskly ascended the winding staircase. Why had he kissed her, and why had his eyes become bitter and hurt when she talked about Gerald? Trying to forget the whole incident, she began to pack her things. Soon they would be in the cottage, and she wouldn't have to concern herself with this rude man and his cold, arrogant ways that upset her so.

※

Three days later Laura and her family were settled in the cottage. Nanny was busy as a mother hen tending to her biddies. She fussed over Ruth, who was placed in the largest of the upstairs rooms. This room had been redone in bright lemon yellow with blue flowers splashed all over the wallpaper. Laura's mother was very content and kept busy helping Nanny with the cooking. The two women competed to start breakfast, but Nanny was always first because her room was downstairs at the back of the cottage and therefore was nearer to the kitchen.

Jenny loved her room because Nanny had fixed it especially for her, knowing that one day she might come here to live. The pink wallpaper was decorated with dolls from different countries. The bedspread was pink gingham with matching curtains. Nanny had lots of shelves built so Jenny could display all of her china dolls.

Jenny loved Nanny, who told her delightful stories about Laura and Gerald when they were children and got into mischief. Nanny had taken Gerald every Sunday to the chapel near Oak Grove where he and Laura had first met. Because Gerald's parents never attended church, they had never met Laura or her family.

Jenny's favorite story was about the time Gerald had wanted to get Laura's attention. Before church one Sunday, he went down by the lake behind the chapel and found a frog. He quietly slipped the small frog into a wooden box in which Laura carried her Bible. When Laura opened the box during the service, the frog jumped onto her lap, and she screamed. Everyone leaped up and ran around, frantically looking for the green menace. No one paid any attention to the minister's plea for calm or his demand that people return to their pews. Realizing he was in trouble, Gerald spied the small tree frog on the hat of Mrs. Winslow, head of the Ladies' Auxiliary. He quickly but gently scooped him up in his hand.

Nanny yelled out to the congregation, "Please, everyone calm down! Gerald has the frog and will take him outside now."

Gerald turned around, hoping to redeem himself. He slowly opened his hand just as Mrs. Winslow swung around to face him. He innocently said, "Look how cute this little tree frog is. He'd never hurt you."

Mrs. Winslow, whose hat had been the frog's perch moments before, took one look. Her terrified eyes rolled back into her head as she slumped onto the pew. Nanny again told Gerald to take the frog outside as she reached into her purse and pulled out smelling salts for Mrs. Winslow, who quickly revived from the vapors. Laura fondly remembered the incident, laughing as she thought back to all of the fun she and Gerald had had as children.

Laura chose the small blue room at the back of the cottage. A tiny balcony had been built that overlooked the garden, which was filled with colorful, blooming flowers. As she stood on this balcony, she realized her fears about returning to the cottage had been unfounded. She felt truly blessed. Gerald had left her their home in his will, and luckily his father had been unable to take the cottage away from her. Fortunately her own father had been thoughtful and planned for the day when she could make it her home after Gerald died. Laura also was very thankful her father had set aside money in a trust for her. The trust funds had since grown enough to allow her, Jenny, and her mother to live here comfortably. She thought only of the good times she and Gerald had enjoyed while living at the cottage and wished he were with her now. As she took a deep breath, the sweet smell of roses came up to her, and she sighed.

As Laura stepped from the balcony into her room, she heard Jenny tapping on her door. "May I come in, Sissy?" she asked.

"Of course," Laura said, as she thought how mature Jenny was acting.

"Yesterday, Miss Saundra visited Oak Grove while I was working with Scamp. She was talking about the ball she's giving so everyone can meet Mr. Hampton. Isn't it exciting?" Jenny exclaimed with a broad smile that revealed the absence of her first lost tooth. "She said you were invited to the ball too."

Laura stiffened as she thought about Bradford. Fortunately she hadn't seen him since they'd left the plantation. Jenny had been there quite often to ride Scamp, but Laura had stayed near the cottage. It seemed Saundra had been seeing plenty of him, though, she thought dryly. But then she thought, *Why do I care?*

"You don't look happy about the ball, Sissy," Jenny noticed, looking puzzled.

"Oh, yes, I am. Since the war there haven't been many balls. I miss the pretty dresses and the gaiety. When I wasn't much bigger than you are now, I watched the grand balls my parents hosted in the ballroom. I was always too young to go to the parties, but Mother would let me stay up late and watch from the landing above the staircase. I always dreamed of getting to go and dance, but then the war came and the balls ended. Would you like to help me get ready before I go?"

SH

"Oh, that would be so much fun!" Jenny responded as she threw her arms around Laura. "May Nanny take me over to see Mr. Hampton now so I can ride Scamp?"

"Yes, you can go. You're not bothering him too often, are you?" Laura asked.

"No, Sissy. He's teaching me how to make Scamp prance and how to show him. He says Scamp is a fine pony and could even win ribbons at the fair."

As she watched Jenny run down the stairs, with her blond curls bobbing up and down, Laura had mixed feelings about Jenny spending too much time with Bradford. Still he had been very kind to her daughter. Laura wondered whether Bradford had figured out Jenny's real identity. If only she could tell everyone about Jenny without the fear of what Judge Taylor would do, she felt her life would be perfect.

Chapter Five

Saundra's Grand Ball

$$\approx$$

On the day of Saundra's ball, Laura let Jenny help her with her gown. The dress was one her father had insisted she get just before he had died. The gown's pale yellow emphasized the golden highlights in her light-brown hair. As Laura knelt, Jenny helped her pull the yellow silk gown over her head. Jenny then helped smooth out the folds of shear material that draped over the dress. The hoopskirt formed a full circle that emphasized Laura's slender waist. After putting on the gown, Laura decided to wear her hair up since that was the fashion. Hinting that she had a surprise for Laura, Jenny retrieved the brush and helped her brush her thick, curly hair. With Ruth's help they then pulled Laura's hair up from the front and sides and piled it loosely on the top of her head into a bun. A few curling ringlets were left to escape and fall down her back.

Soon after Laura was ready, Ruth came into the room, saying, "It's time to go to the ball."

Thinking it was too early to leave for the party, Laura was surprised at her mother's comment. Still, she rushed downstairs to find Bradford, looking very dashing in a black cutaway coat and white tie, waiting for her.

Grinning, Jenny ran up to Laura and revealed, "Mr. Hampton is my surprise." Her smile was so big, and she looked so pleased with herself that Laura didn't have the heart to say that Bradford didn't have to take her to the ball.

Bradford, his eyes laughing, said, "It was Jenny's idea that I be your escort. She knew you had no way to get to the ball without riding in an open wagon."

Jenny's eyes twinkled, as she hoped Laura would be happy she'd thought of the idea. Trying to look pleased, Laura gave her a quick squeeze.

Bradford helped Laura into his carriage and climbed in after her. As he sat back in the seat, he smiled, saying, "Your sister loves you very much. I hope you won't be angry with her because the company she chose for you isn't what you would've picked yourself."

Laura looked up at him. "No. As a matter of fact, I've wanted to thank you for all you've done for Jenny. She thinks the world of you."

"It's too bad her big sister doesn't," he said sadly as he gazed at Laura's pale-yellow dress, which made her striking eyes look more violet than usual, standing out like amethysts on ivory.

Flustered, she replied, "Well, I've never inferred that I dislike you. I mean, it wasn't your fault my father lost his land to you."

Bradford burst out laughing and looked at her with puzzled blue eyes. "I had nothing to do with that. Your father begged my father to loan him the money. From a business standpoint, this was a loan my father never should have made. For personal reasons I've longed to understand why he did it."

With quivering lips Laura explained, "My father borrowed the money for unselfish reasons—to help me." Her eyes seemed to throw sparks at Bradford as she blurted, "You certainly have a morbid curiosity if you want to know why my father lost all his money."

Before Bradford could straighten out this misunderstanding, the carriage arrived at Camellia Hall.

Saundra herself rushed out of the large white mansion to greet the carriage. She flew down one side of the enormous exterior curving staircase as soon as she saw Bradford's coach appear. By the time he had climbed down from the carriage, she was standing on the bottom step, ready to possessively take his arm. "I see my guest of honor has arrived," she said. "You must come in at once to meet everyone. Lots of your Northern friends have already arrived." She turned and said, "Oh, I didn't see you, Laura."

Knowing it was hopeless to try to make Laura understand, Bradford turned away from her and allowed Saundra to lead him into the ballroom. The roomful of guests parted as the hostess proudly led the guest of honor to the center of the room. Laura followed them into the foyer and then into the largest ballroom she had ever seen. When she entered, an intoxicating aroma made her aware of an abundance of flowers; gorgeous flower arrangements were everywhere she looked. There were roses, gardenias, and every other imaginable flower in crystal vases placed around the room.

Ignoring Saundra's snub, Laura entered with her head held high. She turned as she felt a light tap on her shoulder. Facing her longtime friend, she said, "Oh, Charlotte, it's so good to see you. I've missed you!"

"I know you've been busy moving into your new home," Charlotte said, "so I haven't been over lately."

"Well, at least we can visit tonight," Laura replied happily.

"Is that the guest of honor with Saundra?" Charlotte inquired.

"Yes, that's Bradford Hampton, the new owner of Oak Grove," Laura answered sadly. "He brought me to the ball tonight, but I really don't want to ride back with him. Do you think you could take me home after the party?"

"Of course," Charlotte responded. "He's mighty handsome, but I don't blame you for not wanting to be obliged to him. Come on over and join our other friends. They'll love to see you."

Laura quietly walked over to her friends, who were sitting near the musicians. Her dance card was quickly filled with lots of eligible men. Two of them were Bradford's Northern friends who wanted to be introduced to her. Laura enjoyed the dancing and had a lot of fun with her longtime friends as well as Bradford's acquaintances. Yet she couldn't fail to notice that Saundra was dancing exclusively with Bradford and always seemed to be whispering in his ear.

Bradford had felt trapped all evening. He couldn't believe Saundra had signed his name on her dance card for every dance. When it was time for the last dance, he told her, "I've taken my name off of your dance card for this dance. I'm taking Laura home and must dance the last dance with her."

"Well, I signed you up to dance with me for every dance because you're my guest of honor," Saundra said, pouting.

"I've enjoyed the party very much. My friends have too. You were very thoughtful to go to all this trouble, but I must leave now," Bradford said, firmly excusing himself.

Turning quickly to get to Laura's side, he rushed over to find her sitting among a host of admirers.

Bradford appeared out of the crowd to interrupt his friend, who was quietly talking to Laura. "Patrick, go and dance with Saundra. She'll appreciate your company." Without saying a word, he crossed Patrick's name from the last line on Laura's dance card and replaced it with his own. He asked, "May I please have this dance?"

Surprised, Laura agreed.

Before leading her onto the dance floor, he whispered in her ear, "You must pretend to enjoy this so people won't think I'm the one-eyed monster you tell them I am."

She smiled at this absurd comment and relaxed. They floated around the floor with an ease she had never found in a partner before. The smoothness and grace with which they moved made her forget their harsh words. She let him pull her close as they swirled around the floor. Around and around they turned. The pleasant experience ended too quickly as the musicians played their final notes.

Still holding her around the waist, Bradford looked down at her. Laura seemed to snap back into reality and abruptly blurted, "I made arrangements with my friend Charlotte to take me back to the cottage."

Quickly releasing her, he bluntly remarked, "Fine!" Turning, he promptly walked back to Saundra and her smug smile.

Several hours later Laura was glad to be back in bed. As she snuggled under the covers, warmth spread over her body as she remembered being in Bradford's arms and flying around the dance floor. Then she deduced the real reason he was at Oak Grove. He was just trying to humiliate her family. Maybe he was even going through her father's old files she had left in the study. He surely had a perverse curiosity to find out why her dear father had lost all of the money he had borrowed. "Of all the nerve!" Laura muttered to herself. Then she punched her pillow with her fists and fell into a restless slumber.

Chapter Six

A Special Summer Sunday

⚜

The following morning, Laura, Jenny, Ruth, and Nanny dressed for church. As they climbed into their wagon, Jenny turned to Laura and eagerly begged, "Tell us all about Saundra's ball."

"You should've seen Saundra's dress," Laura said, joyfully describing the events of the previous evening. "Her ball gown was a brilliant red and was very striking. The bodice of her dress was off the shoulders. Its giant hoopskirt was the biggest I've ever seen. Rows of ruffles flowed down the sides of the skirt. They flared out as Saundra danced around the ballroom. All the young men flocked to her side to admire her," Laura elaborated. *Especially Bradford,* she thought. Laura didn't add that she had felt taunted by the sly smile Saundra threw her way every time she circled around the room with Bradford.

Laura went on to describe Saundra's many appetizing delicacies. Some she hadn't seen since before the war. "Saundra actually brought in a chef from New Orleans. My favorite dish was the seasoned shrimp with a spicy Creole sauce." Laura explained how Saundra's servants carried the delicious *hors d'oeuvres* on solid silver trays as they served the guests.

With a dreamy look in her eyes, Laura continued, "I felt in awe as I entered the ballroom, which was filled with guests dressed in all the latest finery. I entered through large Corinthian columns into an all-white ballroom. They didn't even need candles because the room was full of light. Gas chandeliers that were full of dazzling crystals produced a sparkling glow that made the room as light as day. The intricate scrollwork around the molding was stunning. Saundra bragged that it took the workers months to complete their work. The ceiling was painted with murals of fluffy white clouds with precious winged cherubs flying around. It appeared that you were gazing into the blue sky when you looked up."

"I can't wait until I grow up and can go to balls like that," Jenny said. "Sissy, you looked so pretty! I know the men must have enjoyed dancing with you." Then she asked shyly, "Did Mr. Hampton dance with you?"

Laura replied, "I danced with a lot of the men at the party and had a fabulous time. Some of my partners were Mr. Hampton's friends. They were very pleasant gentlemen. And yes, I danced the last dance with Mr. Hampton. We did a new dance called a waltz. The dance is considered scandalous by some, but it really isn't. It's actually a lot of fun. The dancers go around and around and around. Mr. Hampton was a perfect gentleman, and I enjoyed him as a partner. He's an excellent dancer, and I really had fun during our waltz." Laura didn't bring up the fact that she had left the ball with Charlotte instead of Bradford, since she didn't want to hurt Jenny's feelings.

Thinking back, Laura realized the reason she was angry with Bradford was because he had largely ignored her at the ball. She was very glad Charlotte had agreed to take her home so she could avoid another scene with him. Laura was tired of his preoccupation with figuring out why her father had invested so poorly.

As Laura's family pulled up to the chapel, they saw Bradford getting out of his carriage. He tipped his hat at them and walked over to join them. Laura tried to look away, but he bowed and asked, "May I escort you ladies into church?" Jenny quickly took one arm and told Laura to take his other arm as they walked together into the church. Nanny and Ruth gave each other knowing smiles as they walked behind the threesome toward the church set on the edge of a lovely lake.

The chapel was small, with three clear glass windows behind the altar. Each window had a cross inside of the frame and looked out onto a crystal blue lake surrounded by cypress trees. The day was bright with the sun shining down on the sparkling water. Stained glass windows along the sides of the church captured the brilliant colors of the glass panels. Laura especially enjoyed the windows, which depicted Mary holding the baby Jesus, Jesus on the cross, and Jesus's resurrection. The beauty of the chapel encouraged the congregation to put aside their earthly concerns and focus on spiritual ones. She'd always gotten so much out of Pastor Jenkins's sermons. She hoped he could help her in her quest to forgive Gerald's parents and allow her to find peace again.

When everyone was seated, the pastor asked the congregation to stand and sing the Lord's Prayer. Laura was amazed at the deep timbre of Bradford's amazing singing voice as he sang, "And forgives us our trespasses, as we forgive those that trespass against us. And lead us not into temptation, but deliver us from evil. For thine is the kingdom, and the power, and the glory, forever and ever. Amen." Laura turned to Bradford and gave him a shy smile. He smiled back, hoping he and Laura could at least be friends. Nonetheless he was slowly realizing he wanted much more from her.

As Laura began to leave the church, several of the parishioners, wanting to visit, came up to her. Bradford overheard one of the women thank Laura for assisting her when her baby was born.

Laura smiled warmly at the newborn baby and asked to hold him. As she cuddled the infant, Bradford thought she had never been lovelier and would make a wonderful mother. He saw a caring side of Laura that was so unlike the shallow women to whom he was accustomed.

After church Jenny whispered loudly in Bradford's ear, "Would you like to come to our house for Sunday luncheon?"

Bradford chuckled, saying, "Ask your mother if that would be okay with her."

Overhearing their conversation, Ruth said, "Of course, Bradford! Please join us. Nanny and I will go back to the cottage to get everything ready. Why don't you, Laura, and Jenny ride back together? Please take your time. We have to get all the food ready," she encouraged with a shy wink.

Bradford turned hesitantly to Laura and asked, "Would you mind?"

Jenny jumped up and down as Laura laughed. "I think it's already been decided."

The day was resplendent. The morning rain had cooled down the woods as they rode along the road that wound its way to the cottage. Light sprinkles could be felt as the trees rocked gently in the breeze, releasing the morning mist. Laura took a deep breath, inhaling the slightly humid air, then released a sigh.

Bradford asked, "A penny for your thoughts?"

Laura grinned. "I just love the woods after a shower. The air is so refreshing. It reminds me of what Nanny calls a 'soft morning.'"

Bradford noticed how truly stunning Laura was with her fair skin, golden-brown hair, and sparkling violet eyes. She looked up at him as he also thought about her strength of character. She had been through the war and the loss of her husband and had still remained caring and warm to everyone around her. Laura was everything Bradford had always wanted in a lady.

Bradford thought about taking her into his arms but couldn't since Jenny was sitting between them. They soon came out of the cool shade of the surrounding oaks and rode to the front of the cottage.

He gently helped Jenny down from the carriage then reached for Laura, lifting her small, delicate figure down before pausing so he could have his arms around her slender waist a moment longer. He wanted to ask her why she hadn't let him take her home last night. If he could ever make peace with her, he felt he could fall deeply in love with her.

Laura quickly looked away when she noticed the longing in his light-blue eyes. Remembering how humiliated she had felt the previous evening as Saundra monopolized Bradford, she turned and abruptly went inside. A thought suddenly struck her—*could she be jealous?*

Barbecued pork, mashed potatoes, lima beans, and fresh corn from the garden were piled high in the serving bowls in the center of the table. Nanny placed a basket of light yeast rolls, along with an apple pie, by Bradford's side. After they said the blessing, Jenny reached toward the center of the table to show Bradford how to spin the turntable. Nanny had to scold Jenny so she wouldn't spin it too fast. Everyone thoroughly enjoyed the Southern-style meal. By the time the pie had vanished, they were all stuffed.

Immediately after the meal, Jenny looked at Bradford and asked, "Do you want to come outside and see my cat Tabby?"

Laura looked at Bradford and was surprised at the pleasant smile on his handsome face. She lightly scolded, "Jenny, Mr. Hampton may have other things he needs to do this afternoon."

He turned to Laura with a gleam in his eye. "I can't think of anything I'd rather do than to escort two beautiful ladies outside to see their cat."

Laura blushed at his compliment. Turning to Nanny and her mother, she suggested, "I should probably stay inside and help clean up."

As Nanny waved her hands, she practically hit Laura with her dishcloth and urged her to go outside with Bradford and Jenny.

Jenny picked up her small parasol and said in her charming Southern drawl, "Southern women know how the sun can ruin a lady's complexion."

Laura also picked up her parasol and smiled knowingly at Bradford.

He agreed, "That must be your secret, Jenny." He then offered one arm to Laura and the other to Jenny as they strolled into the bright sun.

Jenny soon released his arm, skipped ahead, and called out, "Here, kitty, kitty."

Tabby appeared around the side of the barn. Her very plump, gray body jiggled as she ran. Bradford chuckled. "I think you've been feeding Tabby too much."

Laura laughed too. "Bradford, Tabby is going to have kittens within the next couple of weeks."

"Oh," he said as he gently bent down to stroke Tabby's soft fur. The cat wove her body between his legs, showing her approval of the tall stranger.

When Laura saw how gently Bradford treated Jenny's Tabby, she knew he must be a kind, loving man, even though he was a Northerner.

Bradford stood and turned to look at Laura. He paused as he saw her look soften. He was hopeful that, with time, he could break through the wall she had built around herself. Maybe she could finally start thinking of someone besides Gerald.

Jenny grabbed his hand. "Now you must see our fish pond." She tugged at Bradford's hand and pulled him into the garden. He laughed as he and Laura followed her down the flagstone path to a small pond. Jenny smiled as she pointed to her light-brown guppies.

Bradford was very impressed with the fish pond. "Who made this nice pond?" he asked.

Laura sadly said, "My husband wanted to re-create the gardens they had at the Taylors' estate. But he wasn't able to finish digging the pond before he died, so Jenny and I have been working together on the task. We got the plants from the lake and were able to get the guppies there too. Jenny wants some lily pads and some really colorful fish, but I'm not sure where we can get them."

Bradford was saddened to see how Laura looked off into space when she talked about Gerald. Trying to lighten the mood, he turned to Jenny and said, "I have a secret...I know where we can find some lily pads and some goldfish."

Jenny was so excited that she jumped up and down. "When can we get them?"

Bradford faced them. "I'll bring them by later this afternoon if it's okay with you."

He started to leave as Laura looked up at him. She speculated why Bradford was hurrying away. She wondered whether he had to meet Saundra for some reason. Her concern was realized when he added, "I'll go by Camellia Hall. Saundra has an impressive goldfish pond and may have some extra fish she'd be willing to share. I'll go now and see what I can do for your pond."

Jenny was beside herself and said, "I'll be waiting for you to come back."

Laura turned abruptly and walked into the cottage.

True to his word, Bradford showed up later that afternoon with a bucketful of lily pads. Some of them had large yellow blooms; others had white blossoms. He also brought several brightly colored goldfish.

Jenny raced outside to greet him and smiled as she looked in the bucket.

Laura stayed inside, not wanting to see Bradford again that day. She didn't know what to do about her feelings for him. She felt a mixture of guilt and shame, for she had thought she would love only Gerald for the rest of her life. She was, however, confused about the emotions Bradford had awakened in her. Laura didn't know what to do. She felt it would be best if she just avoided seeing him altogether. Anyway, he seemed far too interested in Saundra. Suppressing her interest in him was the surest way to avoid getting hurt again, she reasoned.

Bradford was disappointed when Laura didn't come out of the cottage. Ruth told him she had a headache and was resting. Even though he was unhappy about not seeing Laura, he still had a great time helping Jenny place the fish and lily pads in her small pond. "Look, Jenny," he said. "Now the fish can hide from Tabby." As if following orders, one fish swam under a lily pad. Watching the brightly colored fish swim around and around only to disappear, Tabby crouched by the pond. Every now and then, her paw patted at the water very close to one of the new fish.

"Tabby, you leave those fish alone!" Jenny scolded her cat.

Bradford smiled, "Be sure to come to Oak Grove tomorrow so we can continue to train Scamp for the fair." At long last he mounted his black stallion. As he rode away, Jenny waved good-bye.

As he waved back, Bradford saw the upstairs curtains move ever so slightly. Laura gave him a small wave as she looked out at him. He sighed as he sadly mumbled under his breath, "Will she ever forget Gerald?"

Chapter Seven

An Act of Kindness Goes Wrong

❦

As the days flew by, Laura and her family settled into a pleasant routine at the cottage. She enjoyed working in the garden and around the fish pond. The lily pads were doing well, and she could have sworn the fish had already started to grow. When she saw many new little fish swimming in the pond, she thought maybe they'd had babies. She knew Jenny would be excited!

As the days turned into weeks, Laura rarely saw Bradford. Then, one day when she heard a rider approach, she came around the side of the cottage, wondering who was visiting so early on a Thursday morning. Smoothing out her gown, she strolled to the front, where a visitor would have tied up his horse.

Laura paused when she saw who had come to visit. Bradford had grown tan from all his outdoor activities on the plantation. His bronze skin blended nicely with his jet-black hair, which was slightly windblown from his ride. She caught her breath when she noticed his warm smile. Laura was glad Oak Grove had agreed so much with Bradford. He seemed to fit perfectly into the community too. Laura had heard many stories from her neighbors of his kindness toward them after the terrible drought the region was suffering. He had also infused cash into the local bank her father had started, and the loans helped local farmers replant their crops. Bradford seemed to be warming up to his new life, and Laura thought the change in his personality was very becoming.

Bradford climbed down from his horse and walked around to her. Hat in hand, he bowed slightly and said, "I was wondering if you, Jenny, your mother, and Nanny would care to join me for lunch."

Laura was surprised at his kind offer. She smiled at him as she said, "That would be very nice!"

He hesitated then said. "Will seeing Oak Grove be hard on you? Or would you rather have a picnic?"

Laura paused, thinking of his unexpected kindness about her feelings. She looked up, saying, "I wouldn't mind seeing Oak Grove at all since I'm so happy here. But I think we'd enjoy a picnic more. Jenny especially would like a picnic."

Bradford suggested, "How about tomorrow around eleven o'clock? Would that be too early?"

Laura replied, "That would be a good time. Can we bring anything?"

Bradford smiled. "My cook, Lily, would be offended if she didn't get to do all the cooking. I've told her over and over what a delicious Sunday luncheon you served me, and she wanted to do something special in return."

Humming a tune to herself, Laura went into the cottage. Nanny almost knocked her down as she quickly stood from crouching at the window. Laura laughed to herself as she accused in a stern voice, "Were you spying on me?"

Nanny, turning bright red, said, "Oh, no, Miss Laura. I just saw Bradford riding up and thought I'd better see what he needed."

Patting Nanny's shoulder, Laura said, "In case you didn't hear, we're going on a picnic tomorrow. Did you hear the time of eleven o'clock?" She smiled and winked at Nanny, who blushed again and nodded.

The next morning they were all getting ready to go on the picnic when a neighbor knocked on the door. "The Harrison's eldest son, Abraham, needs some salve," she told Laura. "He accidently burned his hand in the hearth."

Laura had taken the boy's family some preserves recently, and they'd been very thankful for the gift. Not wanting the child to be in pain, Laura quickly agreed to go, feeling certain she could be back before her eleven o'clock engagement. After applying an ointment to the child's hand, she hurried back to the cottage. Heading toward a sharp bend in the road, she heard a team of horses thundering down the road. Trying desperately to get out of the way, she saw Bradford pulling on the reins with all his might. Luckily she wasn't trampled.

After quickly jumping down, Bradford gently pulled her into his arms and whispered, "I'm so sorry. I've got to work on not driving so fast on these narrow roads."

For the first time in ages, Laura felt warm and safe as he held her gently in his arms. Breaking the moment, she looked up and said, "My, but you were in a hurry!"

"I didn't want to be late for our picnic."

"Jenny is so happy and can't wait. I feel the same way," Laura said.

"Let me help you into the carriage, and we'll go get her." Turning to raise her up, Bradford observed, "I'm very glad you weren't hurt." As he lifted her, he admired her shapely ankles as her skirt shifted a little higher than was proper.

Laura, in a ladylike manner, thanked him. Her cheeks turned red as she sensed he had seen her ankles before she adjusted her skirts.

Being a true gentleman, Bradford turned away from her to save her modesty.

When they pulled up at the cottage, Nanny, Jenny, and Ruth were eagerly waiting for them. They were surprised to see Laura sitting in the carriage next to Bradford. Facing Laura, Bradford said sadly, "I almost ran over this lovely lady."

"I'm just too fast for you." Laura grinned, blushing at his compliment. "I'm glad you gave me a ride back to the cottage. Otherwise I would've been late to our picnic."

Smiling, Jenny hopped into the carriage. "This is going to be so much fun!"

The group soon arrived at a lovely spot by the Mississippi River. They spread a blanket on the ground under a majestic oak tree whose mossy branches swept down to the ground. Jenny immediately started to climb a large limb as they put out the food. Everyone relaxed and enjoyed the delicious meal of ham, biscuits, strawberry jam, spiced peaches, sweet potatoes, and sliced tomatoes that Bradford's cook had gone all out in preparing. They especially liked her scrumptious pound cake. After the meal, as they rested on the blanket, Bradford announced that he had a surprise.

With expectant looks the group turned as Bradford reached into his pocket and pulled out a dazzling ring. A circle of lovely diamonds surrounded a sparkling amethyst.

Ruth gasped. "Why, that's my mother's ring. I've been looking for it for ages. Where did you find it?"

"I was going through your husband's desk and felt it in the very back of the drawer. I wanted to return it to its rightful owner." Bradford smiled as he held out the lovely ring.

"I always wanted Laura to have it," Ruth said. "Would you please see if the ring fits her?"

Before Laura could reach over to get it, Bradford took her hand and gently slipped it on the ring finger of her right hand. Laura jerked back and glared at him, her suspicions not allowing her to enjoy the ring at the moment. All she could think of was how he had violated her father's privacy when he had searched through the desk. Why had he done that?

The rest of the afternoon passed with tension in the air. Perplexed, Bradford couldn't figure out what he had done to upset Laura.

As they neared the cottage, Tabby, despite her large tummy, ran in front of the wagon. Jenny yelled, "Look out for Tabby!"

Bradford pulled on the reigns, saying, "Whoa! I can't believe she's gotten even bigger! She must be eating the goldfish I gave you."

Jenny sat up straighter. Looking offended, she said, "I've been counting the fish every day, and they're all there. We even have some new fish babies!" Everyone laughed, and Jenny smilingly added, "Mama said any day now we'll have some baby kittens too. I can't wait. They'll be so cute!"

Chapter Eight

Dark Clouds and High Winds

❦

The next day at breakfast, Jenny announced brightly, "Bradford—I mean, Mr. Hampton—said Scamp is ready to compete in the fair…that is, if it's all right with Mama," she added as she looked wistfully at Ruth, who was quickly agreeing. "He wants me to come over today to practice prancing. Scamp is doing so well. Could you all come and watch?"

The summer had flown by, and the days were becoming cooler as fall approached. Ruth and Nanny were concerned that the fall storms could stop them from making it to the market and buying flour and other supplies. Ruth said sadly, "We're sorry, Jenny, but we can't come today because we've already made plans. We'll come next time."

Looking crestfallen, Jenny turned to Laura. "You can come, though, can't you, Sissy?"

Laura was hoping to excuse herself too, since she needed to do some sewing. She also knew that after yesterday she needed to avoid Bradford, but she felt it would break Jenny's heart if she didn't go. So she agreed. "Of course I'll come. I wouldn't miss it. I know you must be good at showing Scamp. We want you to look like an experienced rider too. We'll tie your hair up into a ponytail so you'll look very professional for the show. I'll also make you a surprise for your debut."

Jenny leaped out of her chair, almost tipping over a large glass of milk. As she ran out the front door, she yelled over her shoulder, "I hear Mr. Hampton's carriage pulling up now. Please be there after lunch. I'm going to practice with Scamp now," she yelled, slamming the door behind her as she ran outside.

Waving to his carriage as Jenny hopped in, Laura laughed as she came back inside to clear the table. She had to admit that Bradford certainly had been kind to her daughter. If only he would stop his relentless probing. Her dear father had only wanted to help her when he borrowed the money. Laura felt resentment that Bradford couldn't let the matter drop.

Seeing her mother and Nanny ride off, Laura spent about an hour straightening up the kitchen. Then she went upstairs to her room. After crossing over to the balcony, she threw open the French doors, hoping to let some light into her room, which was too dark for sewing. Rain clouds were forming on the horizon. She sighed, thinking it was lucky that Nanny and her mother had gone in the opposite direction and that Bradford and Jenny had probably already reached Oak Grove. Because of the growing darkness, Laura moved to the balcony, set up a chair on the wooden overhang, and began to sew.

Time passed swiftly as she bent her head over the small gray riding habit she had decided to make as a surprise for Jenny. Suddenly she heard a faint boom and looked up to see dark, billowing clouds far in the distance. Realizing she had better leave immediately if she hoped to arrive at the plantation before the storm, she put her sewing away in the chest at the foot of her bed and raced downstairs.

Laura rushed to the barn, mounting their other horse. As she left the barn, she kept a watchful eye on the darkening clouds. She figured the storm was still miles away and doubted it would worsen until she reached Oak Grove. Nevertheless, as she approached the woods near the oak tree where Bradford had kissed her, she saw that the giant oak was no longer peacefully shading a spot in the road. Instead the raging winds were wildly whipping its limbs back and forth. The storm with its jagged streaks of lightning was clearly building rapidly.

The horse was skittish as Laura urged her mount into a gallop. The day grew even darker as she continued down the deeply rutted path beneath the canopy of live oaks. Suddenly the wind, with a force Laura couldn't imagine, snapped a huge oak in front of her. Startled, her horse reared up, throwing her to the ground. Stunned, Laura looked up to see her horse racing away from her.

Aching from the fall, she slowly stood. She knew she had to return quickly to the cottage, which couldn't be more than a half mile away. As she struggled to her feet, she realized the wind had been joined by a relentless rain. Laura looked up and saw flashes of lightning brightening the sky. Then she heard loud snapping noises in the distance as she realized the wind was forcefully thrashing the trees back and forth. Large branches crumpled beneath the weight of the heavy trunks of uprooted trees. The noises grew louder as the sky seemed to hurl its full force onto the soggy ground.

Every muscle strained as Laura approached the last quarter mile. Soaked, she staggered over untidy grounds covered with wet leaves and windswept debris. She realized she must have taken the wrong path. Then, as if in a dream, she felt herself falling into an opening in the ground before landing on a cushion of decaying leaves and moss.

As she lay at the bottom of the hole, she prayed, "Oh, Lord, please help me and keep Jenny, my mother, and Nanny safe." She asked for Bradford's safety in her prayer too, since she had been taught to love your enemies. Laura quickly thought she shouldn't deceive God, so she changed Bradford's standing to "friend."

She tried to make herself comfortable in the hole, which Laura came to realize was the old, dry well that someone had dug years ago near the cottage. She speculated that the storm must have blown away the well's protective railing. Straightening her legs to alleviate her cramping muscles, she glanced at the far corner of the well to see two yellow eyes glowing at her in the dark. She stifled a scream as she fell into a state of unconsciousness.

Meanwhile, back at Oak Grove, Bradford took Jenny inside when it looked like a storm was brewing. Gazing up at Bradford with her big blue eyes, she asked him with fear in her voice, "Do you think Sissy is still coming even though there's a storm?"

"Did she say she would?"

"Oh, yes. She promised. And Sissy never breaks a promise," Jenny said.

Bradford reassured her. "I'll find Sissy. Stay here with Lily. She'll take good care of you. She'll probably even let you help her cook if you ask politely."

After running to the stable, Bradford jumped onto his horse and rode toward the cottage. The wind was picking up speed, making it hard for him to make his way through the woods. The heavy rain dripped down the brim of his hat. Barely able to see, he soon lost his way. He kept circling around what looked like the same tree. Suddenly he spied one of the horses from the cottage nervously standing under an oak. His heart sank when he realized there was no rider. In fact Laura wasn't anywhere around. Knowing the horse would lead him back to the cottage, he jumped onto the animal and urged her forward, pulling his horse behind. The way was slow because trees were down everywhere. When he finally arrived at the cottage, he saw a large oak tree lying on top of Laura's cottage, its limbs sticking out of the bay window. He frantically yelled, "Laura! Laura!"

It seemed like hours before Laura awoke to see the sun brightening the gloomy sky. Remembering the yellow eyes, she froze. She dared not even look around for fear that the wild animal might attack. Her eyes gradually adjusted to the darkness. The light from the sun helped her see that she was only about ten feet down. Even so, she knew she couldn't climb out without help because the walls of the old well were straight and slippery. A shudder ran down her back as she realized she would be trapped in this hole until her mother and Nanny returned, which could be hours away. Lying perfectly still, she heard her name being called from a long way off. Gradually the voice grew louder and louder until it sounded as though it came from directly overhead.

Fear constricted her voice. If she cried out, she wondered, would the animal attack? On the other hand, she might lie here for days if she didn't. Realizing this, she screamed, "I'm down here!"

Bradford heard her desperate cry and bent over, shining a torch in the hole. "Laura, are you all right? It looks like you have some friends to keep you company."

With terror in her eyes, she slowly looked around to see Tabby curled up next to her three new kittens. The mother cat had been missing since the previous evening, and Nanny suspected she must have had her litter. Laura burst out laughing when she realized that when she had fallen into the well, she probably had scared the poor mama cat and her kittens even more than Tabby's eyes had frightened her.

Bradford yelled down, "Here! Grab this rope, and I'll pull you up. But first put Tabby and her kittens in this basket I found, and I'll pull them up."

After Tabby and her kittens were safely out of the well, a stiff Laura grabbed the rope. She tied it around her waist and then gripped it with all her might as Bradford pulled her out of the hole.

Laura was stunned at what she saw. Huge oak limbs littered the grounds. Pine trees were snapped in half. As she turned around, slowly eyeing the destruction, she saw a mere shell of her cottage that was barely standing under the weight of a large oak tree. She bent down and picked up an arm of one of Jenny's dolls that had been ripped from its body and tossed to the other side of the yard. She shuddered as she thought of what might have happened if she had made it back to the cottage.

Realizing her thoughts, Bradford put his arm around her shoulders and led her back to her horse. After helping her mount, he walked beside her until they came to his horse, which he had tied to a nearby tree. Looking up at her, he asked, "Will you be okay riding?"

She nodded reassuringly. "I'll be fine."

Bradford and Laura didn't speak as they rode, carefully avoiding the debris. The destruction forced them to move slowly back to Oak Grove. Bradford had lined a basket with soft hay for the kittens and tied it to his saddle. Riding like royalty, Tabby curled up around her new kittens.

Chapter Nine

The Path to Forgiveness

❧

The minute they reached Oak Grove, Bradford helped Laura into her former bedroom and sent for a maid to help her clean up.

After a cool bath, Laura put on one of her dresses that she had accidentally left behind when she moved to the cottage. Laura went downstairs to see Jenny and embraced her. She was very grateful her child was safe. Tears slowly trickled down her cheeks. Not thinking, she clutched Jenny tightly in her arms as she whispered, "I'm so thankful my baby is fine."

Bradford had quietly entered the room and witnessed the scene. As he started to leave the room, Jenny wiggled free and ran up to him, saying, "Is Scamp okay? How are Tabby and her kittens?"

Quickly regaining her composure, Laura turned around to find Bradford's inquisitive eyes staring hard at her. Then he lifted Jenny in his strong arms, as he said, "Scamp is warm and safe in the barn. The stable-boy will take you to see him along with Tabby's new kittens now if you'd like." When he placed Jenny on the floor, she ran out of the room behind the stable-boy. Laura and Bradford heard her chatter far down the hall as she asked an endless number of questions about the kittens.

With Jenny out of the room, the silence was overwhelming as Bradford and Laura stared at each other. Laura turned away to look out of the window, watching the sun's rays struggle through the dark clouds.

Breaking the silence, she said, "Thank you for rescuing me today. I don't believe my imagination could have stood it much longer. I just knew Tabby had to be a rat or some other horrid creature." She continued, "Lily told me the roads aren't that bad, but Mother and Nanny have decided to stay in town tonight. I understand you sent them a message shortly after you found me."

Bradford had been studying her very intensely and replied, "Yes, they're fine. I'm glad they decided to spend the night at the inn. They'll be back tomorrow afternoon. Unfortunately it looks like your cottage was right in the path of a tornado. You and your family are welcome to stay here as long as it takes to get the cottage back in order. Fortunately Oak Grove wasn't damaged at all."

Laura apologized, "I guess we have no choice but to impose on you. I hope we won't be too much of a burden, because it might be a long time before the cottage can be rebuilt."

"Sit down, Laura, for there are some matters I must discuss with you if we're going to live in peace under the same roof," Bradford said sternly.

She sank into a big leather chair by the fire and stared at the flames dancing on the logs. Weary, she looked at him and sighed, "Yes?"

Sitting by her, he said, "First I want you to know I didn't come here to find out why your father lost the money my father loaned him. I knew your father lost a great deal of money by investing in timber. After the war the North wasn't willing to pay a reasonable price for lumber."

Laura stood, her eyes flashing with flames that matched those in the fire. "I will not sit here and listen to you tell me what a poor businessman my father was!"

Bradford commanded, "I'm trying to set straight a conversation we had on our way to Saundra's ball. I guess I'll have to explain a little of my background to you first."

Laura reluctantly sat back in the chair as he proceeded. "My mother died when I was only two. My father was torn apart with grief, since he loved her deeply. Unable to turn that love to me, he became obsessed with making money. All he ever talked to me about was how to become rich. He never let anything get in his way of turning a profit."

Laura was saddened by the picture of his childhood he was drawing in her mind. It explained a lot about his cold, stern attitude. She felt touched that he was exposing himself, which she knew had to be hard for him to do.

A hurt appeared deep in his sad eyes as he continued. "I never had any friends, for my father said I must keep busy studying for the day when I'd take over the huge business dealings he had begun." He added quietly, "Often at other's expense. He never showed any mercy, for he was shrewd and always seemed to know how to beat the other fellow." His eyes turned to hers. "He had never shown any concern for anyone except when he gave the money to your father. When I asked him why he allowed your father to have the money, he would only say, 'My friend desperately needed my help.'

"I have to find out why he broke his cardinal rule," Bradford uttered as his gaze tried to penetrate Laura's mind; he hoped she could possibly shed light on the subject. He so desperately wanted to understand his father's sole act of kindness. Exasperated, he stood, abruptly saying, "Jenny is your child…not your sister. That must have something to do with the money."

The blood drained from Laura's pale face as she looked up into his clear blue eyes. Realizing he knew the truth, she stammered, "How'd you ever guess?"

He said gently, "I guess I've suspected it all along because of the way you look at her. When you spoke of her as your baby, just now, I knew it had to be true. But why have you hidden this from everyone, even Jenny?"

"First you must promise never to tell a soul what I'm about to tell you," Laura said solemnly, looking into his intense eyes.

Bradford sank back down into the chair by her, nodding in assent. Then she began, "Gerald and I were young, and so very much in love, but his father objected to the marriage. He wanted his son to marry someone with wealth and power in order to rebuild what they'd lost in the war. Gerald insisted, however, that we marry, regardless of his father's wishes, and I agreed."

Bradford reached over and squeezed her hand as if urging her to go on. "We were married only a short while before the accident. Gerald's father was angry and had the marriage annulled as soon as he found out his son had died. Several months later I discovered I was going to have Gerald's child. I didn't want Gerald's father to take my baby away. He already had taken so much away from me, and I knew he'd do whatever it took to claim our child, since he now had no immediate heirs. So my mother agreed to pretend the baby was hers. My father borrowed the money from your father, unknowingly to me, so we could become wealthy again and I could finally gain the approval of Gerald's father. I would then be able to claim Jenny as my own, and all would be well."

Bradford, still holding her hand, said, "That explains so much. I guess my father wanted to help yours because he knew what had happened." A small smile touched his lips as he supposed, "It proves he was able to show kindness to a friend, even though he was heartless to so many others. What's the name of Gerald's father? Maybe he's an acquaintance of mine."

Laura, still feeling the strength of his warm fingers on hers, replied, "Judge Gerald Taylor Senior."

"That explains everything," Bradford said sadly. "My father and Judge Taylor were once close friends, but when one of their business deals went bad, they became bitter enemies. I guess my father was still trying to prove his power with money. At least he did help your father out," he added as he continued to hold her long, slender fingers. "After my father died, I went to the Taylors' home to make peace and renew our friendship." Bradford felt her tense up as he noted, "It turns out they're actually welcoming and forgiving people. They all but adopted me as their son."

Unbelieving, Laura stared at him as he continued, "I think if you'd find it in your heart to forgive them, you wouldn't find them the hardened people you imagine them to be."

Quickly she struggled to free her hands as she stood. "After the way they treated me and didn't even bother to get to know me as their only son's wife? Their punishment will be to never find out about Jenny."

Bradford walked over to her and put his strong arms around her. Almost in a whisper, he said, "Quit fighting the past. It's a terrible misunderstanding that never should have happened. War is devastating; it causes people to do things they shouldn't. I want to show you what my mother wrote in her Bible." He bent down and gently placed a small Bible in her hands. He pointed out what his mother had written about forgiveness being the way to true happiness. "I also want you to be happy now, for I—"

He wasn't able to finish his statement, as a raspy female voice interrupted them. "My, my, how cozy," Saundra said as she sashayed into the room, her red hair piled high into a perfect coiffure.

Startled, Bradford and Laura quickly drew apart. His stern voice filled the room as he demanded, "Why weren't you announced?"

Saundra smugly answered, "Since I've been coming here so often, I didn't see any sense in continuing with the formalities. Anyway, weren't you expecting me for the dinner you promised me? I thought we were going to eat alone," she said pointedly, staring at Laura's flushed cheeks.

Embarrassed and feeling she was in the way, Laura excused herself and ran to her room. Exhaustion from the day's events soon enveloped her, and she fell into a deep sleep, oblivious to Saundra's raucous laughter from the floor below.

Upon rising the next morning, Laura went downstairs for breakfast. As early as she was, she realized that Jenny and Bradford had already eaten and were outside preparing for the fair, which was only a couple of weeks away. Yesterday's nightmare when her cottage was destroyed was still vivid in Laura's memory. She knew it was a blessing that no one had been hurt, but she was still saddened to know that a place so special to her was in ruins.

After eating, Laura went outside. Proud as any mother could be, she walked over to stand by Bradford, who was giving his talented student instructions. She was instantly aware of the progress Jenny had made.

Glancing over at Laura, he whispered to her, "You have every right to be very proud of your daughter."

No one had ever said this to her before, and she gratefully beamed back at him. Seeing them smile at each other, Jenny quickly rode up to two of her favorite people.

"Could we please go on a picnic this afternoon?" she asked anxiously.

"Sure," said Bradford, smiling at Laura questioningly.

"I'd enjoy it too," Laura agreed. "I'll go inside and get a basket of food prepared," she said as she went into the house.

She marveled to herself as she thought what a relief it was that someone finally knew the secret she had held in her heart for so long. She busily packed a basket of food, complete with a freshly baked chocolate cream cake that smelled heavenly.

Laura took the basket to the open carriage and placed it on the seat behind Bradford. He jumped down and helped her into the carriage. Once they were underway, they rode off into the deeply shaded canopy road. He turned to Jenny and Laura and asked, "Would you mind going to the cottage before we eat to see how my workers are doing looking through the debris? Hopefully some of your possessions can be saved since it stopped raining right after your cottage was destroyed. Jenny, we can also see how the goldfish pond survived the storm." Jenny and Laura agreed, hoping they could help search for their belongings too.

It didn't take long to reach the cottage that morning. By the time they arrived workers were busily looking for anything salvageable and mounding the rubbish into a large pile to be burned. After getting out of the carriage, Bradford cautioned Jenny to be careful, and helped Laura to the pond. Jenny ran over and said, "Look! It's fine!" The pond was covered with lily pads. Jenny lifted up one of the pads, exclaiming, "I think we have even more baby fish."

Bending over, Bradford lifted a limb that had fallen into the pond. He looked as Jenny pointed out several small goldfish rapidly swimming under another lily pad on the far side of the pond. Laura turned away and walked to the other side of the cottage near the huge pile of rubble.

Circling the pile, she spied the small broom Gerald had made for her. She quickly removed the broom from the edge of the pile of debris and placed it in the back of the carriage. Puzzled, Bradford came up behind her. "If you see anything else, please get it before it's burned. The men found your trunk under the bed, and luckily, it wasn't damaged. It has already been taken to Oak Grove."

Laura turned and thanked him. She called Jenny to come over so they could both look through the pile.

Jenny turned this way and that, looking at the mound of debris. She couldn't see anything that might be important, so she looked up, saying, "It's time to go on our picnic." Laura sadly agreed, realizing that most of their possessions had been destroyed.

Having learned his lesson the day he almost ran over Laura, Bradford drove slowly through the small winding roads framed by lines of pine trees. Finally he pulled up next to a lake filled with swans serenely swimming by.

"Let's stop now," Jenny exclaimed as she hopped out of the buggy. Bradford placed the picnic basket on the ground near Jenny, and she immediately began to finger the food, groaning loudly, "I am *soooo* hungry."

Laughing, Bradford swung Laura down from the buggy, allowing his hands to rest a little longer than usual around her slender waist.

Her soft pink lips parted as she smiled up at him, confessing, "I'm hungry too."

They sat down and stuffed themselves on fried chicken, fresh-baked rolls, and potato salad, finishing the meal with the chocolate cream cake. Finally full, Jenny stood up and declared, "Let's go exploring!"

Bradford and Laura were both so full they told her to run ahead but not to go too far. He turned to Laura and said, "I didn't finish our conversation last night because Saundra interrupted us. Now I'd like to tell you how much I've cared for you since the first day I saw you on the balcony." He took her in his arms and kissed her with a desire that matched her own. It seemed the world was just theirs as the swans peacefully floated by.

As he released her, Laura turned to him and said, "I'll always love Gerald, but—"

Not waiting to hear the end of her sentence, Bradford glared at her as he walked over to the carriage. "You can live with his memories forever. Be sure not to leave this small broom in the carriage. It probably has something to do with Gerald. We'll go now. I won't bother you again," he vowed as he loaded their things in the buggy and brusquely handed her the broom.

Laura said, "Wait, you haven't let me explain."

"All you care about is Gerald, and I'm sure that's the way it'll always be. Let's go now." Bradford looked at the wedding ring she still wore. He chided himself for being such a fool and falling for someone who loved another.

Just then Jenny ran up to the buggy. Sensing something was wrong, even she was quiet. They all rode back to Oak Grove in silence.

Laura wanted to cry, for she knew Bradford would never understand her feelings for Gerald. He wouldn't even allow her to finish her statement. She just wasn't ready to accept the raging emotions that were beginning to stir within her. These emotions had lain dormant for so long. She simply felt she needed more time.

Upon returning to the plantation, Jenny and Bradford walked to the pasture to watch the horses graze. Laura went inside, where Nanny and Ruth warmly greeted her in the parlor.

Nanny said, "We're so thankful the tornado didn't harm you or Jenny. The storm didn't cause much damage in town except for some fallen limbs and debris. So we had little trouble making our way back to Oak Grove."

"Bradford sent us a message last night that the cottage had been damaged and told us to come here," Ruth informed Laura.

Laura sadly said, "The cottage has been totally destroyed. We won't be able to live there until it's been rebuilt from the ground up."

Ruth's face was filled with bewilderment as she cried, "But where will we go? None of our relatives are living."

Laura calmly reassured her, "Bradford has assured me that we may stay here until we find other accommodations."

"He's truly been a generous man. He's especially been kind to our Jenny," Ruth said with a sigh.

Laura's heart cried out as she thought of the distrust she had felt for Bradford for so long. If only he had let her explain that she needed more time to get over Gerald. Trying to think about something else, she replied, "We must do all we can to help run the household so we won't be a burden."

Nanny and Ruth agreed and went off to help Lily with dinner. Laura headed upstairs to assist with the domestic chores.

After straightening up Jenny's room, she decided to dress for dinner. She put on one of the gowns that had been found in the wreckage of the cottage. Luckily it hadn't been damaged because she had stored it, along with Jenny's gray riding habit, in the chest at the foot of her bed. The pale-green gown with its dark-green sash and matching collar accentuated her creamy complexion. The gown's puffy sleeves were very attractive on her slender arms.

As she entered the drawing room, she heard the high-pitched laughter that she knew to be Saundra's. Quietly she entered the dining room and sat at the end of the table, away from Saundra and Bradford. Saundra was so absorbed in what Bradford was saying that she was initially unaware of Laura's entry. As she turned around, she immediately saw Laura.

Laura shuddered as she saw the hate that seemed to glow like hot coals in Saundra's eyes. Saundra was quick to disguise this from Bradford as she said, "Bradford was just telling me you'll be his guest for a short while."

"Yes," Laura replied. "We'll try to help out as much as possible so as not to be a burden."

Until then Bradford had looked at her coolly, but when Laura said how she wanted to help, a faint smile touched his lips.

Saundra, immediately aware of his smile, cattily remarked, "I know Bradford will enjoy having some extra maids around."

Laura stood up, saying, "I guess the help should eat in the kitchen. Excuse me."

Before she could leave, Bradford rose, towering over her. He loudly proclaimed, "You are guests in this house and will stay where you are. Also, would you please ask Ruth and Nanny to join us?"

Saundra was totally shocked at his voracious defense of Laura and her family and tried to appear unconcerned, but deep inside she was seething.

Laura excused herself and went in search of her mother and Nanny, who gladly joined them. Jenny also skipped gaily into the room. After thanking Saundra for the colorful fish and lily pads for her pond, Jenny seated herself next to Bradford, chattering happily about showing Scamp at the fair. Saundra's face turned red as she sat fuming throughout dinner.

Over the next few days, Laura seldom saw Bradford. In fact he seemed to go out of his way to avoid her. When she did see him for brief periods, she was aware of a new aloofness that was increasingly hard to bear. She so wished they could be friends again.

Laura was having fun helping out again at what she still thought of as her home. After the war she and her mother had done most of their own chores; she loved staying busy. Nevertheless Bradford had hired so many extra staff that Laura actually had lots of time to herself.

One day Laura told her mother, "I'm going to talk to Pastor Jenkins. I won't be long." She mounted a horse and waved at Jenny, who was in the corral training Scamp. Laura rode through a shaded lane toward the chapel. The day was cool and pleasant during her short ride. Along the way she thought about what was troubling her and how the pastor might help her. When she arrived, she knocked on the door of the chapel. Pastor Jenkins stood aside and motioned her inside. She followed him into his small office and sat in a chair opposite him. His jovial smile helped her relax as she quickly came to the point of her visit.

"I know you know so much about me and can appreciate how hard it has been since Gerald's death. I want to be able to forgive his family for all they've done to me, but I find it so hard to do so. For a long time, I've been so busy that I haven't thought about my anger and hurt. Now that I'm back at Oak Grove, I've had a lot of time to think, which seems to only make matters worse."

Pastor Jenkins paused before saying, "To be able to forgive doesn't come easy to any of us, especially when we've been wronged as you have. Let me share one of my favorite biblical passages on forgiveness." He then read from Colossians 3:13: "'Bear with each other and forgive one another if any of you has a grievance against someone. Forgive as the Lord forgave you.'"

The pastor advised, "You must change your heart, Laura. When you let go of anger and bitterness, it will free you. Forgiveness takes time. The process is very slow, but the reward will be a freedom that can come only from the Lord."

A small ray of light came though the window of Pastor Jenkins's office, as if to show God's endorsement of the pastor's wisdom. Laura looked pleased. She knew now what she must do. It would take time and would be hard, but she wanted to be free—free from her anger over all her losses, including those regarding Bradford.

Before Laura reached the corner of the churchyard, Pastor Jenkins called her name. After she walked back to the church, he asked, "If you have some extra time on your hands, would you be interested in helping some of the adults in the community learn to read? The teacher we have is presently sick with pneumonia. Reading opens a whole world to people, and I think this would help keep your mind busy. Helping others is rewarding and often helps the giver as much as the person receiving the help."

Laura paused. Then her face lit up. "That's something I can do to help. How many will be coming to the class?"

"Right now we just have a few. Lily is coming from Oak Grove regularly and has made good progress. We're hoping more will join them."

Laura thanked Pastor Jenkins as she walked toward her horse. She already felt her burden lighten as she thought about what she needed to accomplish. Each day she would pray that she could learn to forgive. By doing so she would be obeying the wishes of the Lord and, hopefully, would find the true happiness Bradford's mother had written about in her Bible.

The next evening Laura walked to the church with Lily to meet the adults attending the reading class. Laura found it was great fun to teach such eager students.

When the regular teacher recovered from her pneumonia, Laura became her assistant. Once, when she was leaving to go to the class, Bradford asked her, "Where are you going?"

Laura's eyes lit up as she explained, "I'm teaching a class of adults how to read. It's so rewarding. They're learning quickly. I hope it's okay that I'm using some of your books from the library. I haven't seen you, or I would have asked earlier."

Bradford hadn't realized she was doing this, since he had been trying to avoid her in order to keep his promise not to bother her anymore. "I'm so glad you found something so fulfilling to do with your time. I have no problem with your using the books. I'm very proud of you!"

Laura was pleased with his praise and smiled brightly at him. It was becoming easier and easier to forgive him after all he had done to help her and her family. Now she just needed to learn to forgive Gerald's parents, and her prayers would be answered.

Chapter Ten

Missing!

❦

inally the day of the fair arrived. Jenny was overcome with excitement. She was like a ball bouncing everywhere…house, yard, and stable. Laura could hardly stop her long enough to give her daughter the gray riding habit she had made. Jenny was ecstatic about her outfit and immediately put it on. She enthusiastically ran outside to show it to Bradford. He highly praised Jenny's new outfit before returning to his last-minute preparations with Scamp. Then he lifted her onto Scamp's back and gave her the reins. Jenny sat proudly, with her chin held high, as her pony posed. Laura's face beamed with pride as she admired her daughter.

Later that morning Laura, Ruth, and Nanny rode to the fair. Jenny followed with Bradford so she could help with Scamp.

Laura loved the festive air of the fair. Ladies dressed in brightly colored gowns gathered in the stands before the riding competition. Gentlemen milled around laughing. Several were trying their luck at target shooting. She pushed her way through the crowds to the stands, where she found some good seats for her as well as Ruth and Nanny. They waited anxiously for the events to begin.

A short, stocky man blew a bugle that started the adult competition. After several riders had competed, Laura became aware of Bradford riding into the ring on his black stallion. He rode his horse through all the maneuvers with a noticeable ease. The crowd watched in awe as he easily jumped the highest bar, clearing it by several inches. The applause grew even louder when he received the tall silver cup of victory for first place. Turning his stallion to face the crowd, he smiled as he rode out of the ring, a cloud of dust flying up behind him. After a few moments, Laura saw his towering figure edge through the crowd toward her. Sitting next to her, he whispered, "Jenny will be next. She insisted I sit by you." He looked out over the young girls on their ponies.

Laura immediately saw Jenny and, in her enthusiasm, grabbed Bradford's arm and pointed her out. Feeling him stiffen at her touch, she removed her hand. Glancing up at him, she saw he was looking at her with a distant stare that made her heavyhearted.

Looking away from each other, they turned their attention to the competition. The children had spent many hours practicing for this event. As they skillfully rode through the maneuvers, all appeared confident. The judges would have a tough time deciding who would be the winner.

Then Jenny started her performance. With a special flair, she saluted the crowd as Scamp bowed.

Everyone applauded when she turned her pony around and lightly tapped him with her foot. Scamp immediately pranced with both style and showmanship. Jenny sat straight and tall as her pony broke into a trot and gracefully cleared a low barrier that had been placed in the middle of the field. Afterwards she rode over to the line of children and waited for the judges to make their decision. The crowd was still as the judges announced that Jenny and Scamp were the first-place winners. Laura knew Jenny could never have won without Bradford's patient, diligent training. She turned toward him and saw a wide grin fill his face as Jenny struggled to lift the silver cup that was every bit as big and heavy as his own. Since no one was allowed to leave the stadium until after the mayor's speech, Laura waited restlessly. After the long speech, Bradford turned to face her and saw her struggle for the words to thank him. He gently reached out and placed his fingers on her lips, "There's no need to thank me, for I love Jenny as though she were my own." Before Laura could reply, he stood and went to the stables to get her daughter.

Moments later people surrounded Laura, Ruth, and Nanny to compliment them on Jenny's success. All Laura could do was wonder how she would ever get away so she could congratulate Jenny. Suddenly, over the crowd, she saw Bradford push his way toward her. As he impatiently edged closer, she saw deep lines on his forehead, as though something was particularly bothering him.

He rushed to her side, and said, "Something's happened to Jenny!"

Laura's face turned white as she took the arm he was holding out for her. He skillfully edged her through the crowd so he could talk to her alone. Nanny and Ruth remained behind, trapped by well-wishers enthusiastically offering their congratulations.

"Jenny has disappeared!" Bradford told Laura.

Stunned, Laura could only utter, "What happened to her?"

He spoke as calmly as he could. "It appears that after the show, while we were listening to that boring speech, Jenny returned to the stables. The stableboy said she got into a wagon with a man, and they rode off together. He also said that the driver of the wagon had been in a deep discussion with a lady right before he took Jenny away."

Turning to the crowd, Bradford yelled, "Ladies and gentlemen, may I have your attention? Have any of you seen Jenny Malcolm?"

Hearing the concern in his voice, the sheriff rushed over to Bradford.

The crowd looked stunned. No one had any information; everyone said they hadn't seen her since the competition.

The sheriff spoke loudly to the crowd. "I want all the men to divide up and search in different directions. Start with the homes that are closest to here then work away from the fairgrounds. Report back to the jail tonight. Ladies, please look around the fairgrounds." Speaking directly to Ruth, he said, "We'll do everything we can to get your daughter back. I'll be by Oak Grove tonight to let you know what we discover."

Bradford quickly jumped on his horse and yelled, "I'll head north."

Ruth and Nanny rushed to Laura's side. The three women then ran into the stables to see if Scamp was still there. When they found the pony quietly eating hay, they rushed outside to look around. Finding nothing there, they went through the woods and then on to neighbors' homes close to the fairgrounds. They didn't return to Oak Grove until late that night.

The sheriff knocked on the door shortly after they arrived home. He reported, "So far no one has found out anything. We'll continue the search tomorrow. Don't worry, we'll find Jenny."

That night Laura fell into a fretful sleep, dreaming of Jenny. In her nightmare she could almost touch her daughter, only to see Jenny being snatched away by a big strong man and forcefully dragged to a wagon. Thrashing around in bed, Laura cried out, "Jenny!"

Ruth, hearing her call out, rushed into her room and shook Laura awake. Consoling her, she said, "Laura, Jenny will be fine. Please calm down." She hugged Laura as her only child cried softly into her shoulder.

"Do you think he'd harm her?" Laura asked, wiping the tears from her eyes.

"We must not think such things," Ruth answered firmly. "We must trust God to take care of her."

"Maybe there's some way we could help tomorrow," Laura said, as a spark of hope lit her face. "I'll go back to that stable. Maybe I can identify the woman who spoke to the man who took Jenny."

"Yes, dear, that's the best thing you can do for Jenny," Ruth replied, patting her on the shoulder. "Now go back to sleep so you'll be fresh to start your search."

Before going to sleep, Laura prayed, "Please, Lord, lead me to find the right clues to find my darling daughter." She eventually fell asleep after turning her fears over to God.

In the morning she awakened, hopeful and eager, to begin her search to discover what she could about Jenny's whereabouts. Laura knew she had to keep up her strength, so she forced herself to eat the breakfast Lily had made. After Laura ate as much as she could, she thanked Lily and ran to the stables so she could get into the carriage as quickly as possible. She told the driver to go directly to the stables where the fair had been held.

Upon arriving at the fairgrounds, she got out and walked over to an elderly man who was brushing down a chestnut mare. "Excuse me, sir, but could you tell me if the young man who worked here yesterday is still in the stables?" She had to yell as the old man held a cupped hand up to his ear, straining to hear every word.

"You must mean Joey Blackburn," the old man said very softly. "He only works here on the weekends to earn some extra money."

"Where is he now?" Laura asked as loudly as she could.

"During the week Joey helps his pa out at the grain mill. That's about seven miles down the road."

"Thank you," Laura said, as she hurried to the carriage. After telling the driver where to go, she sank back in her seat, hoping Joey would be able to give her some clue as to what had happened to Jenny.

Soon they pulled up outside of the mill. Frowning, the driver said, "You sure you want to go in there?"

Laura nodded as she climbed down from the carriage. The driver escorted her up the rickety wooden steps that led to a door. After she knocked three times, the door swung open, and a man appeared, his huge frame filling the entire door. "Whatcha want?" he barked.

Taken aback by his rude attitude, Laura replied, "May I speak to Joey Blackburn?"

"My son's busy now," he answered, starting to shut the door in her face.

Laura stuck out her foot to prevent him from closing the door and asked, "When can I see him?"

"Come back at noon. He'll be eating lunch, and you can talk then. What is it you want with him anyway?" the man asked, his big watery eyes looking at her suspiciously.

"I heard he was good with horses and thought he might occasionally help me out at my stables," she offered, grasping at anything she could think of.

"Oh," he said, finally succeeding in slamming the door.

Laura glanced at her watch, realizing she had more than a two-hour wait before Joey would eat lunch.

The dilapidated mill was far from Vicksburg, but a small village lay a short distance up the road. Laura climbed into the carriage and went to the outskirts of the town. She tried to eat some of the food Nanny had packed for her but could swallow only a couple of bites.

Since Laura was getting cold sitting in the carriage, she decided to walk around the small town, hoping this would calm her so she could question Joey effectively.

The walk did nothing to warm her. Still cold and worried, Laura entered the general store. The storekeeper startled her from her aimless wandering through the store. "Ma'am, may I help you? You've been holding that hammer for several minutes. Is there a problem?"

Laura quickly dropped the tool. "I'm so sorry. Please excuse me," she mumbled before quickly leaving the store in embarrassment.

The weather was getting noticeably cooler as Laura saw a dress shop next door. Seeking warmth she quietly entered the small shop. She still had almost an hour before she could meet Joey Blackburn and hoped the dressmaker would allow her to sit by her fire and get warm until it was time to go. Laura's family had been short on funds for some time, and she hadn't been in the shop recently since its gowns were especially costly.

The elderly owner came up to her and asked, "May I serve you? I'm Mrs. Periwinkle. I own this shop."

"It's been a while since I've been here. I have an appointment in an hour, and it's so cold in my carriage." Laura asked, "May I please sit by your fire?"

"Of course, dear. Sit right there by the fire." Once Laura warmed up, Mrs. Periwinkle asked her, "Would you mind looking at a dress I think would be perfect for you?"

Not wanting to appear rude, Laura walked over and fingered the luxurious material that was being made into an evening dress. She lightly touched the lavender gown that shimmered in the sun as the rays came through the shop's bay window.

"Isn't it pretty?" the seamstress commented, adding, "I was making it for one of my customers who no longer wished to have this particular style. It looks as though it would fit you perfectly. I could give it to you for the cost of my labor, since the lady has already paid for the silk. This is a very special organdy silk imported from France," Mrs. Periwinkle added proudly.

"Oh," said Laura, "today I just don't feel like trying on clothes."

Mrs. Periwinkle saw the deep sorrow her customer's eyes held, and said, "Trying on clothes always makes a woman feel better. Come on in the dressing room and take a moment to see how nice this dress will look on you." Before Laura knew what was happening, the cheerful but insistent shop owner had ushered her into the dressing room and had begun to measure her for the finishing touches on the gown, hoping Laura would like it. As she busied herself around Laura, she chattered gaily.

"What part of the county are you from?" the seamstress inquired. Learning that Laura lived in northern Warren County, Mrs. Periwinkle said, "Why, I just finished making several new gowns for Saundra Boulogne. Do you know her?"

After discovering that Laura did indeed know her, she continued. "Seems she was going to a charming town northeast of here called Cameron Falls to visit a judge. She had some very pretty dresses made for the occasion. One was a deep-blue gown with a white bodice covered with lace."

Startled, Laura vaguely remembered a rumor that Gerald's parents had moved to Cameron Falls. Surely Saundra couldn't have anything to do with them anymore. She brushed the thought aside, realizing there could be other judges in that town.

"Look how beautiful you are!" Mrs. Periwinkle said as she looked at Laura. "The dress looks like it was made for you. The pleats on the front panel of the skirt are the latest look, but my patron, Miss Coleson, for whom I made this gown, thought they made her look too thick in the waist. The pleats conceal pockets in which you can put your fan and dance card. For you, the pleats nicely accentuate your slender waist."

Laura turned around and examined herself in the mirror. The shimmering light purple of the lovely silk complemented the ring that Bradford had found and that she was now proudly wearing. The seamstress seemed saddened that Laura didn't appear to like the dress and lowered the price even more. Knowing she owed the seamstress for her kindness, Laura finally agreed to take the dress.

"Thank you for letting me sit by your warm fire, but I have to go now." Laura realized she would arrive at the mill just in time if she left immediately. As she headed toward the mill, she prayed her talk with Joey Blackburn would be successful.

Arriving at the mill, Laura saw a boy with straight brown hair sitting on dilapidated stairs, hurriedly eating his lunch. He looked up as she swiftly climbed out of the carriage and approached him.

"May I speak with you now?" she inquired.

"Yes'm," the boy replied timidly.

"I told your father I'd like you to come to my stables sometime and help. In truth they're no longer mine, but I know Mr. Hampton would welcome your aid, since he was saying just the other day he was short of good help at Oak Grove."

Joey's eyes lit up as he explained, "Working with horses is what I love best."

"Also," Laura quickly continued, not wanting to interrupt his lunch for too long, "could you tell me more about the lady who was talking to the man yesterday when the little girl disappeared from the fair?"

Joey said, "I really can't say anything about the woman since her back was to me."

Laura desperately pleaded, "What kind of dress was she wearing? Did you hear her voice? Any clue at all might save my sister's life."

"Well," Joey mumbled hesitantly, "there was a lock of bright-red hair falling out of the scarf she had tied around her head." He continued, "Her clothes were very fine, as though she was a lady, not a maid."

"Thank you, Joey," Laura said as she squeezed his rough hand. "I think you may have given me just the clues I was looking for."

"But so many ladies could fit that description," Joey said hopelessly.

"Yes, I know," said Laura with a sparkle in her eyes, "but there's one I feel certain it must be. Remember to come to Oak Grove to work at the stables as soon as possible," she reminded him as she got up and went to her carriage.

Climbing into the carriage, she sat down and thought out loud: "Could it be Saundra? Why would Saundra take Jenny? She never seemed to care at all for Jenny and even appeared to dislike her, as she did all children. The dressmaker said Saundra had been visiting a judge in Cameron Falls. Could Saundra be taking Jenny to Gerald's father? But how would she know the judge was Jenny's grandfather?" The notion struck her with despair. There were so many unanswered questions.

As Laura thought about the day's revelations and the information she had learned from the seamstress and Joey, she felt she had at least gotten some inkling of what may have happened to Jenny. Laura never dreamed her best clue might come from her having tried on a dress. It was just like Pastor Jenkins liked to say: "God certainly works in strange and mysterious ways."

When Laura returned to Oak Grove, she ran into the house, calling, "Jenny! Jenny! Where are you? Bradford, are you here?"

Hearing her daughter's voice, Ruth rushed into the hall to greet her. Breathless, her mother said anxiously, "Jenny isn't here, and neither is Bradford. He went north, and I haven't heard anything from him yet. Some of the neighbors who rode south stopped by and said they were unable to find out anything so far. Did you learn anything at all?"

"Oh, dear, where could she be?" Laura cried as her mother followed her into her room. Too exhausted and anxious to eat, Laura put on her nightclothes. Braiding her long light-brown hair, she turned to her mother, who nodded solemnly as Laura informed her, "I learned from a dressmaker and also a stableboy at the fair that Saundra might be involved with taking Jenny to the Taylors."

Sighing, Ruth said, "Saundra has always gotten whatever she's ever wanted. After Mrs. Boulogne died in a riding accident, her father thought that showering Saundra with gifts would make up for the loss both of them deeply felt. I'll never forget the time you had your fifth birthday party, and Gerald brought you a special present wrapped in pink tissue with a white bow. Saundra eyed the present longingly as you opened it and pulled out a china doll with large blue eyes. As you hugged the baby doll, Saundra started crying. Mr. Boulogne tried to comfort her, but she kept wailing. Suddenly you got up and took the doll over to her and let her hold it. Her father later took me aside and offered to buy the doll, but I told him that it was a gift and couldn't be sold. You were a very generous child to let Saundra hold your doll when you were so proud of her."

After pausing briefly, Ruth continued, "Saundra's father kept giving her all her heart's desires. She got a huge playhouse almost big enough to live in when she was only five. She and her father took trips all over Europe. As she grew older, she had no trouble attracting boyfriends, for she was very striking. They always flocked to her side—all except Gerald, who had eyes only for you." Ruth looked up as she said this and was surprised to see that the hopeless look that had always been in Laura's eyes at the mere mention of Gerald's name had disappeared. Puzzled, she continued,

"Saundra wanted Gerald most of all, I think, because he wanted you. She's never forgiven you for having been married to him, even though it was for such a brief time. But I've always feared she would cause trouble if and whenever she could."

Laura finished braiding her hair and looked up at her mother. "Do you think Bradford will be back tonight? I think I'll wait to see if he's learned anything. If necessary I'll go first thing in the morning to Camellia Hall to see what Saundra knows."

"Do you think she'll talk to you?" Ruth asked. "Anyway, why would she take Jenny to the judge's since you, Nanny, Dr. Ellerby, and I are the only ones who know Jenny is yours and that the judge is her grandfather? No one else knows, do they?"

Laura looked away as she realized one other person knew the truth. "She must have found out somehow," she said quickly, hoping Bradford would be back soon.

The next morning was dreary, with dark clouds threatening rain at any moment. A chill permeated the air, so Laura dressed warmly. She decided her gray wool cape with its large hood would be perfect for a day like this.

After dressing she forced herself to eat a quick breakfast, then set out in Bradford's covered carriage for the Boulogne mansion. As she rode to Saundra's, the darkening clouds reminded her of a similar day not so long ago when storms had torn apart her cottage. Laura thought that Bradford had been exceptionally kind to allow her and her family to return to Oak Grove. Progress had been made to rebuild the cottage, but it would take several more months to make it livable again.

The resentment and dislike she had first felt for Bradford had disappeared. Warmth spread throughout her body as she thought of the kiss he had given her the day of their picnic. She felt sure the day had meant something to him too. Suddenly the day seemed to get brighter as she now realized she was in love with Bradford. She had fought her feelings since she had first met him, but she could no longer deny them. One day she would make him realize this. As she approached Camellia Hall, these thoughts fortified her to face whatever lay ahead.

A wet mist started to fall as she climbed out of the carriage and raced up the curving staircase to the massive portico of the mansion. Of all the mansions in Vicksburg, Camellia Hall was the most elaborate. When Mr. Boulogne had come back to assume the position as head of the provisional government, he had spared no expense in making the mansion outshine all the other grand houses in the area. Many of the residents of Vicksburg still thought of him as a traitor, but they also acknowledged his power over them. Saundra's father wanted to make sure no one doubted his new position and authority; she passionately shared her father's ambitions.

As Laura stood before the huge, intricately carved door, she noticed the diamond-shaped glass in the door shimmering like jewels as drops of rain fell down the cut-glass panes.

After a brief wait, a butler, dressed in a blue uniform, opened the door and ushered her into the elaborate parlor. An enormous chandelier with hundreds of tear-shaped crystals hung in the center of the room. After receiving her cape, the butler asked Laura to be seated on a brocaded sofa. Laura faced a large fireplace with marble gargoyles carved into the facing. The fire sent a warm glow into the spectacular room. She tried to relax as she awaited her dreaded meeting with Saundra.

Laura felt she had been waiting forever when Saundra finally appeared at the door and demanded, "What brings you here?"

Laura ignored her aggressive tone and tried to get the conversation off to a friendly start by asking, "This room has been redone since your ball, has it not?"

Saundra, dressed richly in the finest taffeta, sat in a carved chair opposite Laura. "Yes, after the last ball I got tired of the old things, and father had the whole room redone for me," she said. "Even the fireplace has been made over. One of my close friends is a decorator and designed it especially for me. Perhaps you've heard of him? Sir Douglas Donley. He's from England. I met him on one of my recent European tours."

Laura nodded that she had heard his name in connection with some work he had done for the president.

"Yes, he's very famous. I only wish he made more money for his efforts," she regretted with a sigh. "At one time he wanted to marry me, but...never mind. Bradford seemed enchanted with the room the last time he was here." Saundra continued smugly, "We've become quite good friends since he acquired your plantation."

Laura shifted uncomfortably in her chair at the mere mention of Bradford.

"I wouldn't be surprised if he announces something very soon so the world can know of our deep feelings for each other," Saundra said with flair as she twirled one of her long red locks around her finger.

"I didn't know you were betrothed," Laura replied weakly.

With a hint of a stutter, Saundra confided, "Oh, well, it isn't official, so don't say anything to anyone—especially not to him. Bradford's so romantic. He wants to keep it a secret until he feels the moment is right."

Stunned, Laura nodded numbly and promised she wouldn't mention it to him. She'd had no idea that Bradford was in love with Saundra and that he might marry her.

Interrupting her thoughts, Saundra said shrewdly, "Now tell me...what brings you here to call on me?"

Laura had planned on easing into the subject and maybe taking Saundra by surprise, but she knew this was hopeless, so she began, "Did you go to the fairgrounds the day before yesterday?"

"Yes," Saundra said. "Why do you ask?"

"Well," Laura continued bluntly, "a stableboy saw a lady with red hair talking to the man who kidnapped my sister."

Saundra laughed harshly as she stared coldly at Laura. She paused to say, "Certainly you don't think I would stoop to anything so vile? The sheriff already has been here. I told them I knew nothing about what happened. My father is very upset that they even questioned me and warned them not to come back.

Anyway, while we're on the subject, why do we need to play these games?"

"What games?" Laura asked puzzled.

"Oh, the one about Jenny being your sister. Why, I know she's your and Gerald's child," Saundra said pointedly, as her green eyes, like those of a hungry cat fixing on its prey, narrowed into two slits.

"How did you find that out?" Laura asked softly as her face turned deathly white.

"Bradford told me of course. Why should we keep secrets from each other when we're so close? We tell each other everything," Saundra responded.

Laura felt her body go limp. *Could Bradford have betrayed me? Could he have unwittingly told Saundra, who may have participated in the kidnapping? Would he have given away the secret I've held so close to my heart for so long?* The thoughts left her weak as she stood to leave.

Saundra walked with her to the door. "I'm sorry I couldn't give you any more information on the kidnapping of your *daughter.*" Her mocking emphasis on the word "daughter" was surely aimed at provoking Laura.

Laura's driver assisted her into the carriage. As they left Camellia Hall and drove toward the stables on the outskirts of Saundra's estate, Laura felt a jolt on the back of the carriage, as though a heavy object had landed on it. Still stunned from her interview with Saundra, she ignored it. She rode a few yards farther before hearing a tapping noise at the door. Startled, she hesitated to open it, but on impulse slowly cracked the door. Hanging onto the side of the carriage was a tall man soaked to the skin from the pouring rain.

Fear gripped Laura, but then her face lit up as she recognized Tommy Burns.

Laura called to the driver to stop for a moment so Tommy could climb inside. Pushing back his rain-soaked hood, he smiled at her. Laura immediately asked, "How's Aimee?"

"She's so fortunate that your husband was such a brave person to rescue her. She's doing well and doesn't even remember the incident. But I'll never forget how your husband saved my little girl that night, and I'd like to repay you in some way."

Breathless from running after the carriage, he continued, "My wife Julia overheard your conversation with Miss Saundra. She ran and told me everything as you were leaving. Maybe I can give you some information to help you find your little girl."

Laura looked into his kindly brown eyes. She took her wool blanket from around her legs and gave it to him to dry and warm himself.

"I hope I didn't startle you, Miss Laura," he said with concern in his voice, "but I have to talk with you. I've kept up with you over the years, hoping that one day I could help you as your husband helped me. I only wish I could tell you everything, but I'll tell you all I know. A couple of days ago, a good friend of mine told me he'd been hired to drive a child to her grandfather's. He didn't tell me who paid him but said the child's name was 'Jenny.' I know my friend well because he makes daily deliveries from the general store to Camellia Hall."

Tommy continued, "Then my wife told me she overheard you talking to Miss Saundra, and Miss

Saundra said Jenny was your child. I'm so happy you and Mr. Gerald had a child. Your little girl must be very special, for she has such kind and generous parents," he said, smiling at her. "I was immediately alarmed because my wife said you didn't know that Jenny was being taken away. I thought she was your sister, so I didn't understand how Judge Taylor could be her grandfather. Now I know. My friend didn't feel anything was amiss when he agreed to take Jenny to visit her grandparents. So please don't blame him. I was waiting for the right moment to tell you all I knew without Miss Saundra overhearing. Not wanting anyone to see us talking, I felt I had to jump onto the carriage the way I did. Did I scare you?"

"No," Laura said quietly. "That explains a lot, Tommy. I really appreciate your taking this risk to help me find Jenny. What's your friend's name? Maybe he can help us."

"I'd rather not involve him, especially if Jenny wasn't supposed to go. He's a gentle man and never would harm anyone. He has ten children of his own and often takes extra jobs to earn money to support them. He has barely made it after the war. I know he'd never harm your child, and I wanted you to know this above all else. I've got to go now before your carriage takes me too far from the stables. Jenny will be safe with my friend. Please believe that. I'll do all I can to find out who hired him without involving my friend, if that's all right."

As he jumped from the carriage, Laura agreed, thanking him for confirming her suspicions. Then, as the coach became silent once again, tears formed in her eyes. Now she felt certain Jenny was with Gerald's parents, and she would probably never see her daughter again. The cold, dark, gloomy day mirrored her thoughts as she felt she had lost everything…her child, her home, and even the love Bradford might have felt for her. She consoled herself with the thought that at least no one could take away the love she felt for Gerald. Fingering the small gold band she hadn't taken off since the day he had given it to her, Laura tried to feel better, even though she knew all was lost.

Upset, Laura slowly climbed out of the carriage when she returned to Oak Grove. As she entered her bedroom, her mother was waiting for her. Ruth was immediately aware of the sadness in her daughter's eyes. Laura quickly told her that Jenny must be at the judge's house. Ruth tried to tell her daughter that everything would work out and to turn to her faith, but Laura seemed lost in her own thoughts as she absent-mindedly twisted her wedding band around and around her finger.

Chapter Eleven

Wishes Fulfilled

❧

*I*f Laura had known what happened after the fair, her anxiety would have been greatly lessened. Once Jenny won the silver trophy, she rode back to the stables to brush Scamp down. As she got off her pony and put him in his stall, a friendly man approached her. Smiling at her, he asked, "Are you Jenny?"

Puzzled, she responded, "Why, yes sir. How do you know my name?"

"A good friend told me. I've been asked to take you to your grandparents' house for a visit," he explained. With a twinkle in his blue eyes, he added, "You may call me 'Jack.'"

Jenny always envied her other friends, who were able to visit their grandparents. She had longed for grandparents and had wondered why she never saw hers. Even though her mother didn't respond to her questions about where her grandparents were, she always dreamed of meeting them one day.

"I'll go tell my mama I'm leaving," Jenny said happily.

"No," the kindly man said. "Your aunt paid me to get you there as quickly as possible, so we'll have to leave now because we have a long way to go. We'll be traveling until we reach my sister's farmhouse up the road. She has lots of children who I know you'll like. We'll rest there for the night then continue on our way. I've made a bed for you in the back of the wagon if you'd like to lie down. My wife has packed food for you to eat in case you get hungry."

Not wanting to miss a visit she had always wished for, Jenny hopped into the wagon. The aunt he mentioned must be someone else she didn't know, her childish mind reasoned. As they traveled down the road, Jack chattered about all his children. He had ten of them! Jenny was enthralled that he had so many children. She sadly shared that she had only one sister.

"Are my grandparents nice, Mister Jack?" she asked hopefully.

"I'm sure they are, even though I've never met them. Most grandparents love their grandchildren very much," he answered.

After riding until early evening, they stopped for the night at Jack's sister's home. Jenny enjoyed meeting his nephews and nieces and loved getting to sleep in a loft with them. The following day Jack and Jenny drove all day and into the evening until they finally arrived at a stately villa high on a hill. As the wagon entered the circular drive, a man and woman ran from the doorway to greet them. They both immediately fell in love with their grandchild when they saw her darling face peek up from a pallet in the back of the wagon.

As they came closer, Jenny asked, "Are you my grandparents?"

"Yes, we are," Judge Taylor said with a big grin.

Smiling back at her grandfather, Jenny stuck out her arms to him so he could lift her out of the wagon. As soon as her feet hit the ground, she turned and hugged her grandparents, saying, "I've always known you were real and I'd see you one day."

Totally charmed, Jenny's grandfather lifted her back into his arms and carried her into the large parlor. Both of her grandparents were very much aware of how much Jenny, with her blond curls and sapphire-blue eyes, favored their son. After her grandfather put her down, Jenny seemed to come to life, darting around the room and asking what seemed like a million questions. The judge and his wife both felt the painful loss of not getting to know her sooner.

"Grandmother, where will I sleep?" Jenny asked, as she finally sank back on the sofa, her eyelids beginning to close.

"We have a room just for you, so come upstairs and see it," her grandmother said cheerfully, nodding knowingly at her husband.

Jenny was so enthralled with the brightly colored room and all the dolls and toys that she could hardly settle down. Her grandmother removed her riding habit and dressed her in a soft-blue nightgown she had made especially for her. After being tucked into bed, Jenny fell fast asleep, for the journey had been long and tiring.

Her grandmother quietly shut the door and went downstairs to join her husband in the study. He turned toward her as she entered the large room filled with books.

With pain in his voice, he said, "I made a terrible mistake in rejecting Laura. Think of all we've missed in not knowing her and our darling grandchild!"

His wife came over, patted him gently on the shoulder, and said, "We were almost bankrupt at the time, and you needed the money that Saundra could provide if Gerald married her. Also, her father might have reappointed you to your judgeship. We've learned, however, that we were wrong to interfere with our son's decision."

"Yes, I know, but I never realized what Laura meant to Gerald. We never even got to know her or her family, though we lived only a few miles away. We should at least have done that. Then we would've known the money meant very little. I was even able to get a position as judge here without the help of Saundra's father." Pausing, he looked up sadly into his wife's eyes. "Do you think Gerald forgave me before he died?"

Sitting opposite her husband, Mrs. Taylor tried to think of the words to help him forgive himself. Hesitantly she said, "Gerald always did what you told him to do. I think your quarrel was a result of his determination to win his freedom and be a man. Both of you had too much pride. But I believe he forgave you as Laura has now. I also believe he forgave you because he believed in God and knew how important forgiveness is."

The judge looked hopefully at his wife. "Laura must have forgiven us, or she never would have let Jenny come and see us. How can we ever get her to forget what we did to her? Saundra said Laura even told Jenny she was her sister and not her mother. Maybe we can get Laura to come here too. I understand the cottage they were living in was destroyed in a storm and she's temporarily staying with Bradford, who has taken over Laura's family home."

"I hope she'll let us make up for our wrongdoing," Mrs. Taylor said with a sigh. "We'd better go to bed now because I know Jenny will be up bright and early." She added, "I think it's our duty to help Jenny understand who her real mother and father are. Unfortunately it was our doing that led her to believe as she does now."

"As soon as Jenny gets to know us better, I'll tell her everything," the judge agreed. "Now we'd better get to bed, because I think you're right that our little granddaughter will be rising with the sun."

"Wasn't Saundra nice to convince Laura to let Jenny come see us?"

The judge nodded as they went to their room. For the first time in many years, the pain from the loss of their son seemed to fade from their hearts.

The next morning, Jenny squinted as she stared at the soft yellow rays streaming into her room. Confused as to where she was, she sat up and, through half-opened eyes, looked all around her. Realizing she had finally found the grandparents she always knew she must have, she bounced out of bed and ran into the hall. Unsure which room her grandparents occupied, she tiptoed past the huge mahogany doors and down the ornate staircase that fanned out at the bottom. Both of her grandparents smiled as she entered the family dining room at the back of the stately home.

"I'm so glad you were able to get a good rest last night, Jenny," her grandmother said cheerfully. "After you eat these grits and eggs, I want to show you some pretty clothes I made especially for you. It's a good thing, because I couldn't find your suitcase when you arrived. You must've left it in the back of the nice man's wagon."

"I didn't bring one, since I left quickly after the fair," Jenny replied innocently.

Puzzled, her grandmother dropped the subject.

Jenny immediately spoke up. "I looked out my window and saw stables. Do you have horses here?"

"Yes," her grandfather said. The judge was an avid horseman and was pleased to find Jenny interested. "After you finish your meal, I'll take you out to see them. I have one horse you should especially like."

Jenny rapidly gulped down her food, stuffing as much of the savory buttered grits as she could into her mouth without dripping any down her chin.

"Wow, young lady," her grandfather said with a laugh. "We'll have plenty of time. There's no need to rush."

After putting on one of the frilly dresses her grandmother had made for her, Jenny lost no time in finding her grandfather. He took her soft chubby fingers in his large hand and led her down the short path to the massive stables. Jenny had never seen anything like it. Stall after stall was filled with prize-winning race horses. When they reached the far end of the stables, the judge turned to Jenny. "This is My Lady. She's small and very gentle. Would you like to ride her?"

He saw the answer in her sparkling eyes as her blond curls bobbed up and down. "Oh, yes, I can even take care of her all by myself. I'm experienced because I've been taking care of Scamp since Papa died," Jenny said with a mixture of sadness and boastfulness.

After mounting the horse, Jenny rode the mare into the corral. Her grandfather was thrilled to find a child so young riding like a professional. He mounted his own stallion, and together they rode toward an open pasture that lay east of the property.

Chapter Twelve

Bradford's Quest

After Jenny's disappearance Bradford quickly left the fairgrounds. He searched everywhere for clues as to where the mysterious driver had taken Jenny. He was in a panic to do something. Glad the sheriff was rounding up lots of help, Bradford headed north, since the other searchers had gone in other directions.

When he came to a fork in the road heading north, he decided to take the left road. He rode until dark, when he came to a river. Once he reached the ferry crossing, he asked the ferry owner, "Have you seen a child with curly blond hair traveling with a man in a wagon today?"

"I haven't seen any wagons or children all day. If you'd like to stay in that shed over in the woods for the night, you're welcome to do so. No one lives there, so it'll be fine," the man replied.

Disappointed, Bradford replied, "Thank you."

Up bright and early the next day, he returned the way he had come, knowing he had lost a lot of time.

He retraced his steps to the fork in the road. This time he took the other branch. Riding all day, he still hadn't found any clues. After a long day in the saddle, he was tired, hungry, and frustrated. When it was too dark to travel safely, he reluctantly stopped at a wayside inn. Feeling he had lost tremendous ground, he decided to retire early and leave as soon as possible the next day.

The inn he had chosen was in poor shape. Bradford slept fitfully on a hay mattress that swayed in a rickety bed frame that threatened to hurl him to the plank floor with his every move. He awoke to the sound of thunder and rain. After carefully getting out of the ramshackle bed, he dressed warmly before ordering a hearty breakfast. The food he found was, however, similar to everything else in the poorly run inn—leathery, overcooked eggs and weak coffee. After choking down the tasteless breakfast, he had his horse brought to him at the front of the inn.

Before he got a mile down the road, the rain started to pour, penetrating his heavy wool coat. Soon his back was wet from the streams of water running down the small opening in his collar. Lightning flashed all around him, causing his horse to rear and almost hurl him to the ground. Deciding he would have to wait until the storm passed, he pulled up to a small farmhouse near the edge of the road.

A plump woman opened the door and invited him to have a seat by her fire. The glowing logs in her hearth warmed his rain-drenched body. Anxious to get on his way, he was about to thank her and leave since he hadn't heard but an occasional rumble, when she asked, "Would you care for some fresh eggs and strong brewed tea?"

Thanking her, Bradford gratefully accepted the hot meal. Then he inquired, "By any chance did you happen to notice a covered wagon with a man and little girl going this way in the last day or so?"

"Yes, I sure did. It was yesterday morning. It looked like they were heading for Cameron Falls, a small town northeast of here. She was a bonny little girl with blond curls. The man driving the wagon looked like he could be her father, as he had the same blond-colored hair, so I didn't think anything of it. Why? Are you looking for her?" the puzzled woman asked.

Not wanting to go into all the details, Bradford simply said he just needed to reach them as quickly as possible.

Realizing he wasn't going to tell her any more, the cheerful woman began chattering about her family. Bradford was polite and let her finish. As soon as the rain and thunder stopped, he stood up to leave, anxious to be on his way.

Bradford thanked her for her hospitality before continuing his search. Hope filled him as he realized he was at least heading in the right direction. Small drops were still falling from the rain-soaked branches whenever the trees moved with the wind, but he was now warm and eager to go. As he thought back on what the friendly farmer's wife had said, a notion suddenly hit him. He thought out loud, "Jenny must be at her grandfather's home in Cameron Falls!" Giving his horse a gentle tap with his boot, he cantered through the lightly falling mist, hoping to reach his destination without delay.

As the sun sank behind the grass-covered hills, Bradford knew he still had several more hours to go. Finally he reached the Taylors' home. Not wanting to disturb anyone who may have already retired on this damp evening, he knocked softly on the door. The judge opened the door himself and was surprised to see Bradford, whose clothes clung to his body like wet rags as he stood on the porch. Without ceremony the judge quickly ushered his friend into the house and hustled about, trying to make Bradford comfortable. Tired and not wanting to get into a lengthy discussion, he asked the judge if he might have a room for the night.

"You know you're welcome at any time," the judge said. "Hannah, please make Bradford comfortable for the night. We'll have plenty of time to talk in the morning."

Bradford didn't want to confront the judge this late at night. He believed Judge Taylor would hide Jenny if he had indeed kidnapped her. Hoping Jenny was here, Bradford knew he would find out what was going on first thing in the morning. If she wasn't here, he would at least have had a good night's sleep before continuing his search. He soon fell into a deep slumber on a soft feather bed that contrasted sharply to the hard, unstable one he had slept in the previous night.

Chirping noises awoke him from his dreamless sleep. After dressing, Bradford went downstairs to ask about Jenny. The odor of fresh biscuits enticed him to the warm family dining room at the back of the villa.

"Why, good morning, sir," said Hannah, the judge's faithful cook and housekeeper. "You're the first one to awaken on this sunny morning, except for Jenny. She's already up and outside. Would you like some biscuits with the hot tea I'm brewing?"

"Thank you, Hannah," Bradford replied. Her mention of Jenny answered the question that was foremost on his mind.

"She's done wonders for this household. It's as though she's brought sunshine where gloom has been for so long." She continued, "I guess you know she's Judge Taylor's granddaughter. It's a shame we didn't know about her all these years, although I can't blame Laura. If you ask me, the judge had too much pride in dealing with her."

Bradford was stunned to think that the secret Laura had guarded for so long was finally out and obviously spreading like a raging fire being fanned by a strong wind. Realizing he had better not let her feel he was probing too much, he thanked Hannah for the warm, airy biscuits before taking a stroll outside.

Determined to get to the bottom of the matter, he knew he would have to proceed cautiously. If Judge Taylor had kidnapped his own granddaughter, he would be difficult to approach. Knowing Laura would never forgive her father-in-law, Bradford hoped, above all else, that the judge hadn't taken Jenny.

His thoughts were abruptly interrupted when he heard a shrill, "Bradford!" from behind. Turning, he grabbed the soft, wiggly girl and tossed her high in the air. Laughter filled his ears as Jenny wrapped her dimpled hands around his neck so he couldn't throw her again. Hanging on to him with all her might, Jenny said, "I have real grandparents, just like my friends!"

He pried the tight little hands from his neck and looked into the shining eyes that were sparkling like the summer sun shimmering on a mountain lake. Relief flooded through him as he realized she was safe and happy. Swinging her around to his back, he galloped back into the house with her kicking his sides as she cried, "Giddyup, horse."

Once inside he swung her to the floor and asked, "Have you had any breakfast?"

Jenny nodded but admitted that she was still hungry. After eating, she jumped onto Bradford's back and rode him to the stables. She leaped off, raced to the stall that housed My Lady, and climbed up on the gate. Precariously sitting on the edge, she stroked the horse's soft neck.

Steadying her with his arm, Bradford said, "Why, you have a beautiful new horse. Do you think Scamp will mind?"

"Oh, Scamp won't know because I'll keep My Lady here so I can ride her when I visit," Jenny answered.

"Did you tell your mother or sister where you were going before you left?" Bradford asked sternly.

"The nice man who brought me here said it was fine with them that I came," Jenny explained brightly, not feeling she had done anything wrong.

Wanting to understand who was behind Jenny coming to Cameron Falls, Bradford decided to take her back to the Taylors' home where he hoped to get to the bottom of this bizarre kidnapping. Upon entering the house, he was greeted by Mrs. Taylor, who immediately hugged him. "Bradford, I've missed you greatly since your last visit."

Mrs. Taylor told Jenny, "Your friend Sally is waiting to go riding with you."

Jenny yelled, "That'll be fun! Bye," as she ran back outside.

As they entered the parlor, Bradford said tersely, "I didn't come purely for pleasure."

"What is it, Bradford?" Mrs. Taylor inquired with puzzlement in her voice.

"I thought you'd know, but I see I'll have to go into details." Pausing, he continued, "Were you aware that no one in Jenny's family knew she was coming here?"

Mrs. Taylor's hand rapidly flew to her mouth. Her cheeks went pale as she uttered, "No!" while shaking her head. "Why, that would be kidnapping! That explains why Jenny didn't have a suitcase when she arrived. We would never do that, even if it meant never seeing our grandchild."

Totally confused, Bradford whispered under his breath, "Could all this be a mixed-up misunderstanding?" Then, turning to Mrs. Taylor, he demanded, "Who told you Jenny could come to see you? Who made the arrangements to have her brought here?"

"Why, Saundra," Mrs. Taylor shakily replied. Mystified, she elaborated, "She's been visiting us quite often since Gerald's death. She was the girl my husband would have most wanted him to marry." Mrs. Taylor walked under the portrait of her son who had Jenny's sapphire-blue eyes and blond hair, which was neatly combed around his handsome face. "We were desperately in need of money at the time, and my husband thought Saundra would be the solution to all our problems. But," she remembered, as she glanced up at the painting, "from the time Gerald was small, Laura was the only girl he ever loved." Turning her dark-gray eyes toward Bradford's, she solemnly continued, "We made a grave mistake, because we never even took the time to meet the girl our son loved so dearly. If we'd only gone to the chapel with Gerald, things would've turned out differently." She added with deep satisfaction in her voice, "We attend our local church now, and it has brought us close to God." Distressed, she sank into a nearby chair.

Towering over her as he paced back and forth across the floor, Bradford said, "Now let me get this straight. You mean Saundra told you Jenny could come and see you?"

"Why, yes," she said quietly, before continuing. "A few weeks ago, Saundra came here and said she had exciting news. She told us we had a granddaughter. Not realizing it could be possible, we didn't believe her at first. She told us how Laura's mother had pretended to have the baby instead of Laura, so Laura wouldn't be tied down with a child. It made sense."

"Wait," Bradford uttered abruptly. "You mean Saundra told you Laura hadn't wanted her child?"

"Yes," Mrs. Taylor whispered under her breath as she looked up into Bradford's face to see his eyes piercing into hers.

His fists were clenched as he demanded, "Go on!"

"Saundra said she'd arranged for our granddaughter to come spend some time with us. We were thrilled and never thought it would be a problem," she clarified, twisting her handkerchief in her hands.

"Saundra has lied on all counts," Bradford blurted. Turning to Mrs. Taylor, he started to divulge all of her lies, when he realized she was really very innocent in the matter at hand. Taking a seat next to her, he lightly picked up her hand and patted it. His father and Judge Taylor had been friends for years until they had a falling-out over a business deal. After his father died, Bradford had compensated the judge for his financial losses. He and the Taylors thereafter had become increasingly close. Mrs. Taylor had been kind to him when he came to ask for their forgiveness for what his father had done to them, and he didn't want to destroy that relationship.

"Whatever has come to pass, I see you were misled. I'll try to set you straight on these matters as best I can." As his eyes took on a faraway stare, he told Mrs. Taylor all that had happened after Gerald had married Laura. Tears ran down her face as he continued, "After your husband annulled their marriage, Laura found out she was going to have a child. Her fear that you might want to take their child and her pride at having been rejected led her to let her own mother pretend to have Jenny. Even to this day, Jenny doesn't know Laura is her real mother."

I never knew my husband was so angry that he would annul the marriage! No wonder Laura has never forgiven us! Mrs. Taylor solemnly thought.

"I don't know what made Saundra do what she did, but I'll find out," Bradford pledged. His clear blue eyes seemed to turn gray as he seethed in anger.

"Please, don't tell my husband," Mrs. Taylor begged as she stared into the brooding eyes that Bradford turned to her. "He's never forgiven himself for what he did to Laura. Thinking that Laura has forgiven him has made him a new man."

"Right now I'll agree," Bradford said, patting the hand that tightly clutched his. "I feel Jenny must be told who her mother is before a stranger tells her in the wrong way." He added, "And I'd like to do that before I leave. Right now I'll send a telegram to Laura letting her know that I found Jenny and that she's fine."

"Certainly," Mrs. Taylor agreed as she got up, still shaking from the unnerving news. "Won't you stay for a few days at least?" she asked politely.

"I'll stay just long enough to tell Jenny who her real mother is. Then I must get back. Laura loves her daughter very much and will be sick with worry until she learns that Jenny's fine."

"Then you'll let Jenny stay here for a few days after you leave?" she asked hopefully.

"I'll ask Laura in the telegram if she's willing to let Jenny stay a little longer," he explained. "Hopefully she'll give her permission, because I feel Jenny needs to know of your love for her."

At that moment the booming voice of Judge Taylor resounded as he entered the parlor with his granddaughter. "Jenny, do you mean to tell me you've already been out riding your horse?"

Bradford and Mrs. Taylor exchanged knowing glances as the judge entered the room carrying Jenny. He had put on several pounds since Bradford had last seen him. Bradford also was surprised to see the judge's new carefree, even happy manner. It seemed as though a terrible burden had been lifted from his shoulders.

"Why, Bradford, did you rest well last night? We've missed you, my boy," he exclaimed jovially. "Did you know we have a granddaughter?" His round cheeks dimpled when he lovingly looked down at Jenny, who was wiggling out of his arms in an effort to reach her grandmother.

Finally freeing herself, Jenny ran over and hugged her grandmother, whom she had nicknamed "Gran." Witnessing the tender scene, Bradford hoped Laura would let Jenny stay with her grandparents for a few more days.

Knowing how much Laura disliked Gerald's parents, though, he realized she might not allow it. With all his heart, Bradford hoped Laura could forgive them when she learned what had happened. He'd do everything possible to explain the situation to her. He knew, though, that Laura would be very angry that her secret was now out and that Jenny was visiting her grandparents.

After greeting the judge, Bradford rode directly to town to send a telegram to let Laura know he had found Jenny. When he reached the telegraph office, he jotted down his message and read it aloud: "Jenny is fine. In Cameron Falls with Taylors. Will leave Jenny here and come to get you. If not okay, let me know by Tuesday. Bradford." After paying for the telegram, he watched to make sure the telegrapher sent the wire. Bradford then ran some errands for the Taylors before returning to the villa.

Before Bradford had time to mount his horse, the telegraph operator in Vicksburg was writing down the message about Jenny. When the wire ended, the telegrapher neatly tore the message into two pieces and dropped them into the wastebasket. "That was the easiest twenty dollars I've ever made," he remarked to himself.

The days passed swiftly, and Bradford still hadn't found the right moment to tell Jenny about the true identify of her mother. He also knew Laura would be desperate if he didn't return soon. Finally the moment came one morning while he and Jenny were out riding in the brisk fall air. They stopped to build a fire so they could warm up. Huddled together by the blazing fire, Bradford put his arms around Jenny, saying, "Have you seen the picture of the man above the fireplace?"

"Yes," Jenny answered brightly. "He's my grandparents' son."

"What I'm about to tell you may be hard for you to understand, but you must try, Jenny," Bradford encouraged, as he looked down into the innocent eyes staring pensively back at him. "A long time ago, Sissy fell in love with the man in that painting above your grandfather's mantle. As I understand it, they met when they were children, just about your age."

"Nanny told me all about how they played together when they were children and had so much fun," Jenny said. "I know they got married because my Sissy wears a wedding ring. I don't talk about him much, because Sissy gets so sad."

Bradford continued, "I'm glad you know about that. Well, when they grew up, as you know, they decided they wanted to get married. Your grandfather didn't know Laura and picked out someone else for Gerald to marry. Sissy and Gerald married despite his objections. After they were married, Gerald was accidentally killed while bravely saving a little girl who had fallen into a ravine. Laura was very sad, but she did have a little baby who looked very much like him."

All this time Jenny had sat very still, trying to absorb what he was telling her. But when she heard Laura had a baby, she jumped up, saying, "Where's the baby now?"

Taking her small hands in his, he looked into her excited face and explained, "The baby has grown into a beautiful child, and her name is Jenny."

Jenny was a smart as well as pretty child, and she absorbed this very thoughtfully. Looking at first pensive before breaking out in a broad smile, she said, "Laura is my mama!"

"Yes," Bradford stated, relieved. Not wanting to burden her with too many facts, he continued, "I know you'll need time to understand all of this. Your grandfather and grandmother would like you to stay here a little bit longer so they can get to know you even better. You'll be seeing your mother as soon as I'm able to bring her here to be with you."

"I'll have to call Mama 'Grandma' now," Jenny said thoughtfully as she referred to Laura' mother. "Now I have two grandmothers!"

Laughing, Bradford took her into his lap as he gazed into her face, which so closely resembled the portrait above the mantle. He wondered whether Laura would ever forget Jenny's father, whom she had loved for so long.

The next morning, Bradford prepared to leave. He hoped Laura had received his telegram and wasn't worrying too much about Jenny. Knowing what lengths she had taken to prevent Jenny from ever knowing Gerald's parents, he had deep doubts that she would ever forgive him for letting Jenny stay with the Taylors. Since he hadn't heard back from Laura, however, Bradford felt she must have approved his plan to leave Jenny with her grandparents. Quickly pushing aside these thoughts, he dressed in tight black trousers that emphasized his strong, muscular legs. The weather had turned frigid, so he put on a warm fur-lined jacket over a white shirt that contrasted with his tanned skin.

With his self-assured manner, Mrs. Taylor knew why all the women had longed to capture this aloof, extremely handsome gentleman, who was now making his way downstairs to breakfast. So far she knew of no one who'd ever broken through the cold demeanor he had learned to show the world. Somehow, though, when he talked about Laura, there was a warm look that she had never seen in him before. Mrs. Taylor had a strong desire to meet this girl who had captured her son's heart and now Bradford's. Taking Bradford aside, she wondered, "Do you believe Laura would ever consent to come here? Last night my husband said he would like nothing more."

Bradford paused as he looked down at her. "Laura has been deeply hurt. You know the extent of her pain by what she has done to prevent you from ever having an interest in her or her child."

"We were so wrong. If only we could turn back time."

Patting her arm gently, he said, "If Laura ever gets to know you, I feel certain she'd forgive you. I haven't heard back from her, so she must be willing to allow Jenny to stay with you a little longer."

Hope lit up Mrs. Taylor's eyes as she kissed Bradford on the cheek. "You know you've been like a son to us since we lost Gerald."

"Yes," he acknowledged, "and you've been like a mother to me. I'll do my best to help Laura understand."

With that they entered the dining room, where Jenny was energetically eating before her morning ride.

"Slow down, Jenny," her grandfather gently scolded. "My Lady won't run off."

Bradford could see that Jenny had captured her grandfather's heart, and he felt sure that once Judge Taylor took the time to know Laura, she would capture his heart too.

After quickly eating and promising Jenny he would make sure Scamp was doing well, Bradford said goodbye. He rode at a brisk pace on his way back to Oak Grove. He was anxious to tell Laura everything that had happened and hoped she approved of his decision to leave Jenny with the Taylors.

A very early snowstorm had hit Cameron Falls during the night. The day was clear but extremely cold as Bradford rode over the snow-covered ground. His gaze took in the soft-white landscape that surrounded him. He was careful to lead his horse to the high ground, because several years earlier, when he had been exploring this area, his horse had sunk into thick mud while crossing a ditch. Hoping the snow wouldn't slow his progress, he felt he should be able reach Oak Grove by the next afternoon. He had been gone for almost a week, and with that thought, he gently urged his horse to a faster pace.

Bradford made slow but steady progress during the day. After a clear morning, snow began to fall rapidly. His determination to reach Laura as quickly as possible made him insensitive to the signs the weather was sending. The wind whipped the snow around him until it seemed to form an impenetrable white cloud. His muscles tensed from his awareness that the sky was growing darker by the minute.

Blinded by the whirling snow that had turned his cheeks red, he kept tapping his horse's side to keep him moving toward a farmhouse he had spotted on the crest of a nearby hill. The horse seemed to pull to the right no matter what he did, so Bradford trusted his horse's instincts and let him go where he wanted as the sun sank behind the hills to the west.

His hands were numb as he loosely held the reins. After what seemed like hours, his horse stopped abruptly. Still blinded by the whirling snow, Bradford thought he could see a flickering light just in front of him. After jumping off his horse, he sank to his thighs in the snow. Each step took intense effort as he trudged through the thick, white mass. Tired from the long ride and finding it difficult to walk, he inched forward, pulling his horse behind him. When he felt his legs had become little more than frozen masses that he couldn't lift another step, he fell into the side of a wooden farmhouse.

Hearing a soft thud, an elderly farmer came outside to discover Bradford lying facedown in a high snowdrift beside his house. The worried farmer helped the stranger inside and placed him by the blazing fire. Bradford began to recover almost as soon as he was warm, and before long he was able to stand up. He looked down on the kindly couple whose concern for him was obvious in their faces. After introducing himself and thanking them for saving his life, he asked if he might have a place to board his horse and stay the night.

"Of course," said Mr. Brown, "but it looks like you won't be able to travel for a while. This is the earliest snowstorm I can ever remember. If this snow freezes on the ground tonight, it'll be too icy to ride your horse anywhere until it thaws. I'm afraid it may be a while before you can travel."

Weak from exhaustion, Bradford pushed this thought aside, saying, "I have to leave in the morning." He then fell fast asleep on a mat the kind couple had prepared by the fire. They hoped the mat would keep him from feeling the cold stone floor of the drafty farmhouse as he slept.

Upon awaking the next day, Bradford was aware of a chill that numbed his body. Realizing the fire had died to just a few glowing embers, he got up and put several large logs on the dying flames. After poking the logs, the revitalized fire once again heated his chilled body. As soon as he warmed himself, he went to the window. The white scene sent a sense of dread through him as he saw what seemed to be a solid sheet of ice stretching from the farmer's land to the distant hills beyond. Knocking his fist against the windowsill, he knew that all he could do was to wait until the ice melted.

The long, freezing days passed slowly. After four days, the ice had finally melted. Bradford gratefully thanked the kind couple before he anxiously set out once again. He now made good time, practically racing his horse through the slushy countryside. Frequently skirting around large puddles of melted snow, he rode with a speed that he hoped would quickly get him to Laura. He had thought of nothing else this past week and knew his love for her had grown deeper since he had last seen her.

When he reached Oak Grove late that evening, its stillness and gloom made him shudder. Even the light of the full moon did little to change his feeling that something was very wrong. A sense of doom filled him as he approached the dark plantation.

Chapter Thirteen

Laura Fights for Her Life

❈

s soon as Laura returned from her unnerving visit with Saundra, Ruth became aware of her daughter's sense of hopelessness. After greeting her at the carriage, she took her daughter right to her room. Laura refused to eat any lunch. In fact she sat in her room all afternoon, still refusing food. Ruth realized Laura felt she had lost Jenny forever. She didn't know how to break through this impenetrable shield of gloom Laura was building around herself. Ruth had even encouraged Lily to come to Laura's room with a book she was learning to read. Laura usually brightened up when she helped her students, but even Lily failed to revive her interest.

Never having received the telegram Bradford had sent about finding Jenny, Laura grew increasingly upset. Her usually thick, wavy hair hung limply down her back, tangled and matted.

Late one morning, Ruth, carrying a tray, begged, "Laura, please have some food. Nanny made you some ham and soft boiled eggs. I brought it up for you. You need to eat something."

Laura picked at her food as she turned her dull eyes to her mother. She weakly said, "I feel so hot, Mother. Could we open a window?"

"Why Laura, it's snowing out there," Ruth noticed. Rushing over, she put her hand on Laura's sweltering forehead. After taking away the barely touched food, she told Laura to lie down. She got a cool cloth to place on her burning forehead and sent for the doctor.

When Dr. Ellerby arrived later that day, Laura was fast asleep. He examined her without waking her then stepped into the hall to talk with Ruth.

"Your daughter is extremely sick," he reported. "She must be kept quiet. Her fever is dangerously high. We must do all we can to get it down." After instructing Ruth about using snow to cool Laura down, Dr. Ellerby paused, adding, "You be sure to get some rest too." He left feeling sad that he couldn't do more.

Laura seemed to slip deeper and deeper into oblivion. One day merged with the next. She asked constantly about Gerald and ranted about when she was a child. She called out his name in her fevered sleep. Laura's hot hands clutched her mother. Knowing it would do no good to remind her of Gerald's accident, Ruth would only say he'd be coming soon. When her mother assured her of Gerald's imminent arrival, Laura would relax and collapse on her pillow, her hair hanging lifelessly around her head as she tossed continually in her sleep.

Dr. Ellerby came every day and was increasingly concerned about Laura's fevered delirium. Doing all he could, he left one afternoon, adding, "I pray she'll fight for her life, for it's our only hope."

That night Bradford knocked on the plantation door. Nanny let him in since she had been up late, trying to break Laura's fever. Relieved, Nanny said, "Bradford, we're so glad you're back. We had all but given up hope of your returning before it was too late. Did you find out anything about Jenny?"

Immediately sensing something was dreadfully wrong, he reported, "Jenny's fine. I'll tell you about her later. But what's happening here?"

"It's Miss Laura," Nanny replied. "She's dreadfully ill. We can't break her fever. She's gotten weaker every day since Jenny disappeared."

Bradford insisted he be taken immediately to Laura. His heart felt as though it had been wrenched from his chest as he glanced down at the mere shell of the gorgeous woman he knew. Her lovely face was now pale and appeared lifeless. Her hands lay limp and white by her sides. For the first time in his life, Bradford knelt on his knees in prayer, beseeching the Lord to save her. "Oh, please Lord, save Laura. I know I haven't been a faithful follower, but I want to change. I want to open my life to you. I'll trust that, whatever happens, you are in control. Amen."

As he continued to kneel quietly by Laura's sleeping figure, he reached out to brush the hair from her eyes. He was appalled at the heat that radiated from her forehead. Her eyes fluttered open at his cool touch. In her delirium she reached out to him, "You're back, Gerald! I knew you'd come." She sighed and placed her small hand in his. Then she seemed to return to unconsciousness.

A tear rolled down Bradford's face as he dropped her hand. Knowing she was delirious didn't ease the pain that surged through him. As he laid his head on her bed, he felt that thoughts of Gerald would hold her love forever. Still he didn't leave Laura's side. He took her small hand back in his as he knelt by her bed. Waking as the sun was coming up, he was immediately aware that her hand, which he still clutched tightly in his, was now cool. Relief flooded through him as he realized her fever had broken during the night. When he stood to stop the cramping in his legs, he gently removed his hand from hers. Laura's eyes flew open, appearing unusually large in her thin, pale face. No longer delirious, she said, "Bradford, you're back! Did you find Jenny?"

Straightening up, he sat on the edge of her bed and stared down into her large concerned eyes. "Yes, Jenny's fine. Didn't you get my telegram?"

Before he could say any more, Dr. Ellerby entered the room and motioned him to come into the hall. Bradford gave Laura's hand a quick squeeze and left her side.

The doctor took him aside and said, "I'm so glad you're back. Did you find out anything about Jenny?"

"Jenny is safe and happy at the Taylors," Bradford told him. "It was a misunderstanding. I sent a telegram saying that and asking Laura if she would mind if Jenny stayed a little longer with them, but apparently it didn't arrive. Since I didn't hear back from her, I took a chance and let Jenny stay longer," he explained. Frustrated, Bradford added, "I wonder what happened to my telegram?"

In a concerned tone, Dr. Ellerby commented, "I know how Laura feels about Gerald's family, and she isn't going to be happy about any of this. If she gets upset again, she may not live. She's not strong enough to deal with this now. If we tell her where Jenny is, I know how she'll react. She won't stop at anything to see Jenny, and she's certainly not strong enough to make the trip to the Taylors."

Bradford contended, "Laura won't understand why we're not telling her everything now."

"I know, but we'll have Ruth and Nanny help us. They can talk to her too," Dr. Ellerby argued. "I wouldn't put you in this position if I didn't think her life was in jeopardy. Just tell her that once she's well, you'll take her to see Jenny. That should calm her down and give her a reason to recover."

Bradford reluctantly agreed before he reentered Laura's room. He came over to her bed and bent over her as he gently took her hand. "I know you'll be relieved to hear that Jenny is very happy. She said to tell you she's fine and can't wait to see you. We'll discuss everything about Jenny later, when you get your strength back." Bradford gently added, "Dr. Ellerby feels it's very important for you to recover so you won't have a relapse."

"I've been so worried. Can't you tell me where Jenny is and why you didn't bring her back?" Laura pleaded.

"Please listen to Dr. Ellerby's advice, Laura." Bradford continued, "As soon as you're well enough, I'll take you right to Jenny, I promise."

"You will?" Laura asked.

"Of course. Do you think you can eat and rest so you can see her?"

"Oh, yes!" she said. "I'm so relieved Jenny is safe and well. I've been so worried about her. I'll get well as fast as I can." Taking comfort from his presence and words, Laura longed to have him sit by her side and tell her all about her daughter. But she felt her eyes slowly closing in sleep.

Before she drifted off, Bradford freed his hand. "I must see Saundra now," he told her, "but I'll be back soon. Remember all you have to do is to get well. Hopefully it won't be long before you can go see Jenny."

As Laura closed her eyes, Bradford quietly left the room. A tremendous rage filled his heart at the trouble Saundra had caused them all.

After quickly combing his jet-black hair and shaving, Bradford rushed to the stables to get his horse. He arrived at Camellia Hall without delay, since he wanted to get this unpleasant affair over.

After being ushered into the ornate parlor, he impatiently stood by the fireplace, waiting for Saundra's arrival. The gargoyles seem to be laughing at him as he thought she was like most of the women he had known, always plotting to find rich, eligible husbands to satisfy their elaborate tastes. He knew Saundra would like nothing better than to be able to spend his money as she saw fit. It disgusted him, but he'd never seen a woman so determined or one who would go to such lengths to capture his heart and bank account. Filled with fury, his eyes blazed as Saundra entered the room.

Not noticing his mood, Saundra ran over to him and flung her arms around his neck. Then, looking up with longing, she said, "Why, darling, I'm so glad you're back!"

He firmly unwrapped her arms from his neck. Sensing his unwelcoming mood, Saundra backed up and sat in a nearby chair. Bradford suddenly started to pace the floor. His huge frame was taut with anger as he demanded, "Why did you have Jenny taken to Judge Taylor's house without anyone's permission?"

Caught completely off guard, Saundra blurted, "Because I felt if Jenny were with the Taylors, Laura would move there too, so she could be with her. That's where she should be. It's indecent to have her living with you in your home."

"You have no business worrying about whether Laura is in my home," Bradford said, staring at the haughty girl who suddenly jumped up, letting her long red hair fall in disarray over her back. "Who do you think you are? What business is it of yours who stays in my house? I have never considered you—and will never consider you—as my future wife."

"What makes you think that ever entered my mind?" Saundra asked, practically spitting the words back at him. "Don't think you'll ever get Laura, for Gerald will always be the only one in her heart. I know you're aware they had a child together."

Saundra's words echoed through his mind as he remembered the day Laura told him Jenny was her child. Then he turned on Saundra, demanding, "How did you find that out?"

"Why, I overheard you the day of the storm when you were at Oak Grove holding Laura in your arms."

"That's all I need to know," Bradford stated. Then, abruptly turning, he walked out the door.

As he left, he heard her shout behind him, "Laura cares only for her dead husband." Tears streaming down her face, Saundra cried as she slumped to the floor.

❧

Back at Oak Grove, Laura lay restless in bed. She was happy to hear Jenny was fine, even though she felt certain she was at the Taylors'. She couldn't wait to see her and would do everything to get well, but sadness filled her because she felt the judge would never give her daughter back. This thought was devastating. She didn't know how she would get over her loss. Yet she vowed to get well as soon as possible so she could at least see her precious daughter. Knowing the judge was a powerful man, Laura felt sure he would claim Jenny and never let her go. Bradford would do all that was in his power to make sure Jenny was taken care of, but Laura was distraught because of her fear that she'd never be able to live with her daughter again.

As if Laura were in a nightmare, the memories of her visit to Saundra's came back to her as she tossed restlessly, continuing to worry about not getting to live with Jenny again. She was sure Bradford must love Saundra very much if he were so anxious to see her first thing this morning. Because of this, Laura felt he must never discover her true feelings for him and resolved that they must remain just friends. She knew it would be very awkward to be in his home, especially if he were to marry Saundra. Laura prayed for strength as she sadly admitted that neither Bradford nor Jenny would ever be in her life again.

Finally she fell into a restless slumber.

Late that morning, Ruth tiptoed into her room when she heard Laura stirring. She found her eating the lunch Nanny had brought. Thrilled, she asked, "Could I wash your hair when you're through?"

"Oh, that would be nice. Also, could I have a fresh gown to wear? This one feels as if it has grown to me," Laura requested.

Ruth washed her daughter's hair then dried it and brushed it until it glowed. The light from the window bounced off the lovely curly strands. Afterwards she dressed Laura in a soft pink cotton gown with a layer of thin lace covering the entire bodice.

Feeling much better, Laura asked, "Did Bradford say anything more about Jenny?"

"He told us Jenny was fine, and we shouldn't worry about her because she's very happy. Trust Bradford. He's a good man. He wants you to get better so you'll be strong enough to go see Jenny. Dr. Ellerby and I both think he's right. After Bradford told me about Jenny, he left to see Saundra." Ruth added, "Remember that your faith has seen you through so much. Please pray."

"I will," Laura promised.

Chapter Fourteen

The Truth Comes Out

❧

After his visit with Saundra, Bradford was in a foul mood, so he rode around aimlessly, trying to sort out his thoughts. No matter what he tried to think about, Saundra's words about Gerald echoed through his mind.

Upon returning to Oak Grove, he learned that Laura was resting, so he went into his study to catch up on business matters he had neglected during his search for Jenny.

That evening he went up to Laura's room to share supper with her. He was very pleased to see her sitting up in bed, looking cheerful and rested. Ruth had helped her put on a warm robe over her lovely nightgown so she would be presentable for his visit.

He pulled up a chair and sat beside her. "You look much better than you did last night." Admiring the shiny light-brown hair that fell like wisps of newly spun silk over her shoulders, he couldn't get enough of her beauty.

Laura self-consciously shifted in the bed, thinking she must look dreadful after her drawn-out illness. Trying to divert his attention, she asked, "When do you think I'll be well enough to travel?"

Remembering the doctor's warning, Bradford chuckled as he said, "You're hardly well enough yet." Seeing the disappointment blur eyes that threatened tears, he reluctantly shared, "But I'll tell you how Jenny's doing if you'd like."

A warm, gentle breeze, very welcome after the recent fall storm, blew in from the balcony windows. "Could we finish our dinner out there while you tell me?" Laura begged.

"Are you able to walk?" Bradford asked, concern showing in his face.

"Surely I can," Laura said as she quickly threw back the covers and eased her legs over the edge of the bed. She stood up on very shaky legs. Before she knew it, she had fallen directly into Bradford's outstretched arms.

Bradford felt her warm, shapely body under her cotton nightclothes. He stroked her long wavy hair and luxuriated in the moment. Then, realizing she felt nothing for him, he quickly pulled away.

Stunned, Laura looked up into eyes that seemed to be shielding something from her. Not wanting him to guess how much she had enjoyed the interlude, she asked if he would help her out onto the balcony.

The fresh air appeared to wipe away the cold mask Bradford seemed to hide behind. He relaxed and said, "I know you want to know all about Jenny. Let me start by telling you that the people who have her thought they had your permission, so they aren't kidnappers at all."

Shocked, Laura looked up from the food she had been ravenously eating. "What? How could that be?"

Resting his hand on her arm, Bradford quietly said, "Calm down. If this is going to upset you, we'll switch the subject. I don't want you to get sick again."

Laura nodded weakly, signaling him to go on.

Bradford continued, "I only told you so you'd know Jenny wasn't with kidnappers. She isn't at all unhappy. In fact she was riding a horse they gave her when I left. She even has a new friend, Sally, who enjoys riding with her."

"That's wonderful to hear! I've missed her so. I also know a lot more than you suspect, for I was busy after you left," Laura said mysteriously.

Now it was Bradford's turn to be surprised. But before he could inquire into the details, Nanny appeared and told him a visitor was downstairs to see him. Upset at being disturbed, he demanded of her, "Who is it?"

"It's Miss Saundra," she announced.

"Tell her I'll be down in a minute," he stated as he gently helped Laura back to her bed. "We'll continue this later. But right now you're to rest and get your strength back." He left quietly, shutting the door behind him.

Laura relaxed in bed, reliving the all too brief moment when she was pressed up against Bradford's strong, masculine frame. Her blood had surged through her body, awaking senses she'd felt no one could ever rekindle. But she was also frustrated, since she knew he could never return her love for him because he was in love with Saundra. A tinge of guilt also made her feel she was being unfaithful to Gerald's memory. With that she tossed and turned as she fell into a disturbed sleep.

After leaving Laura, Bradford went straight to his study to find Saundra waiting for him. Her gorgeous red hair was piled high on her head as she gazed at him.

"I've come to apologize for the horrid quarrel we had," she said in her honey-sweet voice. "I meant no harm when I took Jenny to the Taylors. The Taylors wrote me a lovely note and thanked me for arranging for Jenny to visit them. They certainly had no problem with the arrangement. Surely we can kiss and make up," she begged.

Ignoring this last remark, Bradford realized the futility of remaining enemies with this girl. She was one of those people who simply wouldn't take no for an answer. So he decided to give her the benefit of the doubt as he eagerly rushed her out the door.

The next morning, as soon as Bradford heard that Laura was up, he dashed up the stairs and entered her room. Sitting on the edge of her bed, he asked, "May I take breakfast with you?"

"Yes," said Laura cheerfully. "Nanny should be up shortly with my tray. I'm sure she will bring you a tray as well."

As Bradford stared into her warm, captivating eyes, he inquired, "Now tell me what you learned while I was gone."

Gazing at him, Laura's eyes rested on his strong muscular hands, which he held tightly clutched near her own. She told him how the stableboy had seen a lady with red hair talking to the man who had ridden off with Jenny, which led her to suspect Saundra. Omitting her quarrel with Saundra, Laura told him how one of Saundra's servants had told her he knew Jenny was at the Taylors' and wouldn't come to any harm.

As Laura said these things, Bradford clutched his hands in frustration until his knuckles turned white. Relaxing his fingers by parting them, he gently took her hands and rested his around hers. He knew, although Laura had gotten better, she was still a long way from being completely well. As he entwined her long slender fingers among his masculine ones, he said, "Don't worry about what you found out. Jenny can't wait to see you and show you her new horse. As soon as you get your strength back, I'll take you immediately to see her."

"But that may be a long while." Laura sighed as she adjusted her pillow and sat up higher in her bed.

"I think you can get better faster than you realize. For someone so petite, you're one of the most determined and strong-willed people I know," Bradford said, smiling at her. "When Dr. Ellerby says you can make the trip, we'll leave." Placing two fingers on her protesting lips, he lightly stroked her cheek.

Nanny entered the room, interrupting the couple. After placing a tray next to Laura, she smiled and asked, "Bradford, may I bring you a tray too?"

"That would be very nice, Nanny. Thank you."

Bradford and Laura exchanged pleasantries, mainly talking about all the things he had learned about Jenny while he was with her. "Do you know she even got to sleep in a loft with lots of other children?" he asked.

"Oh, she must have enjoyed that. Please tell me more. I want to hear every detail!" Laura said, smiling.

Bradford talked on for several more minutes about Jenny as they finished eating the delicious breakfast of country ham, grits, and freshly baked biscuits. He left after the meal, letting her sleep.

Laura was able to regain her strength quickly because she was determined to see Jenny as soon as possible. During this time, Laura and Bradford usually took their meals together. They enjoyed talking about Jenny and getting to know each other better.

After only a week, Bradford heard a light tapping on his study door. "Come in," he quietly said, keeping his head down as he looked at the business papers before him.

Flinging open the door and running into the room was a flushed and healthy Laura. "I'm much better," she declared. "I've even felt well enough to help Lily with her reading," she bragged. As Bradford looked up at her, she added, "Dr. Ellerby believes I'll soon be well enough to make the trip to see Jenny! He suggested horseback riding to build up my stamina and said I can go for a ride today if I wish."

Looking doubtful but realizing her determination, Bradford said, "I'd better go too."

Laura laughingly said, "I'll be fine, but I would enjoy the company."

Bradford's mood lightened. Pushing his papers away, he stood up, and they walked to the stables together.

After choosing a very gentle horse for Laura, they mounted and rode into the dazzling sunshine that bounced off the trees and barn. After riding a short distance, Bradford insisted they return. Laura was grateful, for little as she wanted to admit it, she was breathless from their ride.

The next day they rode again. This became a regular habit over the following days. Each day Laura was building up her strength, ever hoping the doctor would permit her to make the trip to see Jenny.

Laura was increasingly excited that the time was growing near when she could see her daughter again. Bradford warned her not to push herself, though. She knew he was right, but she also sensed something was bothering him. She felt sure, however, that whatever was concerning him had nothing to do with Jenny. Laura was confident he loved Jenny and only wanted what was best for her. He wouldn't allow her daughter to be in a bad situation, so Laura had to be patient and put her mind to getting stronger.

If his concern wasn't Jenny, then it must be Saundra, Laura thought. Surely Saundra was unhappy that her fiancé had taken in Laura and her family. Laura's only lingering doubt was the growing realization that her love for Bradford had bloomed so much that she feared he would guess it any day. "Maybe he already has guessed my feelings?" Laura wondered out loud.

Nanny realized Laura had feelings for Bradford the next day when she walked into Laura's room.

Laura was getting ready to go for her morning ride and was taking an extraordinary effort to brush her curly hair so that it would be perfectly styled. Nanny noted, "'Tis been a long time since you took such pains to look your best." A grin filled her face as she knowingly looked into Laura's sparkling eyes.

As Laura realized Nanny knew her secret, her face immediately clouded over. Nanny walked over and gave her a quick hug, saying, "Wipe that worried frown off your face, for I'm not one to tell things that are only hunches."

Relieved, Laura hugged her back then went into the hall to get her wrap. Nanny always insisted she take it whenever she rode. Laura had thrown it over a chair outside her room so she wouldn't forget it. Holding her shawl, she started down the stairwell. As she reached the landing, her eyes locked with Bradford's.

Their eyes met for a moment as he looked up from the foot of the curving stairwell. Not expecting to see him at that moment, Laura hadn't shielded her feelings. Usually she was careful to guard her expressions so he wouldn't know how much she cared for him. But this time a slight smile touched her lips as their eyes met. A deep radiance shone from her face as her heart pounded wildly in her chest. Caught completely unaware, Laura fought to get her emotions under control as she descended the stairs.

When she reached the last step, Bradford took her hand in his for one brief instant as he gazed into her eyes. Laura's heart cried out for fear he couldn't fail to notice how she felt, because her love for him must have been written all over her face. She knew he would probably ask her to leave Oak Grove immediately if he felt she were in love with him, for Saundra would surely be angry and jealous.

Slowly dropping her hand, he turned to her, asking, "Well, are you ready to go?"

"Yes," Laura replied, happy that the moment had passed, and he hadn't asked her to leave—at least not yet.

"I thought we might ride to your cottage and see how the work is coming," Bradford said.

"Oh, I would enjoy that," Laura said enthusiastically. "How far along are they?"

"Several more months, and they should be finished," Bradford said thoughtfully.

Laura was lost in thought, as she realized that if he married Saundra, the only place she would have to go would be the cottage. That would be fine, but she didn't like the thought of living so close to Bradford and Saundra.

Trying to put this thought in the back of her mind, she walked with Bradford to the stables. "I think I'm going to be well enough to see Jenny very soon." Her eyes sparkled as she added, "I'm just so anxious. It helps to keep busy, though, until I can go. Do you realize I've never given you the grand tour of Oak Grove?"

"No, you haven't. When I first arrived you weren't happy with my being here," Bradford said with a mischievous glint in his eye.

"Oh," said Laura, pretending indignation before bursting out in laughter. They mounted their horses and set out for the cottage.

The day was quite warm for late fall. Laura was bundled up with mittens, a wool hat, and a loosely woven shawl pulled tightly about her shoulders.

As they entered the woods, Bradford drew his horse up beside hers and commented, "You certainly shouldn't get chilled today."

Laura agreed. "Nanny insisted I wear all these clothes. She's so afraid I'll have a relapse."

Bradford turned in his saddle and looked at Laura, suddenly realizing she was no longer the invalid everyone still assumed her to be. She was as healthy as ever. He was hoping that when Dr. Ellerby came today he would decide she was well enough to travel. Bradford knew the time was coming when he would have to tell her everything. Laura would be so upset that she probably would never forgive him for letting Jenny stay even one extra day at the Taylors' home. He wished Laura had gotten his telegram. He would have brought Jenny back immediately had she replied and let him know that she didn't want Jenny to remain behind. Since he hadn't heard from her, however, he had assumed Laura approved of Jenny staying with them a few more days. Dread filled him, as he knew how terribly upset she would be at him when the truth came out about who had Jenny. It would certainly end their close friendship, which had been one of the happiest times in his life.

Sensing Bradford's mood, Laura quietly rode beside him. She wished she could ask him what he was thinking. Maybe he was hoping the cottage would be finished soon so he could marry Saundra. Quickly pushing this thought from her mind, she was determined to enjoy the day. She spurred her horse up ahead of his.

Not wanting to be left behind, Bradford quickly matched her pace. Before they knew it, they were in the clearing in front of the cottage.

Bradford helped Laura down from her horse and turned toward her. "Well, what do you think?"

"Why, it's charming!" she exclaimed. "I never liked the old shed-like roof that hung over the front door. And look—there are now two bay windows instead of one. They give the cottage more symmetry and style. Who has done such wonders to a place I already thought was almost perfect?" she asked in wonder. Concerned, she whispered, "Can we afford the extra work?"

Bradford smiled. "Your trust did very well this year, so don't worry about the money. I guess if I'd had my way, I would've been an architect. I was always drawing and making model buildings that were very detailed even when I was little. Father thought it was a good hobby but not suitable for a profession."

Laura was enthralled with this unknown facet of him. She turned to admire the cottage. Now she began to notice small details he had skillfully changed. She slowly walked around the cottage, marveling at the decorative trim over the windows. As she looked at the cottage, she was pleased to see her balcony was now at the front of the house. It was similar to the one at the plantation, with two French doors that opened onto a large overhang. An open latticework railing accentuated the glass panels on the French doors.

Turning toward him, she exclaimed, "This is how the cottage always looked in my dreams!"

A smile slowly spread across Bradford's usually stern expression as he commented, "I built it especially with you in mind."

"Thank you," Laura replied. "You've done a superb job. Can I see the inside?"

"Well, the workmen are just starting inside. They hope to be finished in early spring. Maybe we can come back then and see it together," Bradford hoped.

"Yes, that would be nice," Laura said as he helped her over a rough area in the yard where the garden used to be. "Oh, let's see how the goldfish pond is doing." Bradford looped her arm in his as they walked to the pond.

Laura clapped her hands together. "Look how good it looks! I'm so glad. I wish Jenny could see it. Do you think the doctor will give his permission today for me to travel?"

"I don't see why not! You're as healthy as ever, and I know Jenny is going to love seeing you. We'll leave first thing in the morning if he approves."

When they returned to Oak Grove, Laura said, "Now it's my turn to show you around."

Bradford agreed but insisted they have a light lunch first. Nanny cheerfully prepared them sandwiches, which they ate on the patio.

"Now where should I start our grand tour?" Laura said. "I guess I'll begin with the grounds, since we're outside. My great-grandfather brought this land in the early 1800's. He owned one of the first mercantiles in Vicksburg, which did very well. Then, after his father passed away, my grandfather built a small house on the property close to where Oak Grove now stands. My father worked very hard starting his bank. He later inherited this land and the small home from his father."

Bradford asked, "Was your grandmother as fond of the balconies as you are?"

"Yes," Laura said. "Grandfather had one built especially for her on the second floor. Then, when my father built Oak Grove, he made sure my mother had one off her room. As a matter of fact, all of the upstairs bedrooms have access to the pillared gallery.

"Now let's go inside. I'll show you the downstairs first." Laura led the way as they entered the hallway. They proceeded into the large parlor, which displayed a portrait of a jolly-looking man with a gray beard. "This is Grandfather Malcolm," Laura continued, smiling up at the painting and adding, "He was a warm man and dearly loved horses. I guess Jenny gets that from him."

Bradford commented, "The fireplace must be of Italian design. Why did your father pick that style?"

Laura smiled. "My parents went to Italy for their honeymoon. My mother's parents did very well financially. They gave her a generous dowry when she married my father. My parents bought the marble and several of the furnishings in Europe while they were there. These things reminded them of that time in their lives, so I'm glad they were saved during the war. Have you discovered the secret room in the study?" Laura asked mischievously.

"No," Bradford remarked, appearing extremely curious.

Laura led the way into the richly paneled room where Bradford's paperwork was neatly distributed throughout. She walked over to the bookcase and removed one of the Shakespeare volumes. After moving the book, she pressed a button, and an entire panel slid away, revealing a room the size of a small closet.

"When I was little, I used to pretend I was a spy and listened in on meetings," Laura reminisced. "It's very small, but I suppose an adult could hide inside it for a short while."

"Oh, my," Bradford said as he stepped up to peer inside. "It's such a creative place to hide important valuables. Does anyone else know about this secret room?"

"Only my mother and I know, as far as I'm aware," Laura said. "Fortunately, during the war my father kept his gold here, which he later used to recover financially. Without the gold he wouldn't have been able to restart his bank because, as you know, Confederate money was worthless."

As they climbed to the second floor, Laura quickly changed the subject, since she didn't want to delve into her father's financial problems too much. Continuing the grand tour, she explained, "Your room was my grandparents' room. They lived in the newly built main house with us after my father completed Oak Grove."

"Is your mother's suite where she stayed while your father was alive?"

"Yes." Stepping inside the room Laura pointed to a four-poster bed and remarked, "That's where General

Grant slept when he was here. My parents had a connecting suite, and now Jenny sleeps where my father used to stay. Over the years we had changes made to the second story. Now let's go to the most exciting place of all—the attic with the cupola!" she exclaimed.

Before they started to the third floor, Nanny called, "Laura, Dr. Ellerby's here."

Laura excused herself with excited anticipation. "I'll be right back. Please hope it's good news," she said, as she went to her bedroom so the doctor could examine her.

After examining her and seeing how well she was doing, Dr. Ellerby stepped into the hall to speak with Bradford. "She's well enough to travel!" he said. "She seems to be back to her old self. She's amazing to have recovered so quickly."

When Laura rejoined Bradford, she was beaming happily. "I'm so excited. Dr. Ellerby said you can take me to see Jenny! Can we leave first thing in the morning like you said?"

Bradford responded, "We should be ready to go then. I believe we can get all the arrangements made if we work quickly. Why don't you show me the cupola, and then we'll start packing?"

Together they climbed the steep staircase to the third floor. The attic door swung open as the rusty hinges groaned loudly. Dust lay thickly over the trunks and old furniture. Laura opened a small door in the center of the room. This led to a set of spiral stairs. She had to squeeze the sides of her hoopskirt together to fit into the small winding stairwell. She quickly ascended the stairs to the cupola. She had an extra bounce in her steps because of her excitement about finally being reunited with her daughter.

Bradford followed close behind. They wound higher and higher until they came to a small square room that looked out over the grounds. A chimney passed through the center of the room and out through the roof. Each of the four walls had two large multi-paned windows, allowing them to see out from all sides. The view of the grounds and the river beyond was breathtaking.

As they came to the top step and entered the room, Laura said, with a gleam in her eyes, "This was my favorite place to come as a child." Facing Bradford, she explained, "My father had the cupola built around the chimney. His parents had had a chimney fire when he was little. So he was always worried about fire. With a cupola, if a fire started they could open this small door and pour sand down the chimney to smother the fire. But to me the cupola represented much more. I could come up here and look out over what was my whole world." Laura threw out her delicate hand, pointing to the Mississippi as it slowly wound its way downstream.

Bradford turned toward her. "I've always wanted a cupola. I'm so glad Oak Grove has this one. It reminds me of something you'd find along the Northeast coast. There we call them 'widows' walks' since the popular myth holds that they were used by wives whose husbands had gone to sea. The women would stand on them anxiously watching for their husbands to return. Often the husbands didn't make it back, so they got the name 'widows' walks.'"

Bradford looked around, closely studying the fine points of the architecture. He was fascinated by the room's construction.

Tugging on his sleeve, Laura regained his attention as he wistfully said, "You had such a wonderful childhood growing up here. If I'd lived here when I was little, this cupola would have been a great place to spy on pirates coming down the river."

They were both laughing as they started back down the tightly winding stairs. When they reached the bottom of the stairs and were back in the attic, Laura led him to a large white chest. Together they knelt by the chest as Laura slowly opened its intricately carved lid.

Turning toward him, she glanced over the attic. "Before we move back to the cottage, I'd like your permission to go through these things and sort out our ancestral keepsakes. If there's anything of value, I'll leave it," Laura said in a serious tone.

"It's all yours," Bradford offered. "Now tell me what's in this trunk."

"You probably won't be interested," Laura said, suddenly embarrassed. "It contains some things I had as a child."

"I'm very interested," Bradford responded as he looked deeply into eyes, which sparkled with glowing anticipation.

Laura pulled out several of the clothes she had worn as a child. They were very practical clothes that were feminine but also made for an active child. She looked at a dress she had worn when she was around five and said, "Why, this would fit Jenny now. I can't wait to see her!"

As she reached down for a scrapbook, Bradford placed his hand lightly on her arm and turned her to face him. In a deep, solemn voice, he said, "I believe the time has come for me to tell you everything about Jenny."

Laura looked into his face and saw his pain as he uttered these words. She had tried not to think about Jenny being at the Taylors', because she dreaded what that meant for the future. She knew Bradford had said she was fine. Also, she knew Jenny would be cared for if she were at the Taylors'; however, the fear she had of Gerald's father was still very real to her.

As she faced him, Bradford began, "I know you've guessed where Jenny is. She's with her grandparents. She has brought so much joy into their lives that Gerald's parents have fallen in love with her."

"But," Laura exclaimed vehemently, "they have no right!"

Bradford gently put his fingers on her lips to stop the flood of words from bursting forth. Then he explained, "Saundra heard us talking in the study and overheard you say Jenny was your and Gerald's child."

"Oh, so you didn't tell her?" Laura happily sighed as relief flooded through her.

"No, of course not." Bradford continued, "Somehow Saundra got the idea that Jenny should be with Gerald's parents. Saundra even told them you said it was fine for Jenny to visit."

"Of all the nerve!" Laura exclaimed as she flung her hands up, sweeping dust over them.

"Now wait and listen," Bradford said, trying to calm her down. "Jenny was taken to the judge's house by a nice man Saundra hired. When Jenny arrived, the judge and his wife took her to her own room, which they had fixed especially for her. Judge Taylor loves horses and even gave her one when he discovered she enjoys riding as much as he does. All this time they thought it was fine with you."

"When you found her, why didn't you tell them it wasn't fine?" Laura said, her eyes flaring.

"Laura, Mrs. Taylor begged me not to because the judge has suffered regret all these years, and now he's like a new man. He believes you've forgiven him," Bradford clarified. "Jenny loves them, and I felt she should get to know them while I explained things to you. Then, when you didn't answer my telegram, I thought you were fine with her staying a little longer. I got caught in an ice storm, or I would've returned sooner. If you hadn't been ill, I would've taken you right then to see Jenny. The Taylors have even extended an invitation for you to live with them. The judge was hoping you would even join them for Christmas."

"It's an invitation I'll never accept!" Laura said in a rage. "So you side with them." She shook with anger as she quickly stood up. "Gerald's father brought all this on himself. You don't know the humiliation I went through when I had to tell my friends that my father-in-law, who hadn't even bothered to come see me, didn't approve of me. Then there were the years of fear that he would take my child. Finally the worst of all was not having my own child know I'm her mother. I've prayed to forgive him, but I don't want him to be part of our lives…ever!" Laura shouted. She rushed from the attic, dropping a small book at his feet.

Bradford sat on the floor, realizing his worst fears were coming true. Laura had been through too much to forgive Judge Taylor completely. He glanced at the small book that lay open at his feet. It was a diary Laura had written when she was a teenager. Not wanting to pry, he closed it just after he happened to see: "I will love Gerald to the end of time." He carefully placed the diary back in the white chest and quietly walked to the study.

Bradford met Ruth in the stairwell and told her everything. He bent over and gave her a gentle squeeze as he sadly said, "Laura will need you now."

"Laura has been through so much because of the Taylors," Ruth told him. "I don't know if she can ever forgive them, but that's something we'll have to let her decide for herself. I only hope and pray that God will heal her heart. Don't blame yourself, Bradford. I feel you did what was right. Jenny definitely needs to know Gerald's side of the family."

He thanked her and descended the stairs to the study then quietly shut the door behind him.

Laura stretched out on her bed as she looked out the windows. Tears had left her eyes swollen and red. All the grief she had kept inside for so many years had finally been released, and calmness gradually settled over her after the explosive venting of her rage. Slowly she got up and went onto the balcony. As the breeze lifted her hair off her back and caressed her red cheeks, she thought back to a conversation she and Gerald had had about his father right before his accident.

She could almost hear Gerald speaking as she reminisced. "My mistake all these years was not letting you get to know my family," he'd said. "I don't believe they ever even saw you." He put his arm around her as he continued, "My father is stubborn, but I know that when he gets to know you, he'll realize why no one else could replace you in my life."

Laura thought that maybe she should at least meet his parents. Christmas wasn't that many weeks away, and she could at least be with her darling child. At that moment it was as though God was pointing the way for her to go. She made up her mind to put the past behind her. She felt the answer to her prayers was to open her heart to total forgiveness.

Laura combed her wind-whipped hair and checked to see that her eyes were no longer red. Then she quietly went downstairs to tell Bradford that tomorrow they would go as planned to meet Gerald's parents and see Jenny. As she reached the study, she realized Bradford must have stepped out for a moment, so she sat down to wait. Then she heard voices coming from the hall. Not wanting to see anyone but Bradford, Laura quickly stood up to leave. She immediately realized she would have to meet whoever it was if she went into the hall. After her trying day, she was in no mood to talk to anyone. She impulsively reached up and grabbed the book that hid the secret button. After pressing it, she slid into the small hideout, closing the door behind her.

Soon the voices grew louder, and Laura realized Bradford was talking to a woman. As she heard their footsteps enter the study, the voices became quite clear; she was quick to recognize Saundra's stilted drawl.

"Well, Bradford," Saundra asked, "when should we announce our very exciting news to our friends?"

"Next month," Laura heard Bradford state.

She knew they must be speaking of their engagement. She had hoped that Saundra had lied about their upcoming marriage, just as she had lied about Bradford exposing her secret about Jenny. At the realization that Saundra had actually been telling the truth about her relationship with Bradford, Laura's heart sank.

Then she heard Saundra say, "Now give me a hug and a kiss to seal the deal."

During the quiet moment that followed, Laura imagined Bradford ardently kissing Saundra. Finally she heard them leave. Laura's legs were cramped from stooping so she wouldn't hit the ceiling. Feeling all around for the button to open the door in the secret room, Laura began to panic. She couldn't find the release button. After a few minutes, she finally remembered the button was behind her. When she gently pressed it, the door swung open. She walked out and quickly closed it behind her.

Reading a document, Bradford walked back into the study. Surprised to see her, he asked, "How did you get in here?"

"Well, I…" Laura paused.

Bradford didn't seem to hear her. "Well, have a seat," he said. "I was just going over the deed to some land I'm purchasing."

"I've come to say," Laura said, hesitantly, as she sat down, "that I'm sorry for my behavior in the attic."

Bradford put down his papers and walked over to her chair. He sat by her as she slowly continued. "Jenny does need to know Gerald's family. I think it's best that I meet them too. I'll probably stay with them until the cottage is ready," she conceded, averting her eyes from his.

"You and Jenny can stay here as long as you want, so you don't have to live with them," Bradford offered.

"You mean they'll let me have Jenny?" Laura almost jumped out of her seat in her excitement.

"Yes, she's yours forever," Bradford stated firmly. "I thought you knew that. I'll make sure Jenny is never taken away from you again!"

Laura relaxed and knew that as long as she would get Jenny back, she could endure anything—even living with Gerald's parents until the cottage was ready. She decided she wouldn't impose on Bradford anymore, especially since he would be announcing his engagement soon.

"When can we leave?" Laura asked as she looked into shining eyes, which smiled into hers.

"Tomorrow morning," Bradford said. "This is something that shouldn't have been put off this long. But we needed to wait until Dr. Ellerby said you were strong enough to hear the truth about Jenny and make the trip. Maybe Saundra did us a favor after all," Bradford added mischievously.

Laura ignored this remark as the dread of facing Gerald's family filled her. "I'll pack now and be ready to leave early tomorrow morning."

Chapter Fifteen

A Journey to Confront the Past

❧

$\mathcal{B}$efore she knew it, a rooster crowed in the barnyard. Laura, now awakened, energetically got up and began to dress, taking care to choose a conservative but attractive traveling suit. She decided to wear her pale-blue linen jacket. It was warm and also gave her dress a touch of elegance. She felt the pretty clothes would give her the extra confidence she needed to meet Gerald's parents. She also decided to wear her hair up so she would look more fashionable. After smoothing out a few wrinkles in the gown, Laura pulled the front of her hair straight back into a large knot at the back of her head and secured it with a blue ribbon. Taking one last look at her room, which would never be hers again, she sighed and walked into the hall.

Preoccupied, she collided with Bradford, who had dressed for the trip in a double-breasted frock coat, carrying his hat and gloves. "Oh, excuse me," Laura lightheartedly said, glancing up at him.

Bradford looked at her hair pensively as they proceeded down the hall. He had seen her wear it up only occasionally and missed the flowing, curly strands that usually fell down her back.

Laura interrupted his thoughts as she inquired, "How far is the Taylors' house?"

Bradford replied, "Well, it should take us approximately a day and a half. We can stay the night at an inn about halfway there. Have you told your mother and Nanny you're leaving to see Jenny?"

"Yes," Laura said. "They'll come next week. Mother felt it would be nice for me to get acquainted with Gerald's parents on my own."

Bradford noticed her face turn pale with these words. Giving her a reassuring smile, he led her to the dining room, where they ate a filling breakfast with Nanny and Ruth.

Before they left for Cameron Falls, Laura's mother took Laura aside and said, "I feel all the tragic events that have led to this moment will be resolved by your going to the Taylors'. I know it'll be one of the hardest things you've ever done, but it'll be worth all your efforts." As she hugged her daughter, she whispered, "I love you, dear. Please tell Jenny how much I've missed her." She gave Laura a little squeeze as she advised, "Please open your heart to forgiveness. Remember what it says in Luke 6:37: 'Do not judge, and you will not be judged. Do not condemn, and you will not be condemned. Forgive, and you will be forgiven.'"

Laura nodded and returned her mother's warm hug. "I will, Mother. You've been such a wonderful mother to me." Then she turned and hugged Nanny.

Before leaving she ran into the kitchen to see Lily. "Please keep practicing your reading, Lily. You're doing so well. Mother said she'd help you if you have any questions."

Lily thanked her, promising, "I'll keep reading. Be sure to give Jenny a hug from me."

After helping Laura into the carriage, Bradford signaled the driver to proceed before swinging into the seat across from her and quickly shutting the door to keep out the brisk wind.

The swaying motion of the carriage soon soothed Laura's jittery nerves. As she relaxed, she moved next to the window to view the countryside. As they rode along, she pointed out different landmarks to Bradford.

"Oh, look, there's Camellia Hall. I guess Saundra is sorry to see you leave," Laura remarked as she turned toward him.

Thinking to himself about all the trouble Saundra had caused, Bradford replied gruffly, "I'm sure she has plenty to occupy herself with."

Deciding they must have had a quarrel about his making this trip, Laura sighed. "I hope this trip hasn't ruined any of your plans."

Looking puzzled, Bradford said sharply, "What do you mean? I had no other plans."

Not expecting to have upset him, Laura quickly changed the subject. "This is as far as I've ever come. My father didn't enjoy the rocking and swaying motions of a carriage, so we stayed at home. This is really an adventure. I'd love to travel and see what London, Paris, and Rome are like."

"You mean you've never been to London?" Bradford asked. "London is such an intriguing city with its hustle and bustle, but with a charm that's truly English. I'd enjoy showing it to you one day."

"Oh, I'd love that," Laura said, sadly realizing that this could never happen and wondering silently what Saundra would think of Bradford's comment.

"What lake is that?" Laura inquired, as she pointed out her window to a glimmering body of water surrounded by weeping willows that drooped gracefully near the water's edge.

Bradford came up to the window beside Laura as he replied, "That's Lake Misty. It's so scenic that the governor built a country house on the far side of the lake. Look carefully, and you'll see it now."

Laura saw the white house tucked beneath the swaying willow trees. "It's enchanting." As she turned her head to get a closer view, she rubbed her cheek against Bradford's in the tight interior of the rocking carriage. The thrill of his warm cheek against hers made her long to stay by him. She turned toward him and, for a brief moment, saw a warm glow in his usually distant expression. Suddenly, the glow faded, however, and he turned away.

"I guess I'd better relieve the driver. Be sure to call me if you need anything at all," Bradford said. After signaling the driver to stop, he got out, slamming the coach door behind him with a crash.

Laura felt a loss at his absence and, losing her earlier interest in the landscape, decided to nap. She awoke as the carriage pulled up to a roadside inn.

Bradford opened the door and gently helped her down from the carriage. As they walked into the inn, the innkeeper said as he bowed, "Please come this way for your evening meal."

Since she'd eaten only a small amount of food during the trip, Laura was ready for dinner. The men in the tavern parted to let them pass. As they followed the innkeeper, all eyes seemed to be on Laura as she entered the room. Tall and muscular, Bradford looked disapprovingly at the men who stared at her. As he followed her to their table, the men at the bar sheepishly looked away from the glaring stranger.

"Please have a seat," the innkeeper said as he pulled out a chair for Laura. Looking at Bradford, he added, "You'll be served right away."

Tired from the long journey, Bradford told Laura, "I hope you got a lot of rest on the trip over. Hopefully we'll be able to make good time tomorrow."

"I just can't wait! It'll be a joy to have Jenny back in my life," Laura said, trying to forget her uneasiness about meeting Gerald's family.

While discussing the picturesque scenery on their journey, Laura and Bradford ate a delicious meal of chicken and dumplings, cornbread, and pecan pie. The tasty meal and pleasant conversation allowed them to ignore the rough crowd at the bar.

The innkeeper rejoined them as soon as they finished their meal. Taking them to their rooms, he scurried about, trying to impress his customers. "I've obtained the two most suitable rooms in our charming inn for you. I hope you'll be very comfortable," he said, leading them to the second floor. With a flourish he threw open the first door. "I feel this room will please the lady. My wife will be available to help her in any way she can." He turned to Bradford. "Your room, sir, is directly across the hall. Please let me know if I can be of any further assistance." He bowed deeply and gave them a broad smile.

Laura's room was indeed charming, with lace curtains hanging at the window and a large feather bed dominating its center. Even so, Laura felt a bit uneasy and asked Bradford, "Will those people downstairs be noisy all night?"

"Yes, I'm afraid we're right over the bar. But after today's journey, I don't think I'll have any problem falling asleep," he mumbled wearily as he turned toward his room.

After dressing in her nightgown, Laura climbed into bed and sank amid a plump mountain of feathers. For several minutes she tossed and turned, soon realizing her error in having slept so long during the afternoon journey. As she lay in the dark room, the rowdy voices from downstairs encouraged her uneasiness. She knew it was hopeless to try to sleep, so she lay there listening to the nighttime noises. As the hour grew very late, she heard the men from downstairs slowly pound their way up the wooden steps. They clumped noisily down the hall. Occasionally she would hear angry words as one of the men unexpectedly stumbled into a wall or a chair as he made his way to his room. At long last it appeared everyone was in bed. The total silence made Laura nervous as she tossed and turned. Then she lay perfectly still as she heard muffled steps slowly and carefully climb the stairs one by one. They weren't at all like the loud, boisterous ones she had heard earlier. She strained to listen as the light steps halted outside her door. Laura froze as she thought she heard a key being inserted into her lock.

Moonlight reflected on the shiny brass of her doorknob. She could actually see it being turned with a careful ease so as not to make a sound. The door slowly and silently swung back, and Laura faintly saw the glimmering blade of a knife tightly clutched by a wicked-looking man dressed in dark clothing. Fear gripped Laura. She tried to scream, but nothing came out as tightness immobilized her body. Finally her loud scream pierced the air, and she jumped up, before quickly rolling under the bed. The assailant frantically searched for her among the covers. She felt her heart pounding as she gasped for air, hoping the man would leave before finding her under the bed. Praying to God to save her, she saw the intruder crouch on his hands and knees before looking under the bed. She edged away from the intruder as far as her trembling arms and legs would allow, as his hands groped under the bed searching for her. Soon she felt his cold fingers grip her leg. As he tried to pull her out from under the bed, she fought with all her strength, kicking at his hands with her free leg. This only intensified the man's anger, as his icy fingers dug deeper into her tender flesh.

Laura made another desperate attempt to scream. As her dry lips parted, her piercing scream ruptured the still night air. The assailant uttered an ugly word and jerked her leg again. She hung on to the bed frame with all her might. Splinters from the roughly hewn bed dug into her fingers, but she knew she was clinging on for her life.

Bradford called, "Laura!" as he dashed into the room. Her assailant quickly released his grip and ran out the door, rudely pushing Bradford aside.

Half asleep, Bradford rushed forward, continuing to call out her name.

"I'm under the bed," Laura cried softly.

Since she was still in shock, Bradford carefully took her hands from the bed rail. He slid her out from under the bed and pressed her shaking body against his. His long fingers stroked the tear-wet hair that fell over her trembling frame.

"It's all right now. He's gone and can't hurt you," Bradford soothingly whispered as he gently rocked her back and forth in his arms.

"He was going to kill me," Laura muttered. "He was going to stab me with that knife."

"No," Bradford said reassuringly. "I think he was after your mother's diamond-and-amethyst ring. I noticed several men at the bar staring at it when we first arrived. I'm glad you're enjoying wearing it, but maybe you shouldn't wear the ring around strangers."

"I never thought it to be valuable to anyone but me," Laura replied as she studied the diamonds shimmering around the deep-purple stone.

"I believe it's worth quite a sum. All the diamonds are large and have a perfect blue-white color," Bradford speculated.

"Here—you keep it with you. I don't want to attract that kind of attention again," Laura stated as she slipped the ring off her finger and laid it in his hand.

"You won't have to worry except when we're traveling," Bradford reassured her, lifting her head from his shoulder. "Will you be all right now?"

As his muscular arms started to pull away, she began to tremble. Bradford felt her entire body vibrate through her gown.

Laughing, Laura replied, "I guess my body has given me away. I would like to appear braver. How did the man get a key to my room?"

Bradford looked into her fearful eyes, which looked like those of a deer that had just been chased by a mountain lion. "What do you mean he had a key?"

Laura shakily replied, "I wasn't asleep and heard the key turn in the lock."

"We need to find out how the intruder got a key. I'll get a blanket and sleep on the floor by the door," Bradford replied when Laura started to protest.

Just then they heard a cough as the landlady shuffled into the dimly lit room carrying a lantern. "What's been going on in here? From downstairs the scraping noises sounded like someone was rearranging all the furniture. Who was screaming?"

Instantly cheered by the gruff but friendly woman, Laura told her all the horrors she had just endured. Being used to rowdy customers, the landlady wasn't afraid and announced she would stay with Laura so no harm would befall her.

Bradford asked the landlady, "How did that man get a key to her room?"

The landlady held up the key. "He must've taken it off the hook when my desk clerk took a break. Whoever it was dropped it in the hall when he fled. So there's no way he can get in now. I'll protect the lady. Never fear." She waved a heavy-looking rolling pin in the air. "I brought this with me just in case." Placing her hands on her sturdy hips, she unflinchingly stood by Laura.

Bradford winked at Laura as he left the room, leaving the formidable landlady to tuck Laura into bed. After searching the grounds in vain for signs of the intruder, he returned to his room. Facing the hall with his door open, he fixed his gaze on Laura's door for the rest of the night, wondering if something else lay behind the assault.

Morning light soon filtered into the dim room as Laura stirred. The episode of the previous night faded as though it were part of a soon-to-be-forgotten nightmare. When she awoke, the landlady's pallet was empty. The sound of clattering pans and the smell of frying bacon gave Laura a clue as to the woman's whereabouts. Laura dressed in a lovely muslin gown with a brocaded bodice decorating her pale-pink dress. Then she put on her black velvet cape and joined Bradford downstairs at a small wooden table by the fire.

Bradford studied Laura's clear violet eyes under her long lashes as she sat down beside him. Seeing no sign that she was still distressed over last evening, he asked, "Well, are you ready for the last stretch of our trip?"

"I've missed Jenny so much! I just can't believe that I'll get to see her today. Whatever else lies ahead has been carefully stuffed into the bottom drawers of my mind," Laura admitted with a slight shake in her voice.

Noticing the catch in her voice, Bradford said, "The way you describe Gerald leads me to believe he's definitely a product of his parents. I feel certain you'll agree soon," he threw in with a mischievous gleam as he awaited her reaction.

"If you think for one minute that I'll ever like them, you're wrong!" Laura fumed, leaning forward and upsetting the cup that rested near her elbow.

As Bradford helped her mop up the spilled coffee, he said with a laugh, "I hope Gerald's father knew what he was doing when he invited you to come."

"Well, I hope so too," Laura agreed, realizing Bradford just wanted her to stop pitying herself. She knew she must face the Taylors with resolve and dignity, not fear. Fortified with courage mixed with a little pride, she was ready to face whatever lay ahead.

Bradford climbed into the carriage after her and stretched his long muscular legs onto the cushion across from her. As she quizzically glanced at him, he explained, "I was up all night making sure no one tried to get into your room again."

Laura looked into his tired eyes as they were closing and whispered, "Thank you."

All day long the carriage bumped along, seeming to hit every rock and pothole in the country lane, but Bradford slept peacefully. It was hard for Laura to pull her eyes from his sleeping form. When she was with him, she always had to maintain a mask over her feelings. But now she could openly gaze at his long, angular face. She studied the thick black hair that was neatly parted to the side. His high-arched eyebrows gave him a dignified, confident appearance while framing clear blue eyes that now rested peacefully.

Laura took one of the blankets from the rack over her seat and laid it over him. As she finished turning down the edges of the coverlet, a thought struck her: This was the last time she would ever be alone with him. She wondered when Bradford's wedding with Saundra would occur. Hopelessness enveloped her as she stood to keep the blanket from slipping off when he rolled over. Just as she tucked in the corners, the carriage hit a deep hole in the road, throwing her into his arms.

Still half asleep, Bradford wrapped his arms around her, softly caressing her back. Stunned from the fall, Laura struggled to stand up.

Misinterpreting her reasons for freeing herself, Bradford was now totally awake, and said coldly, "Pardon me."

"It was my fault," Laura stuttered, "I…was trying…to fix…the blanket." She stated indignantly, "The buggy must be going too fast."

Feeling that Laura must be repulsed by him, Bradford sat numbly in the corner of the carriage. Tension filled the coach as she fought for words to end the misunderstanding.

Before she could find them, the driver yelled, "Whoa! We're here."

Bradford regained his composure and quickly flung open the carriage door. The cold wind swiftly enveloped the carriage as Laura drew her black velvet cape closer to her and climbed down the coach's steps. Turning to Bradford with sorrowful eyes, she started to speak.

Before the words came forth, a cheerful sound reached Laura's ears—a sound she had longed to hear ever since Jenny could talk. Disbelief flooded her face as she turned to see her smiling child running down the hill toward them.

"Mama, Mama," Jenny yelled as she stumbled, falling facedown into the tall brown grass. Quickly picking herself up, Jenny ran a little more cautiously toward them.

When Jenny reached them, she rushed straight toward Laura with her arms wide open. "Oh, Mama, you've come! I've missed you so. You'll like Gran and Grandfather so much. They even gave me a real horse!"

Jenny reached over, pulling Bradford close to Laura so she could hug both of them. Pressed up to Laura's cheek, Bradford felt the warm tears that were flooding down her face.

"Why are you crying, Mama?" Jenny asked, puzzled.

"The tears are for the happiness I feel seeing my little girl," Laura stated, relishing the words *my little girl* on her lips.

Laura glanced up at Bradford, who had wiggled out of Jenny's grasp and was turning to get back into the carriage. "Aren't you going to say hello to Judge and Mrs. Taylor?" Laura inquired, wiping the tears from her cheeks. "Please come," she appealed. Her pleading eyes looked at him with a mixture of fear and sadness that he was leaving.

"Yes, I guess, I should," Bradford stated hesitantly, swinging her bags down from the carriage. They all then proceeded up the hill toward the Spanish-style villa.

Laura was bursting with questions. Foremost in her mind was how Jenny had come to know the truth. She knew, however, this was not the time to ask.

As they reached the villa, Mrs. Taylor quietly opened the intricately carved wooden door. Laura paused as she studied the tall, stately woman whose grayish-blond hair was piled high on her head. She held her head in a proud, almost arrogant manner. But upon closer appraisal, Laura was quick to catch the friendly twinkle in her gray eyes.

"Oh, Laura," Mrs. Taylor said, immediately taking Laura in her arms. "I've longed for this day for years."

When Mrs. Taylor turned to greet Bradford, she was quick to sense his tense mood. As she led them down the hall into the library, she asked how their journey had been.

Laura replied politely, trying to relax before experiencing that fateful moment she had long dreaded when she would meet Judge Taylor. As they turned into the book-lined room, Laura immediately came face-to-face with Gerald's father. She was taken aback by his short, rather robust figure. She had expected a tall, stately gentleman. With a wide grin filling his face, he gestured for them to sit by the fire. "Please have a seat."

Laura seated herself and then found herself smiling back at him.

The judge was nothing like she had ever dreamed he would be. His round face was framed by dark-brown hair combed over to conceal a balding head. His cheeks were ruddy. His brown eyes were as clear and alert as those of a man half his age.

Judge Taylor approached Laura, lightly kissing her hand, and said, "It's a pleasure to finally meet my only son's wife and the mother of my darling granddaughter."

Laura had expected a cold, hard man and had never planned to forgive him for what he had done. Suddenly, however, she found herself melting under the charm of a man who was so like Gerald in personality.

As Judge Taylor started to say more, Jenny, who had been tugging on Laura's hand for the past few minutes, said, "Let's all go see My Lady."

Everyone agreed and headed outside. "Please come this way, and I'll show you the stables," the judge said. Along the way, he explained to Laura how he had reestablished his fortune. He told her how he had found a few of his prize horses after the war and was able to rebreed his stock. After his horses had won a few races, his reputation as an expert horse breeder spread throughout the countryside.

The impressive stables were a very practical but also an artistic structure. As they approached the arched entrance, the judge turned to Bradford and proudly said, "Bradford designed them for me as a favor. Several of my friends were so impressed that they contacted him to get the plans so they can erect similar buildings."

Stepping into the stables, Laura turned toward Bradford and asked, "Did you design the villa too?"

"Yes," he admitted, this time no longer preoccupied. "The judge likes Spanish architecture, so I gave the huge veranda a Spanish look by placing the same arches over it as you find in the stables."

Laura was quick to notice the mosaic tiles that framed the smooth arches matched those she saw on the front of the villa. "Have you been to Spain too?" Laura inquired in awe.

"When the judge asked me to create an authentic Spanish villa, I traveled there for a few weeks to compile some notes," he admitted.

"You'll have to see the gardens Bradford designed in the back," Mrs. Taylor bragged. "They're truly spectacular."

Laura looked at Bradford, who seemed to have slipped back into his quiet mood. She walked silently by his side as the others walked farther into the stables. Stopping, she touched his arm and casually turned toward him. Almost in a whisper, she uttered, "You have tremendous talent. Don't let it go unused any longer."

Bradford's eyes flared, thinking back to how she had rejected him in the carriage. He asked, "Why do you care?"

Taken aback, Laura, no longer able to meet his demanding look, felt defeated and turned quickly on her heels. Leaving Bradford, she rushed to join the others, who were engrossed in admiring Jenny's horse.

Later that evening, after an elaborate meal, Bradford stood to thank his host and hostess, saying he had to leave before dark. Laura wanted to run after him and plead for forgiveness for whatever she had done to anger him, but instead she remained seated in the elaborately carved chair, nervously stroking the gold brocaded cushion. She watched as Jenny eagerly ran over to Bradford. He knelt so she could squeeze his neck before he rode off. Minutes after his departure, Laura was already feeling his absence. She turned toward Gerald's family, hoping that they'd be glad they had invited her for an extended stay.

Chapter Sixteen

The Ominous Threat

❧

*G*rinning, Mrs. Taylor reassured her visitor, "I know you're very tired, my dear. Your room is right next door to Jenny's. Let me take you there now."

Laura took Jenny's hand, and all three climbed the marble staircase with its elaborate wrought-iron banister. When they reached the top stair, Jenny ran ahead, shouting, "Come see my pretty room!"

The colorful flowered wallpaper and the shelves full of dolls and horse statues delighted Laura.

"Gran got this for me last week when we went into town," Jenny explained as she held up a china pony. "Doesn't it look like Scamp?"

"Oh, you shouldn't have done so much!" Laura exclaimed.

Mrs. Taylor faced Laura as she replied, "Jenny is such a miracle to us. I so wish we could have come to know her earlier. Please let us spoil her—and you," she pleaded with a sparkle in her eyes. "Now, Jenny, let's show your mother her room."

Laura followed Mrs. Taylor and Jenny next door to a spacious room with an oak canopy bed. On one wall a large window provided an expansive view of the lake below. "This is so lovely!" Laura replied as she turned and gave Mrs. Taylor a warm hug.

Smiling, Mrs. Taylor said, "I know you must be very tired. So I'll let you get ready for bed."

After Mrs. Taylor left, Laura helped Jenny onto her lap. Sitting on the edge of her bed, she noticed, "My, how you've grown! I'm just so happy to see you."

As Jenny's eyes started to droop, she sweetly looked at Laura as she murmured sleepily, "You're my very own mama. I'm so happy! When will Nanny and Grandma come?"

"Next week," Laura replied, fighting the urge to find out how Jenny had learned she was her mother. "Now off to bed," Laura urged as she took Jenny to her room, helped her into her nightclothes, and tucked her into bed. "Sleep well, my darling daughter."

After unpacking, Laura dressed for bed. As soon as her head met the down pillow, she fell into a restful slumber. During the night she woke up and decided to check on Jenny. Seeing that she was resting peacefully, Laura returned to her room. As she stopped in front of the door, however, terror seized her as she saw a man tiptoeing through her room. After slipping a few silver items into a large black sack, the man climbed out of the window, completely unaware of her presence.

As soon as Laura's heart stopped pounding, she rushed to her window and slammed it shut. When she tried to lock it, the bolt seemed to be loose. From her window, she saw the intruder in the moonlight, jumping from the arbor and running out of the yard. Feeling sure the thief was gone, she ran back to make sure Jenny was still safe. After she left Jenny, she quietly returned to her room. Then she lit a candle and inspected her room. Nothing seemed to be amiss. Concerned, she kept looking. Except for a few stolen items, everything seemed to be exactly as she had left it. Then her eye caught a small white note pinned to her pillow. Neatly written in a delicate feminine script, it read: *No one is happy that you are here. Leave immediately or you may not like the consequences.*

Laura's immediate reaction was that Mrs. Taylor had written the note. But she quickly put that thought out of her mind. Why would Mrs. Taylor have invited her to come only to threaten her? Maybe she hadn't liked her after she had arrived? Thoroughly confused, Laura fell back into a restless sleep. Her mind kept remembering the glimmer of the moonlight off the blade of the knife she had seen at the inn the night before. Had the knife been meant for her? Tonight this intruder didn't have a knife, but he seemed equally intent on frightening her.

The early-morning sun streamed into the room as Laura arose after her fretful sleep. Not wanting to alarm Jenny, she decided that she had simply allowed her imagination to run away with her. She felt sure it was just a coincidence that what had happened at the inn had happened again here. She decided only to mention the theft of the items to the Taylors and not tell them about the threatening note. Perhaps she would pick up clues as to the person responsible for the note.

Once Laura got out of bed, she put on a light-yellow dress. She went into Jenny's room and asked, "Do you need help getting ready?"

Jenny was awake and dashing about, trying to find something to wear. "Look at this pretty pink dress Gran made for me!"

Laura smiled. "It's very nice. Please, come over here so I can help you put it on." After Jenny was dressed, they went downstairs to the Spanish-style dining room. Large tiles formed a colorful blue-and-white pattern on the floor of the sunny room. As they ate breakfast, Jenny and Laura sat at a cozy table that overlooked the gardens. Jenny's grandfather soon joined them. He lightly squeezed Laura's arm then bent over to give Jenny a pat on her head.

Grinning at them, he asked, "What would you two ladies like to do today? I know what Jenny wants to do. Laura, do you enjoy riding as much as Jenny does?"

Laura grinned at the judge and decided he would have to be a superb actor to have anything to do with the note. Relaxed with this insight, she said she would love to see the gardens and then go for a ride. When Jenny stepped out of the room, she told him about the intruder.

Judge Taylor was startled. Before leaving to ask his head gardener if he had noticed anything unusual, he turned to Laura. "If you'd like, why don't you go on outside and explore the gardens? I find I can relax better there than anywhere in the world. We'll get to the bottom of the robbery." Concern filled his face as he confided, "I wouldn't want anything to happen to you or Jenny."

Laura excused herself and stepped outside onto the cool lattice-covered patio. Wisteria vines had wrapped their long branches into the lattice, blocking out all but the smallest rays of sunlight. After walking a few more steps, she left the cool, shaded patio and stepped into the bright sunlight. Enjoying the warmth of the sun, she wandered farther into the garden. The sun glimmered off three rectangular pools that were like mirrored stepping-stones that led down to the dark-blue lake. The first pool was on the same level as the villa and was surrounded by small yellow flowers. The second pool was much lower on the hill but could be reached by descending ten tiers of mosaic steps. The third pool was on the same level as the lake. From the top it looked like it was quite a ways down, but the multicolored flowers that framed the pools made the trip worthwhile. Laura quickly descended the steep stairs. When she reached the third pool, she sat on a marble bench that overlooked the duck-filled lake. She enjoyed watching the ducks bob around the lake as they swam toward her. She tightly wrapped her cape around herself, as the air had suddenly become very chilly.

After sitting for a while, lost in her thoughts, she jumped when she heard footsteps behind her. Laura quickly turned, coming face-to-face with an elderly woman.

"You must be Laura, the mother of Jenny," the proud, forceful woman stated briskly. "I'm the judge's sister, Mrs. Temple, and I live over there." She pointed to a small house near the lake. "I saw you sitting here from my kitchen window."

"Yes, I'm Laura. I'm pleased to meet you," Laura said.

Sitting beside Laura, she continued, "I haven't seen much of anyone since your child arrived." Laura was immediately aware of Mrs. Temple's bitter tone as she stared into the woman's cold eyes. "You'll have to come over and meet my son. My husband died years ago. We lost our vast acreage after the war. My brother purchased our land and will hold it until we can buy it back from him. I'll expect you to come to dinner tomorrow night at six o'clock. Now I must get back. It's too chilly for me out here." Mrs. Temple hurried off as quickly as she had come.

Laura was surprised to learn that the judge had a sister who was living so close to him. She seemed to be a very strong-willed, almost brusque person. Contemplating whether or not to visit her, Laura ascended the tile steps that led back to the villa.

Upon entering the dining room, she saw that the judge had already left. Laura poured herself a cup of coffee and seated herself so she could enjoy the majestic view.

Smiling, Gerald's mother entered the room and remarked, "Well, it seems I'm the last one up. May I join you for some coffee? We have so much visiting to catch up on. If you aren't too tired, please tell me all about your wedding to Gerald, the cottage Bradford said you and Gerald lived in, and Jenny's birth."

Laura filled her in on all these details and was touched when tears appeared in Mrs. Taylor's eyes as she told her of Gerald's heroic efforts on the night of his death. Laura was puzzled, though, that Mrs. Taylor never mentioned the annulment in their conversation. It was as though she were completely unaware of it. Or was she simply too polite to do so? Maybe she didn't want to bring up something so unpleasant, Laura reasoned.

"Thank you so much for filling a void in my life. I've long wondered what happened after Gerald left our home. Now that we've finished our coffee, I'd like to show you some special treasures that were his," Mrs. Taylor said. As they headed down the long hall to the sounds of their footsteps echoing on the cool tile, she added, "First I'd like to show you a painting."

As they entered the huge sitting room, Laura looked above the fireplace. She immediately froze as she gazed up into Gerald's eyes, masterfully captured by the artist. His deep-blue eyes actually seemed to be smiling at her. The artist had also perfectly depicted his hair—blond bangs neatly combed to the side. After a momentary silence, Laura whispered under her breath, "This painting is just the way I remember him."

"Yes, isn't it an amazing painting?" Gerald's mother remarked. "Whenever I miss my son, I just come in here and look at his portrait. Now I'd like for you to come up to a special room, dear."

As they wound their way through the hall and up the stairs, Laura remarked, "When I was by the lake this morning, I met the judge's sister."

"Yes," Mrs. Taylor said, as coolness entered her tone. "She's lived here since she lost her farm. When her husband died several years ago, we bought the farmland from her, and she came to live near us. They had fallen on hard times after the war and were going to lose the property. The judge received a new judgeship, and we were able to buy her land, which gave her the money she needed to continue living here. We thought we were doing her a favor, but she feels the loss of the land very deeply. I try to give her a lot of attention, but it seems I can't please her enough. Maybe you can visit her. She loves company. Perhaps she won't be so lonely if you spent a little time with her."

"She invited me to dinner tomorrow night. Would that be a good time for me to go?" Laura inquired.

"Yes. In fact I'd be very thankful if you'd go see her. Since Jenny came, I feel that I've neglected her."

After turning left at the top of the staircase, they entered a large room that faced the front of the villa. The room was filled with heavy, masculine furniture.

"This was the furniture Gerald grew up with. When we left Vicksburg after the war, I couldn't bring myself to part with any of his things, so we brought them with us." She moved over to a large chest and bent down. After prying open the heavy lid, she motioned for Laura to sit beside her. Laura sat on the floor, and they began to go through the mementos of the person they both had loved. When they got to the bottom of the chest, Mrs. Taylor reached in and pulled out a small box covered in velvet. After opening it, she gently handed it to Laura. The box contained a ring with diamonds that sparkled with brilliant fire. Mrs. Taylor said, "I gave this to Gerald to give to you when I first learned he wished to marry you. It was my mother's wedding ring. He was in such a hurry that he must have forgotten to take the ring. Now I'd like you to have it." Mrs. Taylor seemed to pause as she stared at the ring. After a few moments, she slowly turned and looked at Laura's hand. "I notice you still wear the ring Gerald gave you."

"Yes," Laura replied, glancing down lovingly at her wedding ring.

Mrs. Taylor continued wisely, "You're so young. I know some man will want to buy you his own ring one day. If it's all right with you, we'll give this ring to Jenny."

Laura agreed, realizing that Gerald's mother had accepted her son's death far better than she had. As they closed the trunk's heavy lid, it was as though they were closing the lid on the past so Laura could face the future. Turning to Mrs. Taylor, she asked her if the judge had told her about the theft the previous evening. Since the judge hadn't seen his wife yet that morning, Laura told her what had happened.

Startled, Mrs. Taylor let out a gasp. Gripping Laura's hand, she asked, "You weren't hurt, were you, dear?"

Laura gently reassured Mrs. Taylor that she had been checking on Jenny during the robbery and was coming back into her own room when she saw the robber leave. She told Mrs. Taylor that the thief didn't even notice her when he climbed out the window.

Mrs. Taylor looked concerned as she stated, "This is just awful. I'll have strong locks put on your door and window as soon as we can go into town to get them. I'm not concerned about the trinkets that were stolen, just that no one harms you or Jenny."

Laura now felt sure that neither of Gerald's parents had anything to do with the break-in, but she wondered what was behind the robbery and who had written the note.

Both of the women turned and left the room. As they proceeded down the ornate staircase, Mrs. Taylor said, "I guess you saw the gardens when you met Mrs. Temple."

"Yes," Laura replied. "They're so beautiful! Bradford never gave me any idea that he was so talented in designing landscapes and villas."

Mrs. Taylor confessed to Laura as they reached the hall, "I've tried everything possible to make him realize he should pursue his talents, but he just won't listen. He only built the villa for us because we're so close. His father was such a kind, loving man when his wife was alive. After she died, however, he became preoccupied with money. I was never able to understand how that could happen. Several years back my husband and Bradford's father, James, went in on a business venture together. Bradford's father bought the land and made improvements before my husband became involved. Therefore he felt he should collect more of the profits when the business was sold. My husband disagreed because the influx of cash he provided made the business a viable operation. He therefore believed the partners should share equally. That's when the two friends had such a big falling-out." Sighing, she added, "I guess we all have our weaknesses. Bradford was so thoughtful to come after his father died and pay my husband his fair share. Bradford also made sure we knew how sad he was that the misunderstanding had ever happened. He's such a good man," she commented, smiling shyly at Laura.

Turning away from Laura, Mrs. Taylor acknowledged, "I know you'll want to see Jenny now, so I'll go instruct the cook about dinner. Jenny should be down at the stables with her grandfather. They're so much alike," she noted with a twinkle in her gray eyes as she looked over her shoulder. She smiled at Laura as she continued toward the kitchen.

Laura went out the heavy carved door onto the front veranda. She quickened her step as she saw Jenny gallop toward her on her brown mare. Jenny skillfully rode up beside her, saying, "Isn't My Lady friendly?"

Laura patted the soft brown nose that nuzzled her hand. My Lady was certainly a fine horse with a little spirit but not enough to make her unsafe for a small child.

Just then the judge came up behind them. "I hope you don't object to my letting Jenny have a full-grown mare. She told me you had only allowed her to ride a pony."

"My Lady is just the sort of horse I would've picked out for Jenny," Laura reassured him. Even so, she was glad he felt her opinion was important.

"Come into the stables now, and I'll find a horse for you."

Laura followed him into the cool stable. The smell of fresh hay filled the moist air. The judge passed several horses before he stopped before an alabaster-white mare that shined from a newly brushed coat. He said, "I recently bought her. She doesn't even have a name yet, so you can name her if you will, since she'll be yours."

"She's beautiful," Laura said in awe. She hadn't owned her own horse since the war, when her father had sold all their livestock, except for one plow horse. After the family recovered financially, her father had gotten Jenny's pony and a few horses for their wagon, but Laura still hadn't had a horse just for her own use. She stroked the white mane gently, thinking aloud, "I think I'll call her 'Snowdust'. She's so white; she's the color of newly fallen snow."

"Very nice name," the judge said with a deep, jolly laugh. "Now I'll saddle her up, and Jenny can show you around the grounds."

As soon as Laura climbed into the saddle, she felt perfectly in tune with her new horse. Snowdust trotted easily after Jenny's horse through fields covered with winter grass.

Laura pulled up beside Jenny as they rode toward the lake. As she glanced at the lake, she saw Mrs. Temple's home. Feeling certain she could make out a figure pressed against the window, she waved. Whoever it was must not have seen her, for the person quickly turned away, letting the curtain fall back in place. Perplexed, Laura turned her horse toward the opposite side of the lake. Jenny and Laura enjoyed riding around the lake before heading toward a grove of trees. When they finally reached their destination, they rode up under the trees. As she slid off her horse, Laura said, "Let's tie up to this tree."

Jenny pulled up beside her, saying, "Okay, Mama. I think My Lady's tired. Can we eat now?"

After having ridden all morning, they dismounted and unpacked their light lunch. After eating, Laura hugged Jenny as they sat on a blanket under trees bared by the early snowfall.

Laura was very glad to have this precious time alone with her daughter. Caressing Jenny's blond curls, she asked, "Have you enjoyed visiting your grandparents?"

"Oh, yes, Mama," Jenny said, beaming. "I can't wait to tell all my friends about having grandparents just like they do!"

Laura laughed. "I guess you did feel sort of left out."

"Yes, but now I have two grandmothers and a grandfather, plus a mama!" Jenny exclaimed as she squeezed her mother's neck.

Laura felt now was the perfect time to ask the question that had been bothering her since she'd arrived. As she stroked Jenny's curls, she softly asked, "How did you discover that I'm your mother?"

Jenny looked up with eyes shining. "Bradford told me that when you were young, you married Gerald and had a baby. And I'm the baby! Gran showed me his painting over the mantle, and loves to look at it. Bradford said my daddy died soon after you married, and you decided to let Grandma be called my mama," she said, a slightly puzzled tone in her voice.

Laura was thankful when Jenny didn't ask why but instead asked, "What was my daddy like?"

As Laura looked into the eyes of her child, so like Gerald's, she said, "First, as you can see in his painting, he looked very much like you do. We grew up near each other and played as children. I know Nanny has told you about lots of our childhood escapades, like the time he put the frog in my Bible box. When

I grew up, I knew he was the one person I could love forever." A faraway look came into her eyes as she continued, "We lived in the same cottage where you and I lived until the storm destroyed it. Your father was a kind, thoughtful person. When he heard about a little girl, Aimee, who needed help, he never hesitated. Your father tied a rope around her waist, and Aimee's father was able to help her out of a deep ravine. Unfortunately the rope broke while her father was pulling your daddy out, and he fell. Did Bradford tell you that?"

"Yes," Jenny said. "He must have been very brave."

"Yes, he was." She stood and gazed out over the shimmering water. A few ducks slowly floated across the lake. Trying to lighten the conversation, Laura said, "Nanny and your grandma will be coming next week. Won't it be nice to see them?"

"I've missed them so much. I can't wait!" Jenny continued as she mounted My Lady. "Let's ride the other way around the lake. There are some caves and a big waterfall I want you to see."

After Laura climbed into her saddle, she and Jenny rode toward the far end of the lake. They soon came to a large, rocky hillside with water rippling over its sides and falling into the lake. Laura was instantly enraptured by the beauty of the sight.

Jenny led the way up a short, rocky path to the right of the waterfall. She got off her horse and tied it to a tree. Motioning for Laura to do the same, she said, "We'll need to walk the rest of the way to the waterfall." After climbing over a huge boulder, they finally reached the entrance to an old cave.

Having never seen a cave before, Laura was enthralled. At the same time, she was leery to enter a narrow hole in this dark hillside. Warning Jenny, she said, "You know not to go into caves unless someone is with you who knows how to get out, don't you?"

"Oh, Grandfather told me all about that. He took me into the big room but said it's like a maze beyond there, and I should never go any farther into the cave. Would you like to see it?"

Laura supposed that no harm could come if they ventured in just a short ways. Darkness closed in on them as soon as they moved beyond the entrance. Daylight filtered into a large circular room as they rounded a corner. Light seeping through a crack in the wall illuminated the bluish-gray walls. The domed roof gave the impression of size, even though only a few people at a time could squeeze into the space. Cold and dampness filled the air, making Laura shiver.

"I believe we'd better leave, for it's getting late," Laura nervously muttered as she groped along the moist walls, feeling her way out. As soon as the sunlight hit her face, she was glad they were now breathing warm, fresh air again, for the cave had given her an eerie feeling. Not wanting to show her fear to Jenny, she cheerfully said, "That was a real adventure. Now let's ride back to your grandparents' home."

Letting the horses run free, they quickly arrived, appearing just in time for the evening meal. Jenny was excited and told everyone about exploring the cave.

Judge Taylor firmly warned, "That cave is very intricate and dangerous. Sadly I've known of two people who went in and never returned. So remember, don't ever go beyond the first room."

Jenny and Laura promised, and they all continued the meal in a lighter spirit. After dinner, Laura decided to retire early, so she went upstairs with Jenny. After bathing her daughter, Laura settled her down by telling her a few stories about the time when she and Gerald were children. Then she tucked her in, saying, "Sleep tight," before quietly going to her own room.

As Laura prepared to get into bed, she lit the candle on the nightstand in order to reread the threatening note from the previous evening. Frustrated, she realized she had learned nothing new. Her only clue was that the message had been written in a feminine hand. At least Laura felt confident the Taylors were innocent. Laying down the note, she gazed out the window into the darkness beyond, and grudgingly admitted that solving the mystery of the author of the note would have to wait until another day.

Chapter Seventeen

Could Gerald Be Alive?

❈

$\mathcal{F}$inding it impossible to sleep, Laura started to read a novel she'd found in a bookcase by her bed. Since the novel moved very slowly and did so in a most uninteresting way, she felt herself getting extremely sleepy. Knowing Jenny had probably kicked off all her covers, she decided to check on her before going to sleep. Pulling her warm robe over her green cotton gown, Laura moved through the dark hall into Jenny's room. The house seemed so still and quiet that she assumed it must be much later than she'd imagined.

A soft light from the full moon illuminated her daughter's room enough to show Laura that Jenny was indeed uncovered. After pulling the covers over Jenny and giving her a quick kiss, Laura tiptoed back into the hall. Her eyes were now totally adjusted to the dark hall, and she was quick to catch a flash of movement in her room. She froze in the doorway as she recognized the man who had been in her room the night before. He seemed to be feeling around on the bed, searching for her. As though he sensed her presence, he quickly ran in her direction. She felt his warm breath on her cheek as he came to her side. Before he could touch her, however, Laura heard a voice near her window yell, "Halt!" The loud shout from the second man caused the intruder to shove her to the cold tile before running down the hall.

Dizziness overcame her when she hit her head. She lay on the hard tile, fighting to stay conscious. Laura tried to see what had happened to the two men who had rushed past her. Moonlight streamed into the window, making her aware that the tall, thin man who had frightened the intruder away had returned and was now leaning over her. He asked, "Are you okay?"

"Yes, but I need to make sure Jenny is safe," she replied anxiously.

"I'll check on her. Let me first help you into bed."

Then, as she gazed into his face, just visible in the moonlit room, her heart lurched. As he placed her gently in her bed, she thought this could only be one person. As unconsciousness enveloped her, Laura whispered, "Gerald?"

❧

When Laura raised her throbbing head from her pillow early the next morning, she vaguely recalled the events of the previous evening. In her dreamlike state, Gerald had saved her from the man who had broken into her room. Her pulse raced as thoughts of her husband kept haunting her. Could he possibly be alive? But why would he have hidden himself from her and his family all these years? "It had to have been a dream," she said aloud. As soon as she saw the Taylors, she would tell them about the intruder returning. *Why is someone after me?* she wondered.

Soon the whole house was stirring. Jenny came into her room, saying, "I'm all dressed and ready to go downstairs. Why are you still in bed?"

Laura replied weakly, "Jenny, I'm feeling a little lightheaded this morning."

"I'll run and tell Gran. I hope you get better, Mama."

Mrs. Taylor came in looking very concerned. "How are you doing, Laura?" she asked. "Jenny said you weren't feeling well."

Laura replied, "There was a second break-in. I don't think anything was stolen this time, but the man knocked me to the floor in the hallway. I'm still a little dizzy from hitting my head on the tile."

Mrs. Taylor was horrified. She walked over to the window then said, "This window has been pried open, and someone broke the lock. I'll send the staff to town right now to get the strongest locks they can find. This will be done immediately!" Mrs. Taylor added with concern, "I'll also tell them to remove the arbor leading to your window and put new locks on all the outside doors."

Helping her with her breakfast, Mrs. Taylor sadly stated, "I'm just so sorry this has happened again! If only I had sent someone yesterday to put new locks on your window and door, this could've been prevented."

"Please, don't worry. I'll be fine," Laura said, as she patted her hand.

Laura's head stopped aching soon after breakfast. She didn't mention to anyone that the person who had saved her looked just like Gerald, as she knew it must have been a dream. She decided to keep her experience of seeing her deceased husband to herself, since she doubted the incident was anything more than an illusion. Someone who looked just like Gerald must have saved her, Laura reasoned, and she was determined to find out who it was.

When the help returned from town, they wasted no time installing heavy steel bolts on Laura's window and door. They also removed the arbor, which made her feel much safer. Laura only wished these extra precautions could have been taken the day before.

Judge Taylor came to see her later that morning with his wife. As he came up to her bed, he stated, "I just don't know what's going on, but I've told my head gardener to be on the lookout."

Still upset, Mrs. Taylor kept repeating, as she wrung her hands, "Nothing like this has ever happened at the villa before." Clearly they were both very disturbed about these unsettling events.

Jenny had also been coming into her mother's room on and off all morning to check on her. After lunch, she asked, "Would you like to ride with Grandfather and me to a neighbor's house?"

Still feeling weak, Laura said sadly, "Jenny, I'd better not go. You go and have fun with your grandfather." As Jenny left the room, Laura remembered her engagement with the judge's sister that evening. She dreaded the dinner because she felt sure that Mrs. Temple resented her presence. *Could she be plotting to scare me off?* Laura wondered. Surely Mrs. Temple couldn't be that resentful about the recent inattention of the Taylors, she reasoned.

Laura tried not to think about any of this while she spent the afternoon writing a lengthy note to her mother, hoping she would receive it before leaving Oak Grove. Having finished her letter, Laura decided she should also write Bradford. She remembered the cold look he had given her when he had abruptly left the Taylors not that long ago.

She longed to have their friendship return. In her letter she thanked Bradford for bringing her to the Taylors' home. She also said he was wise for encouraging her to visit them and told him how kind and generous they were. She mentioned how happy Jenny was and how much Jenny missed him. Longing to tell him about the prowler, she added a line about the intruder and said that new locks were now on her window and door. Just letting Bradford know about the situation made her feel safer, as though he were there to protect her. Then, hoping Bradford would enjoy hearing from her, she sealed the letter.

Darkness was descending on the sunlit day, so Laura decided to dress for dinner with Mrs. Temple. She chose a pink gown that complemented her thick, curly, golden-brown hair.

Mrs. Taylor was standing in the hall as Laura came out of her room. "Won't you please join me at Mrs. Temple's house?" Laura invited with a plea in her tone.

"You'll be fine, my dear. I'll have our head gardener walk you over." Mrs. Taylor added, "My sister-in-law can appear very gruff, but she isn't as curt as she appears. Anyway, I wasn't invited, and she doesn't like guests to appear unexpectedly. She has only Sara to help her, and it would upset her plans if I were to come. How are you feeling?"

"Oh, my rest made me feel much better. Thank you," Laura remarked cheerfully, not wanting to worry her about the events of the previous night. She especially didn't want to sound crazy by claiming that Gerald or someone who looked like him had saved her. She knew it had to have been a dream.

Mrs. Taylor introduced Laura to her gardener, Todd Granger, and asked him to escort her to her sister-in-law's house. It was still light outside, so Laura thought it unnecessary, but Mrs. Taylor insisted. Todd was a large man and very pleasant. As they walked along, Laura was so absorbed in her thoughts that she failed to notice the beauty of the reflecting pools where the afternoon sun sent small glimmers of golden light sparkling on their rippling surfaces. Trying to be con-genial, Laura turned to Todd and asked him, "Do you have any children?"

"Oh, yes, miss. I'm Sally's father," Todd replied. "She loves playing with Jenny. My daughter's a little older than yours, but when she isn't helping my wife, Hannah, in the kitchen, she's playing with Jenny. They quickly became friends because they both like to ride horses."

"Oh, Sally is such a great playmate for Jenny. We really didn't have anyone at Oak Grove for her to play with. I'm so glad she and Sally have become such good friends." Laura turned to him as they came up to the door of the cottage. "Thank you so much, Mr. Granger."

"Please call me 'Todd.' Send someone to get me when you're through so I can walk you home," he requested, smiling pleasantly.

"I'll do that," Laura said, knocking on the front door of the home. She realized the cottage was much smaller than it had seemed from farther away. Mrs. Temple opened the door herself.

"You're right on time. I like promptness. You didn't wear a wrap. Aren't you cold?" Mrs. Temple asked with concern.

"It is a little cooler than I thought," Laura admitted as she surveyed the cozy room. She seated herself in a chair by the fire. The warmth from the vigorously blazing flames reached every corner of the charming room.

Mrs. Temple misinterpreted Laura's assessment of her home and defensively said, "I take no charity from anyone. I paid for this home with my own money, and I don't need any of my brother's money to live on."

Bewildered, Laura shifted uncomfortably in her chair. Suddenly she froze as a man entered the room. Her eyes locked with his. Every feature of his face was identical to Gerald's. He even wore his blond hair combed neatly to the side. His twinkling blue eyes surveyed her as he answered her unspoken observation. "Yes, Gerald and I look alike," he told her. "We were always able to fool people. We could even trick our mothers if we dressed in each other's clothes." He grinned just like Gerald would have grinned.

Mrs. Temple shrugged. "I could always tell you from Gerald, for you were much more handsome. Have a seat, Mark, while I see if Sara is ready with the supper."

When Mrs. Temple left the room, Mark walked over and sat opposite Laura. She was still slightly trembling because of his uncanny resemblance to Gerald.

Mark, sensing her uneasiness, tried to discuss causal subjects by asking her how her stay had been at the Taylors'. After gaining her confidence, he asked, "Are you all right after last night? I'm so glad I came along when I did. As I was walking by your bedroom, I saw a man climb up the arbor and go into your window. That's when I rushed in after him. I couldn't catch him, however. After I left you in your bed, I checked on Jenny, who was sound asleep. When I went by my uncle's today, I saw they were removing the arbor. I'm very glad they're taking precautions."

Laura relaxed quickly in Mark's company and said, "Thank you for checking on Jenny after you helped me. The night before last, the same man stole some items from my room. I didn't say anything about how I was saved because I thought I had dreamed about seeing Gerald. I especially didn't want Jenny to worry, so I've tried not to get everyone upset about what has happened the last two nights. With new locks on my door and window, and the arbor removed, I should be safe now."

"I'll be sure to keep an eye out for you when I'm here," Mark told her. "I'm sorry I haven't been able to meet you sooner, but I've been helping my uncle with the farm he owns north of here. I stay in the farmhouse where I grew up and come to visit my mother when I can get away. I wasn't even aware of your arrival at first, although I have met your delightful daughter."

As he was talking, Mrs. Temple reentered the room and soon monopolized the conversation. "All this land was once ours. After my husband died, we were forced to sell off portions of the estate. I guess we were lucky we could keep it in the family by selling it to my brother." She regretted with a deep sigh, "I had especially hoped Mark would inherit the farm one day. My husband and I worked so hard to develop it that I hate to see it in someone else's hands—even my brother's."

Uncomfortable with the topic of the conversation, Laura was glad when Sara, a pretty blonde, announced that supper was ready. The meal was delicious and attractively prepared, even though Mrs. Temple found many unfair reasons to criticize the tasty roast that had been cooked to perfection.

As soon as an acceptable time had passed after the meal, Laura excused herself, saying she had to leave. Mark insisted that he escort her to his uncle's house.

The cool air was a relief after being in Mrs. Temple's stuffy house. As Laura and Mark walked slowly by the lake toward the garden steps, he reflected, "My mother has had to struggle. Losing the land she and my father built up has made her very bitter, but underneath her unpleasantness, she's actually a warm person. I hope you can get to know that side of her."

Laura felt at loose ends as to what to say as they reached the bottom of the mosaic stairway near the reflecting pools.

Mark gently took her arm and invited her to sit on a small stone bench. He loaned her his coat as he sat by her.

A gentle breeze blew Laura's hair as she turned to look at his face. At first she had thought he was Gerald, but upon closer scrutiny, she now realized that he was not Gerald. Somehow all these years she had felt that Gerald would come back to her, but now, as she studied Mark's face, she knew she had been living in the past. The love that she now felt for Bradford had been shrouded in guilt that she wasn't being faithful to her dead husband's memory. Perhaps if she hadn't been so confused, Bradford might even now be by her side instead of preparing to marry Saundra. As Laura looked out toward the stillness of the lake, she knew that Gerald was gone forever and that she now had to live in the present.

Chapter Eighteen

The Judge's Special Condition

❧

eep in thought, Laura continued to gaze quietly at the dark lake. She looked up to see the stars shining brightly in the clear night sky. She realized these same stars were twinkling over Bradford who now was far far away.

Mark, sensing her somber mood, asked, "Are you thinking about last night?"

Laura somberly responded, "No, I was just realizing something I should have recognized a long while ago. If I had, I might not have lost a person I dearly care about. Oh, forgive me for going into my problems. I still haven't thanked you for saving my life last night."

"Actually I only told you part of the reason I happened to see the intruder climb through your window."

"I never considered why you were there. I was only thankful you were there at the right time," Laura admitted with relief.

"Well, I do owe you an explanation, which I hope you'll keep to yourself for the moment," Mark requested nervously. Laura nodded and gave him her full attention as he began. "Sara and I are in love and would like to get married. My mother is very much against the match, however, even though Sara comes from a fine family, which, like many, has endured unfortunate financial setbacks since the war. Her family lives in a home near my uncle's. I was walking her home after she cleaned up following dinner. It only upsets Mother if we're together, so Sara and I leave after my mother retires for the evening. We were walking in the garden when I saw the man climbing through your window. I went in after him, and I'm sure you remember the rest. If only I had succeeded in capturing him," he lamented.

Laura now thought back to the looks that Mark and Sara had exchanged during the meal. "I know how you and Sara feel," she advised, "but the worst possible way to handle this is to run off. You can try to explain firmly to your mother that you're going to marry and tell her that she can accept it or not. You should, however, be open about your plans. If you don't stand firm, your guilt and secrecy might destroy the love you and Sara feel for each other. I know that many people's lives would be different had I known this and not run off with Gerald."

She paused, deep in thought. "I have a plan!" Laura jumped up excitedly. "If you'll trust me, I believe I can help you."

Mark looked puzzled but promised Laura that he and Sara would not elope. "I hope your plan works," he said as he stood up.

"I feel certain it will. But if it doesn't, you'll just have to be firm with your mother," Laura advised.

Mark laughed. "She can be very stubborn, but I know now you're right."

He took her arm and escorted her up the steps. Laura knew she had a good friend in Mark. Thanking him for the use of his warm coat, she returned it and smiled at him as he watched her enter the side door. When she was almost inside, he waved good-bye and promised to let Todd know she was safely home.

The villa was dark and still as Laura walked inside, her footsteps echoing throughout the hall. She noticed a small beam of light filtering from beneath the door of the judge's study. She stopped outside the door and decided now was the time to set her plan in action, for Mark and Sara might not have much patience. After tapping lightly on the mahogany door, she soon heard the approach of heavy footsteps. When Judge Taylor saw it was Laura, he flung the door wide-open and motioned her inside.

"I've been hoping for a chance to talk to you, but it seems like the right time never comes," the judge said as he helped her into a leather chair by his desk. Pushing aside a mound of paperwork, he said with a chuckle, "It seems my desk is in a constant state of disarray."

"Maybe I could help?" Laura stated eagerly. "I used to write letters for my father."

"That would be so helpful!" the judge exclaimed. "I've been meaning to get through all this myself, but there never seems to be enough time."

"I'd be glad to help you in the morning," Laura offered willingly, knowing this would give her a chance to ease her plan for Mark and Sara into motion.

"Thank you so much. I'll be here around nine o'clock, and we can start sorting out this mess."

Laura grinned. Before leaving, she commented, "By the way, I've been to see your sister and her son, Mark."

The judge looked pensive as he reflected, "I wonder what's bothering my sister? I sure wish I could find out. Maybe you could help. Never mind. I don't want you to worry about this," he consoled a thoughtful Laura.

"I guess I'd better leave now since it's getting late. But I'll be here in the morning," Laura promised brightly as she turned to leave the room.

"Wait," the judge said as she faced him. As he looked into her shining violet eyes, he said, "I want you to know that I never annulled your marriage to Gerald. The note I sent to you was a cruel, heartless attempt to ease the pain I was feeling for my loss. I never even told my wife I wrote such an insensitive note to you. I hope one day you can forgive me for sending you such a letter. Legally your marriage to Gerald has always existed."

Laura's eyes sparkled as she fought back the tears that threatened to pour down her cheeks. Looking up at him, she whispered, "Thank you for telling me this. It means so much to know you never destroyed my marriage to your son. I forgave you the minute I saw how much you cared for Jenny." Then she warmly hugged her father-in-law and quietly left the room.

The evening air had turned noticeably cooler by the time Laura was ready for bed. She made sure the window was tightly bolted and climbed into bed. She wanted to take no chances, especially with Jenny in the room next door. With the arbor gone and new locks installed, she was able to rest without any disturbance from intruders.

Waking up refreshed the next morning, Laura dressed in a simple navy-blue gown that was perfect for the business she was about to undertake.

Jenny rushed into her room soon after Laura was dressed. "Would you like to go to town with me and Gran this morning? We're going to do some Christmas shopping. Santa Claus will be coming soon."

"I'm going to help your grandfather with his paperwork, so I can't go this time," Laura said. "I know you'll have fun with Gran, so you go ahead. I'll be anxious to see what you buy when you get home."

"Oh, we'll have loads of fun!" Jenny exclaimed. "Will Grandma and Nanny be coming soon?"

"Yes," Laura replied as she knelt and hugged Jenny, "in three more days. We've both missed them, haven't we?"

"I wish Mr. Bradford was coming too." Jenny said, wiggling free and rushing down the stairs.

As Laura knelt there, she knew that she too would enjoy seeing Bradford again, more than anything. She wondered whether he and Saundra had already married.

On this thought Mrs. Taylor came from behind. "Did you drop something?"

Laura stood up and explained that she had been hugging Jenny, who had just rushed off.

"Oh," Mrs. Taylor chuckled. "Jenny is so active. It's hard to keep her still long enough to hug her. By the way, I have this letter for you."

As Laura took the letter from her, she immediately recognized Bradford's neat, masculine script. She knew it was impossible for him to have received her letter and written a reply so quickly. She reasoned that he must have written her a letter soon after he left. As she held the letter close to her, she wanted to rush into her room and open it, but she knew that doing so would be impolite. Instead she placed the cream-colored envelope in the pocket of her skirt and went to breakfast with Mrs. Taylor.

After the meal, Jenny and Gran left for town, and the judge and Laura went to his study. Laura was quick to learn exactly how the judge wanted his letters written and his business forms sorted. They went right to work. Judge Taylor sat at his large mahogany desk while Laura sat facing him in a chair, sorting and stacking papers. Little was said as they concentrated on the work at hand. As noon drew near, he suggested they get a bite to eat. During lunch, which they ate in his study, Laura said, "Mark certainly resembles Gerald."

"Yes," the judge replied. "His mother is so proud of him. I hope she doesn't make the same mistake I made with my son." As he saw her look up at him, he said regretfully, "If I had only taken the time to attend chapel and had gotten to know the wonderful girl my son cared so much about. Back then I only cared about money. Things are different now. Since

I've found God, my life has been so much richer in ways that money can't buy. I only wish my sister could discover this."

Laura blushed at his warm words toward her. Then she looked puzzled.

The judge saw her look and clarified what he was saying. "My sister wants Mark to marry a rich heiress so he can buy back the farm she sold me years ago. She doesn't realize the land isn't nearly as important as Mark's happiness. I wish I could help her understand this. I've even offered to give her the farm back, but her pride keeps her from accepting my help."

Laura asked a question to which she already knew the answer. "Is Mark in love with someone?"

"I believe he is. It seems to me my sister has a girl working for them. Let me see...I know...her name is...Sara. She's very pretty and would be perfect for Mark, but her family is no longer wealthy, and she was forced to get a job helping my sister."

Laura was surprised that he knew so much about Mark.

Sensing her puzzlement, the judge explained, "Mark and I have been very close since his father died. He's a fine young man. I only hope my sister doesn't drive him away. I've tried everything to make her realize the mistake she's making." The judge added in a hopeless tone, "Now there seems to be something bothering my sister. Oh, well. I hope I haven't been burdening you too much with your new family's problems."

Laura put down her cup of tea and turned toward the judge. She paused, realizing this wasn't quite the time to tell him her plan for helping Mark. Instead she commented, "I'm proud to be considered a member of the Taylor family."

Smiling, Gerald's father took her hand. "The Lord has certainly blessed me." He turned to look at his desk as he complimented her. "You've helped me so much. I can't believe all of the progress we've made!" They then returned to their work, both deep in thought, pleased at everything they'd accomplished.

Late that afternoon the study door burst open. Jenny ran in carrying a big basket full of presents covered with a cloth. "Look what we got!" she stated proudly. "I've gotten presents for Grandma, Nanny, you, and Grandfather for Christmas. You can't see them until then, though, so I covered them with this cloth." Jenny grinned as she turned to Gran, who held out her hand to her.

"After dinner we'd better wrap your gifts," Gran said, "so they'll be ready to put under the tree. Now it's time for dinner."

As they all walked toward the dining room, Laura asked, "Did you get any gifts for yourself?"

Jenny sweetly announced, "No. I was trying out what they taught us in Sunday school last week. It's better to give than it is to receive."

They all said how proud they were of Jenny as they sat down to a delicious dinner.

That evening, after her busy day with the judge, Laura quickly got ready for bed. She anxiously took out Bradford's letter. As she clutched the message, she thought of him. Suddenly a pained expression filled her face as she realized this might be an invitation to his wedding. After quickly tearing open the envelope, she dropped the remains of the envelope on the bed and began to read.

Dearest Laura,

How do you like living with the judge and his wife? I hope you find them as kind and generous as I have. Given time, I know you will have them wrapped around your little finger, just like Jenny has done.

Laura smiled and read on.

I have lain awake several nights since I left the judge's house, thinking seriously about the advice you gave me. I don't know why you suggested that I become an architect—maybe you knew I would have work to do in London, and you would be rid of me.

Laura clutched the note as she cried out, "Oh, that man!"

Whatever the reason you advised me, I have decided to give it a try. I'll be at 1123 Aksarben Drive, New York, if you need me for any reason.

Yours truly,
Bradford

p.s. I hope it isn't as cold there as it is in New York. Have a Merry Christmas!

Laura briefly looked at the address as she mulled over the letter. So he hadn't gone back to Saundra. Then a sobering thought occurred to her—maybe Saundra was in New York too.

"Oh, well," Laura muttered, thankful the letter wasn't a wedding invitation. "At least I've succeeded in getting him to pursue his talents when everyone else has failed. Now maybe Bradford can follow his dreams and find fulfillment." With that thought on her mind, Laura fell into a deep, dreamless sleep.

Over the next few days, Laura grew to know Gerald's father very well as they worked side by side. In many ways he was like Gerald—kind and thoughtful. She had grown fond of him and was so happy that they had been able to spend time together. Now she knew the true blessing of forgiveness as she let go of the anger that had raged inside her for so many years.

One afternoon, after working very late, Laura surveyed the neat desk. Behind it the judge beamed. Laura said, "My, I do believe we've accomplished a lot."

"I never thought I'd see the inlaid monogram on my desk again," the judge said with a chuckle. "You deserve a medal for rescuing my desk!"

Laughing, Laura said, "It's nice to feel I can do a little something to repay you for letting Jenny and me stay here while our cottage is being rebuilt. Tomorrow you'll also be hosting my mother and Nanny."

"I'm looking forward to meeting your mother and seeing Nanny again," the judge said, gazing at her thoughtfully.

Sensing his solemn mood, Laura wondered, "Is anything the matter?"

"Oh, no," the judge said with a smile. "I just don't know how to bring up a subject I'd rather ignore. No one enjoys thinking about the time when he'll no longer be on this earth, but I want you to know that you and Jenny are our new heirs and will inherit our estate when my wife and I die. I had a new will drawn up earlier this week while I was in town." Shifting in his chair, he proceeded, "I've also set up a trust to begin immediately so that you can live as you're accustomed either here or in your ancestral home. I have another surprise for you. You now own Oak Grove."

Laura's glowing eyes stared into the judge's eyes as he chuckled. "Yes, Bradford sold Oak Grove to me just before he left. He suggested it himself, saying that he knew you loved it and that's where he felt Gerald would want you and Jenny to live."

Tears of happiness streamed down Laura's crimson cheeks as she quietly said, "I never expected my home would ever belong to my family again. My mother will be so happy. My family's roots go so deep there; I never realized how land becomes such a part of you. How can I ever thank you?"

The judge put his short, stocky hand in hers, as he said, "You forgave me and have made my life worthwhile again. By the look in your eyes, I can tell you'll want to return to Oak Grove soon." As Laura started to protest, he said, "I understand, but I'd like you to stay here long enough for me to host the largest ball ever given in the county. I want to be able to introduce my daughter-in-law and granddaughter to all my friends."

Wiping her eyes, Laura readily agreed. "Jenny's birthday is in the spring. Maybe we could have it then?" she suggested.

"That's a perfect idea!" the judge said as he began mentally to plan the party.

Laura interrupted his thoughts. "Maybe I have no right to say this, but I believe I know what's bothering your sister and how we can help her and Mark."

"Please go on, dear. I'm very eager to hear what you have to say."

Laura carefully thought out her exact phrasing as she began, "I know your sister is deeply feeling the loss of her property. I can see how someone could lose sight of more important things in order to get his or her land back." The judge nodded as Laura continued. "You just said Jenny and I are your new heirs. Does that mean your sister won't inherit anything?"

"She has a little money left to her by her late husband as well as the money she got from the sale of the farm. I feel she could do quite well living where she is now." As the judge said this, his eyes brightened as he realized, "That's why she's been moody ever since she found out about Jenny. She knew I'd leave everything to you and your daughter, which means she won't get her farmland back. Now I guess she feels it's hopeless unless Mark marries an heiress."

Laura nodded as she softly suggested, "Jenny and I would never feel comfortable taking the farm that means so much to her."

Judge Taylor stood and came around the desk to face her. He leaned his stocky frame against the slick surface of the polished desk. Stroking his chin, he promised, "I'm going to put the property in a trust for Mark. He can immediately begin to work the land for himself. I'll leave the farm to him as my nephew in my will. My sister can't refuse that offer. If she argues that it should go to Jenny, I'll tell her that you have no desire to live there and that I want the land to remain in the family. I am, however, going to insist on one stipulation..." The judge's brown eyes twinkled as he paused for a moment. "...that Mark marries the girl of his choice in the near future."

Laughing, Laura said, "What a great idea. Maybe they can announce their engagement at Jenny's birthday party."

"Perfect." The judge grinned. "I'll tell my sister tomorrow. She's stubborn, but I don't see how she can refuse. Now we'd better get ready for dinner. It'll be nice to meet your mother and also see the special woman who helped raise Gerald. I never wanted to dismiss Nanny, but we had very little money at the time, and I had no way of keeping her on staff."

After dinner everyone retired early since they expected the next day to be busy with the guests arriving. Anxious to tell Mark the good news and eager to see her mother and Nanny, Laura drifted off to sleep.

The night was warmer than the previous evenings had been, even though they were still in the fall season. Laura had been sleeping with her window tightly shut and firmly bolted to avoid another break-in, so she woke up very early, needing some fresh air. She decided to go ahead and get up, even though the sun hadn't risen. By the time she had dressed, the sun was just peeking over the hills. She chose to go for an early ride on Snowdust. She hoped she would run into Mark so she could tell him what the judge was going to do for him. More than likely he was still asleep, like she should be.

Laura tiptoed quietly downstairs. As she walked into the humid morning air, she realized that it was still a lot darker than she'd expected. The arched stable loomed mysteriously up ahead as she slowed her pace. At first she thought her imagination was playing tricks on her when she saw a shadow dart inside the building. Feeling she had simply imagined this, she entered the stables. The quiet early-morning air felt very eerie. Suddenly Laura froze. Sensing that someone was staring at her from behind, she shivered. Momentarily she didn't know whether to turn and run or scream. The quiet of the morning seemed to descend upon her as she remained still, aware that at any moment the shadowy figure might jump out of the dimness at her vulnerable body. She knew how a lamb must feel as a wolf is stalking it.

In a flash Laura felt a cold hand cover her mouth. She struggled as someone pulled her toward the back of the stable. In the instant before her attacker had a chance to push her down, she noticed a pitchfork leaning against the wall near her leg. As her body was roughly thrust forward, she slipped her left arm around and grasped the pitchfork. With anger she thrust it with all her might into her attacker's foot. His scream filled the early-morning air as he released her. He limped away as fast as he could, disappearing into the woods. Laura stood against the wall, noticing the blood on her leg where the pitchfork had punctured her flesh before hitting its target.

"Hello. Who's in here?" a familiar voice cried out as Mark, his face full of concern, rushed to her side and examined her leg. "What happened, Laura?"

"Someone jumped on me from the back of the stable!" Laura said.

"This is the second time I know of that someone has tried to harm you. Why would anyone do such a thing?" Mark demanded.

Laura paused as she considered the possibilities. The only person who could profit from her being out of the way was Mark's mother. Was that why he was here now? Could he have known that her attacker was going to harm her? Laura pushed these thoughts aside as she saw the concern in his eyes. Looking at him, she was certain he could never have played a part in any plan to get rid of her. "I don't know what's going on." Laura reassured him, "Don't worry. I'm going to tell the judge so he can get to the bottom of this, but please don't alarm everyone, because it'll only scare Jenny."

As Mark bandaged her cut with fresh gauze he found in the stable storeroom, he reluctantly agreed. "It looks deep. I'm afraid you'll need stitches," he said. "Let me get you to your room, and we'll send for the doctor. What are we going to tell Jenny about the wound?"

"We'll think of something that won't frighten her, but we'll also let her know to be careful about any strangers that she might meet."

"I'll only do this if you promise not to go anywhere after dark without a chaperone," Mark said.

"I will from now on," Laura agreed, standing up on her aching leg. The pain surged through her as she tried to bend her leg in an effort to walk. Attempting to hide the seriousness of her injury, she said, "I have exciting news to tell you."

"First let's get you seated," Mark suggested, helping her to a bench next to the wall. After easing her down, he placed her leg on a small wooden stool he found in a cluttered corner of the stable.

Taking the weight off her leg made all the difference, and Laura was able to begin with the enthusiasm she felt. "Your uncle is giving you all the surrounding farmland when he dies. The land will be placed in trust for you to begin using immediately."

Momentarily, almost unnoticeably, a puzzled frown passed over Mark's face. Then he brightened. "That's just what Mother wants!" But then he turned away from her, muttering, "Mother said this is your land now, and she'll never take it unless something happens to you and Jenny." His face was pale as he turned back to Laura. "You know I could never take something that should be yours."

Laura advised him, "It's fine. I have no use for the land. Judge Taylor bought my home near Vicksburg for Jenny and me. He's also providing funds so Jenny and I can live quite comfortably there for the rest of our lives. I told him I have no need or desire to have this property.

Since he wants a family member to care for it, I suggested you. That's why I know all about the judge's wishes and feel free to let you know." Laura leaned forward with a twinkle in her eye. "But there is one condition."

"What's that?" Mark questioned cautiously.

"That you get engaged to the girl of your choice and soon!" Laura exclaimed gleefully.

"My uncle is a genius! Mother can never refuse that offer, knowing what she'd be giving up." Mark beamed at her, saying, "Thanks. I knew you had a plan, but I didn't think it would work out so well."

"The judge made it all possible! He's a generous uncle and father-in-law," Laura said.

After helping Laura to her room, Mark rushed to get a doctor. Once the doctor stitched her deep wound she lay in bed until she heard the house stirring with activity. When the judge came to see her, she told him everything that had happened.

Holding her hand, Judge Taylor said, "Don't worry, Laura. I'll get Todd to look out for anyone who appears suspicious. We'll also get some of the staff to stand guard at night. We're going to catch whoever has been doing these things to you. I'll tell Jenny, but I promise that I won't let her get too upset about what has happened to you. I'll warn her to be very careful and avoid strangers. In the meantime I'm going to have someone escort her when she and Sally go riding. I'll make sure everyone knows so they can be on the lookout. I'm just so sorry this happened to you, dear," the judged added solemnly.

Propping up her leg helped it feel much better. Laura was soon able to get around with only a slight limp, and even went downstairs for lunch. Everyone expressed concern for her leg, but Jenny's excited restlessness about the arrival of her grandmother and Nanny was a welcome distraction.

"Will Grandma be here soon?" Jenny asked as she stuffed an oversized piece of ham into her mouth. Not waiting for an answer, she jumped up, tipping over a glass of lemonade as she rushed to look out the window. Returning dejected because she didn't see a carriage, she quietly helped mop up the spill. Then, seconds later, she asked, "Will they be here soon?"

"Jenny, dear, it could be late tonight before they arrive," Gran replied patiently. "Why don't we go upstairs and put on one of the new outfits I made you? That way you'll be presentable when your grandmother and Nanny arrive."

Sufficiently distracted, Jenny skipped out of the room, yelling, "We'll be right back!"

Laura and the judge laughed together, agreeing Jenny had more energy than they all did combined. Laura told Judge Taylor that Mark had been kind to help her after her accident. "I hope you don't mind, but I let him know what you planned to do about his inheritance. I also filled him in about having to marry the girl of his choice. He's really pleased about that stipulation!"

"I'm glad you told him, since it was your news to tell. You were first in line to receive the land. You're very kind and generous to let Mark have it. You've been such a blessing to our family," the judge remarked.

Shortly afterwards, they heard a team of horses pull up outside.

Recognizing Nanny's cheerful laugh, Laura slowly rose and limped to the window just as her mother was climbing down from one of Bradford's best carriages. Before Mrs. Taylor could fully open the door, Jenny rushed past her. Her leg throbbing, Laura returned to her chair to wait for the visitors to come inside.

Jenny received warm hugs from the new arrivals, who oohed and aahed over her outfit. She carefully took their hands and led Nanny and Ruth to Judge and Mrs. Taylor. She introduced everyone, saying, "I know Gran and Grandfather already know Nanny. This is my other grandma." Everyone was pleased to see and meet one another. They then followed Jenny inside. Laura carefully got out of her chair and gave her mother and Nanny a big hug.

When Jenny left the room, the judge and Laura told Ruth and Nanny about the attacks. He said, "I suspect a deranged person is on the loose. You need to be cautious."

The women were very upset that Laura had experienced several attacks, but were also glad that she wasn't injured more seriously than she was. They promised to be on the lookout for anything unusual.

Laura's mother and Gerald's mother were immediately at ease with each other as they talked about their granddaughter. Meanwhile Nanny hustled off to "inspect" the kitchen and meet Hannah.

⚒

As the weeks passed, they settled down, blending perfectly into the routine at the villa. Fortunately no one seemed to have any problems, and no more attempts were made on Laura's life. She again wondered whether Mark's mother had been behind the attacks that were, perhaps, aimed at scaring her off. She speculated that maybe there would be no more threatening episodes now that Mrs. Temple had secured her son's inheritance. Even so, Laura remained cautious, keeping her promise to Mark not to go anywhere after dark without an escort. Her mind was also distracted because Christmas was rapidly approaching.

Chapter Nineteen

A Christmas Celebration

❧

"Laura, would you and Jenny like to help me find a tree for the parlor?" Judge Taylor asked as they finished breakfast one morning.

"That would be great fun. I know Jenny would enjoy the search," Laura replied, smiling pleasantly at him.

As the judge pulled the wagon to the front of the villa, Laura and Jenny, who were all bundled up, hopped in. The horses, with shiny new bells on their harnesses, jingled away as they trotted into the woods.

An animated Jenny leaned far out over the edge of the wagon, looking for the perfect tree.

"Wow, young lady, you're going to fall out," Laura said as she quickly grabbed Jenny's coat.

Jenny scooted over and said, "Let's all sing 'Jingle Bells' since the horses are making those jingling sounds." Squirrels, trying to get out of the way of their wagon, ran up and down the road as the joyful singing and the jingling bells disturbed the peace and stillness of the forest.

Just as they finished singing, Jenny yelled excitedly, "Look over there." Pointing to a clearing in the woods, she said, "There's the tree we should get!"

Judge Taylor handed the reins to Laura as he bragged, "That's a beauty! Here, hold the reins. I'm going to chop down the tree Jenny wants."

Jenny said she would help too, but the judge warned, "Please stay in the wagon. This ax is very sharp." Smiling at his granddaughter to ease his stern warning, he began to chop down the enormous tree.

Jenny yelled, "Timber-r-r-r!" as the tree fell away from the wagon. "Can I help load it into the wagon?" she asked.

"Hop down and grab the top. I'll grab the trunk," her grandfather said.

"Oh, this is heavy." Jenny grunted and groaned as she lifted her end.

"You're very strong, Jenny. Thanks for your help," the judge said, giving the tree a final boost. The tree landed with a loud thump in the back of the wagon.

As they pulled up to the villa, Nanny, Ruth, and Mrs. Taylor ran outside to see the tree. The judge and Todd placed the tree in its wooden stand in the parlor. It was larger than they had initially thought, its top almost touching the twelve-foot ceiling.

Nanny took Jenny's hand and said, "Let's go into the kitchen and make popcorn garlands to hang on the branches."

"Come on, Gran and Grandma. Come help us," Jenny called as she ran into the kitchen.

"This is going to be the best Christmas we've had in a long time. Thank you so much, Laura," the judge said, beaming.

That night after dinner, the entire household went to church for the Christmas Eve pageant in which Jenny was going to be an angel and one of her china dolls was to be the baby Jesus.

"Hold still, Jenny, while I tie your wings on your back," Laura said.

Jenny loved her wings as she flapped them, trying to fly.

"Careful, Jenny, the wings might fall apart," Laura warned, watching one of the goose feathers float to the floor.

"Oh, my, I'm shedding," Jenny teased.

"Then, we'd better go, before you're featherless," Laura said with a smile.

The Christmas Eve pageant was a very special event for Laura. She watched the play, proudly glowing as Jenny stood very still over the baby Jesus.

After the play, the congregation was invited to the villa for candied apples and hot apple cider. Afterwards the guests enjoyed singing Christmas carols. The visitors admitted they had a great time but left early because the children needed to be in bed for Christmas.

"Can I please stay up a little longer?" Jenny begged as she yawned.

"Santa Claus is coming tomorrow, so you must get ready for bed now. Here's your stocking. Would you hang it up?" Laura asked.

Jenny turned to her grandfather as he hammered a nail in the mantle. "Would you please give me a boost?" she asked.

"I would enjoy doing that so much!" After helping Jenny hang her stocking, he said, "Now run along, so you can be up bright and early to see what Santa brought you."

Laura followed Jenny upstairs and tucked her into bed. Jenny begged her mother for a story about the time when Laura was little. So Laura began a familiar story. "When I was young and the war was going on, I clearly remember the Christmas when Santa Claus didn't come. Your grandma said even he couldn't penetrate the Union blockade of 1862. But I wasn't too sad, because she had lovingly made me a small doll from corn husks. It was the only gift I received that year, but it meant a great deal to me. I still have it, and I believe you've even played with her. Oftentimes you realize it isn't the number of things you get that counts. I don't think you need to worry tonight, however, because there's no blockade, and Santa Claus will have no trouble coming to see you. So sleep tight," Laura encouraged as she bent over and gave Jenny a kiss.

Laura decided to go to bed early too. As she lay in bed, she wondered what Bradford was doing. *Was he with Saundra?* That sad thought was the last one she had before falling asleep.

As soon as the sun peeked into Jenny's room, she ran into Laura's room to wake her up. "Wake up, Mama, it's time to go downstairs," Jenny whispered into her mother's ear.

"It's so early," Laura said groggily.

"I went downstairs and saw that Santa has come," Jenny whispered back.

"Jenny, what did you see?"

Excited, she replied, "Lots and lots of gifts!"

"Okay, let me get dressed."

They soon walked down the stairs holding hands. When they saw the tree, Laura was amazed. She had never seen so many beautifully wrapped gifts.

"What took you so long?" Gran asked, smiling up at them as she sat on the sofa with the judge.

Since they hadn't noticed them sitting by the tree, Laura and Jenny both jumped.

Jenny's grandfather had lit all the candles, which made the tree look spectacular. The silver foil ornaments that Jenny had made brightly reflected the light from the shimmering candles. "I guess we were more excited than Jenny," Jenny's Gran said with a laugh.

Jenny wondered, "Should I wake up Nanny and Grandma?"

"Of course," her grandfather said. "They wouldn't want to miss seeing you open your gifts."

Jenny quickly came back with two very sleepy people.

Jenny wanted everyone to open the gifts that she and Gran were giving first. Holding out her first gift to Laura, she said, "Open it, Mama."

"Oh, Jenny! It was so nice of you and Gran to get a gift for me!" Laura tore off the colorful paper and pulled out a new pink parasol with lace fringe around the edge. "I love it and will carry it when I go out!"

Then Jenny rushed over to the judge and told him to open his present. Her grandfather placed her in his lap as he opened his gift. "How did you know I've wanted this pipe for quite a while? Did Gran give you a hint?"

Jenny smiled. "Gran helped me out since I wasn't sure what you'd like. I like the smell of your pipe." Her grandfather gave her a squeeze as Jenny turned to her Grandma. "I got you a very special gift too," she boasted.

"Oh, Jenny, it's just what I wanted. A new sewing basket! Thank you so much," Grandma Ruth said.

Jenny ran to Nanny. "Can you guess what Gran and I got you?"

Nanny was very pleased with her new red apron.

"I helped embroider the flower on the top," Jenny proudly announced.

Finally she held out a gift for Gran, who was thrilled when she opened a painting of daffodils—her favorite flower. "When did you get this?" she asked, surprised.

Jenny replied, "I painted it."

As Jenny tore into her mountain of gifts, Laura had an enjoyable time watching her family share such a special occasion together.

Mrs. Taylor stood and came over with a small, brightly wrapped gift. "This is from Bradford. He wanted it to be here for Christmas and had it specially shipped to you."

"Oh, my," Laura said as she gazed at the small package. Carefully tearing away the wrapping paper, she saw what looked like a jewelry box. She opened the small velvet box to find a delicate gold cross.

"Oh, it's lovely!" she said as everyone gathered around her.

"Let me help you put it on, Mama," Jenny said. As she stood on a chair, she placed the necklace around her mother's neck and carefully fastened the small clasp.

Gently fingering the cross, Laura said, "I hope he received my gift in time for Christmas." She thought of the scarf she had lovingly knitted for him. She hoped that he would wear it and that it would keep him warm in the cold New York winter. Then she looked down as a white note drifted into her lap.

Dearest Laura,

I hope you are having a special Christmas with Gerald's family. I know they love you dearly and want only the best for you and Jenny.

Remember what my mother wrote in her Bible: "Forgiveness is the key to happiness." Always keep your faith.

Yours,
Bradford

A tear touched her cheek as the words made her realize how truly blessed she was.

At that moment the judge stood up and announced, "It's time to make our deliveries." Grabbing their coats and baskets full of cakes, toys, and special treats, everyone went onto the veranda. What a sight met their eyes. Two of the horses had small branches tied to their harnesses to look like antlers. Happily they climbed into the wagon to take gifts to their less fortunate neighbors.

After the family returned from delivering the presents, Jenny ran to meet Sally. The girls spent the rest of the day playing with their new toys.

As dinnertime drew near, Mark and his mother entered the dining room, joining the Taylors and their guests for the heavenly-smelling Christmas feast. Nanny had made a huge turkey with all the traditional side dishes, including the famous Taylor stuffing with currants.

Mark walked over to Laura's side. Smiling down at her, he whispered, "Merry Christmas." There was no time to talk, but Laura could tell from his smile that Sara must have accepted his proposal. Mark's mother even came up and gave Laura's hand a squeeze. Certainly this Christmas had been a very memorable one with her new family.

Chapter Twenty

Welcome and Unwelcome Guests

⫸

The months flew by. . . . Everyone relaxed since no more suspicious activities had occurred at the villa. Still Laura remained a bit uneasy because all the attacks had been directed toward her, and no one had been apprehended. She tried to forget about the incidents as she helped plan the Taylors' ball to celebrate Jenny's birthday.

The whole villa was turned upside down when spring cleaning got underway in preparation for Jenny's party. Nanny supervised the staff as they removed every speck of dust from any surfaces that could be easily inspected by prying eyes. Ruth often went shopping with Mrs. Taylor. They seemed to enjoy being together, which made Laura especially happy. They frequently came back from their expeditions with all kinds of fruits, nuts, sweetmeats, and other delicacies for the party.

Laura decided the birthday cake would be a triple-layer vanilla cake with pink icing. Swans would appear to be swimming on the top layer of the cake, with a lake made of light-blue icing sprinkled with coconut. Streamers would flow from the back of each swan down to the table. Each streamer would then be attached to a party favor. She felt Jenny would enjoy such a special cake because she loved pretty things.

The Taylors had decided to have the celebration early in the evening. After the birthday party, Jenny and her friends would play games while the adults danced.

Mrs. Taylor asked Laura to write the invitations. Laura's leg had taken a little longer to heal than expected since the injury was more serious than they'd initially thought. Therefore she was glad for the excuse to sit while she wrote personal invitations to everyone on the long list.

Once, as she was pausing to relax her cramped hand, she thought of Mark. She had seen him only briefly at the Christmas dinner and hadn't yet found out about his engagement. Ever since then, Laura had wondered how it had gone when he proposed and whether he had told Sara about getting the farm. Dreamily she hoped they would announce their engagement at Jenny's party. Laura made up her mind to try to find him and see what Mark and Sara's plans were.

That afternoon Laura passed the reflecting pools on the way to Mark's mother's house. To her surprise a cheerful Mrs. Temple answered the door. "Why, Laura, come in," she exclaimed enthusiastically. Laura took a seat near a window that overlooked the fields in the hope she would see Mark. Not seeing him, she nervously turned to face Mrs. Temple.

Laura was soon able to relax as Mrs. Temple said, "My brother told me the reason he's leaving the farmland to Mark is because of you. I hope you never regret giving up this fine land, but thank you." A little of her old gruffness crept back into her voice as she continued. "Of course I know if Mark had had more time, he could have found a more suitable wife, but I guess Sara will do. She's staying at her home until the wedding. I hated to see her leave. It's so hard to do all the work by myself. I have to admit, however, that she's a hard worker, so Mark should never have to complain about that."

Laura fought back her laughter at this last comment. It was just like Mrs. Temple to keep thinking that Mark was being dragged into this marriage. With a straight face, she asked, "Is Mark here? I wanted to ask him some questions about the party."

"So much fuss over a child's birthday. I just can't imagine. No, Mark hasn't been here in a while. He should, however, be back at any time since he's through with his work on the farm."

"Well, I guess I'd better get back and finish the invitations," Laura said as she left.

Enjoying the view, she slowly climbed the steep stairs by the reflecting pools. As she reached the terrace, Mark approached her from the covered patio.

"Laura," he said, "I've been looking everywhere for you. My uncle said we can announce our engagement at Jenny's birthday party. Sara and I will be married soon after that! I owe it all to you," he exclaimed as he bent down and warmly hugged her.

Over his shoulder, Laura was startled to see Bradford coldly staring at them as they tightly embraced. Totally flustered, she separated from Mark and said, "Oh, Bradford, I wasn't expecting you."

Holding out his hand to Bradford, Mark said, "I'm Judge Taylor's nephew, Mark Temple. I've always wanted to meet you, but whenever you came to visit the Taylors I was at the farm. I've heard so many nice things about you," Mark said, with awe in his voice. Shaking hands with Bradford, he added, "It's a pleasure to meet you."

Bradford smiled. "My, you look just like the painting of Gerald that's hanging over the mantle."

"Yes. Even Laura thought I was Gerald's ghost when we first met. Well, I guess I'd better be getting back to work. It's nice to meet you," Mark said as he left, whistling a cheerful tune.

Laura turned to find Bradford's eyes searching her face. "I guess you're wondering what I'm doing here."

At the moment Laura didn't care; she was just thrilled to see him. She tried to appear as casual as she could, saying, "I hope whatever the reason is you'll stay for Jenny's birthday party."

"Mrs. Taylor mentioned something about her party. I'd like to be here for that." Then, carefully studying her face, he remarked, "Mark could almost be Gerald."

"Yes," Laura replied, changing the subject. "Have you gotten many of your designs done while you were gone?"

"I've done a lot of work in New York, and I'm planning to leave for London soon. As a matter of fact, I should be there now, working with the Metropolitan

Board of Works on the architectural designs for the Duke of Norfolk's summer home." Then, looking down into her eyes, he commented, "But I felt something was far more important for me to do here."

Puzzled by this last statement, Laura asked, "How's Saundra?"

Casually Bradford glanced away, saying, "I haven't seen her since I left your plantation," he said, emphasizing "your."

Laura's eyes sparkled with relief and joy as she realized they hadn't married.

Thinking she was grateful for the return of her plantation, Bradford stated, "Now you don't have to worry that anyone will control your ancestral home except you."

Sparks of purplish light glowed in her eyes as she looked into his clear blue eyes. "I owe you so much for selling Oak Grove to the judge. Now my mother can return to her home."

"Seems to me that you were the one who most resented my ownership," Bradford said with a laugh.

Laura looked down, a deep crimson filling her cheeks. "Maybe I did overreact. My father always said my feisty spirit would get me into trouble one day."

"Your father knew you well. My prediction was right too. From what Judge Taylor tells me, you have him wrapped around your little finger."

Laura looked up to find Bradford staring off, as though he had remembered something very painful. "Well, I won't keep you," he said, as he walked in the direction of the stables, thinking about Laura hugging Mark.

Laura entered the villa as though in a dream. *He's back!* she thought to herself. *And he hasn't married Saundra yet. Maybe that was why he looked so sad at the end of our conversation.* She hoped she would have more time to see him in the coming week. She remembered the cross he had given her and reminded herself to thank him for it. She'd worn it every day since Christmas.

Laura's happiness was soon crushed when Saundra arrived that evening after dinner. Bradford was at the stables to see Jenny's new horse when Saundra flounced into the dining room. Her red hair was swept up high on her head into a fashionable bun. Her green eyes darted about, anxiously searching for Bradford as she greeted Judge and Mrs. Taylor. As she continued looking over her shoulder for Bradford, she casually threw a greeting to Laura and her mother.

Turning to Mrs. Taylor, she said, "I was visiting some of your neighbors when I heard about the soiree you're having. From what I hear, it's going to be a fabulous ball." Saundra assertively asked, "I hope you don't mind if I attend?"

Not knowing how to respond, Mrs. Taylor replied hesitantly, "If you wish."

Laura, having no desire to converse with Saundra, excused herself and went to her room. She sat at her dresser, tucking in the few strands of hair that had escaped the chignon she'd been wearing since her arrival. As she carefully gazed at herself in the mirror, she realized that pulling her hair tightly from her face and parting it in the middle did nothing for her long, slender face. While fashionable, the chignon seemed to detract from her high cheekbones. It also made her expressive eyes appear too large. She grabbed the bun, which was attached to a lace cap at the back of her head, and let the long strands fall loosely down her back. Regardless of fashion, this was how she knew she looked her best. She then combed the freed locks until they were smooth and silky.

Still restless and knowing it was too early to go to bed, Laura got up to take a walk. She decided to stay near the villa since it was just beginning to get dark. Without an escort, she was intent on keeping her promise to Mark that she wouldn't go anywhere alone after dark.

As she stepped out of the side door, Jenny yelled, "Watch My Lady jump."

Laura walked toward Bradford, who stood by the fence waiting for the jump. As she approached, she saw his eyes studying her hair. His usually aloof eyes were hard to read, but Laura felt sure she saw a brief softening as she drew near.

After Jenny made the jump, Bradford told Laura he wished to speak with her. He asked Jenny to put My Lady in the stable since it was getting too dark to practice. He then walked with Laura toward the lake. As they strolled, Bradford said, "Jenny has the ability to be a champion rider. Do you think you can handle that?"

Laura smiled up at him. "I've grown up around people who love horses. I believe I can continue to encourage her."

After they stepped behind a hedge, Bradford turned to her. A worried expression filled his eyes as he looked down at her, "You wrote in your letter that someone tried to get into your room. I wish I'd gotten your letter faster so I could've been here sooner. How many times has this happened?"

Laura tried to be casual, replying, "A few. Nothing has happened recently, so I think whoever did it is gone." Fingering her gold cross, she turned to him saying, "This cross means so much to me."

"I've often thought of your strong faith and wanted you to have it. I've really enjoyed your scarf. It's kept me very warm this winter."

Suddenly he turned her to face him. He gripped her shoulders as he pleaded, "Please, Laura, tell me everything about what happened."

Laura told him about her first night in the villa and about the note that was left on her pillow. She further explained how Mark had saved her the next night. Laughing nervously, she said this was when she had thought he was Gerald's ghost. Finally she told Bradford about the most recent attempt in the stable and how she had escaped by using a pitchfork.

Bradford was very serious as he promised, "I'm going to find out what's going on before I leave here." Then, as he searched her eyes, he asked, "Why didn't you tell me Mark is engaged?"

Totally confused, Laura replied, "I don't see what that has to do with anything at all."

"I just don't want to see you get hurt," Bradford said as his hands fell from her shoulders. He turned away, looking out over the lake.

Laura was stunned to think that Bradford believed she could be in love with Mark. Wanting to clear the air immediately, she turned to face him when she heard a piercing "Yoo-hoo."

Saundra's heavy hoopskirt swayed with the motion of her hips as she sauntered up to them. Upon arriving at Laura's side, she said in her too sweet voice, "Jenny told me you were over here with Bradford." As she turned her green eyes toward Laura, she noticed her long golden-flecked strands of hair falling loosely over the bodice of her dress. "What a quaint hairdo. You had a much more mature look with the chignon you were wearing earlier. Now you look like a child."

"That was uncalled for, Saundra," Bradford said. "You're a guest here in Laura's in-laws' home. I believe you should act with better manners. As a matter of fact, I think her hair looks stunning."

"Well, excuse me," Saundra said huffily. "I had no idea you could be considered one of my hostesses, Laura. The air is getting damp. Maybe I should retire. Would you mind escorting me?" she insisted, smiling seductively at Bradford as she extended her arm.

Bradford reluctantly took her arm as he led her inside. Laura followed them back to the villa but decided to go to her room for the evening, knowing her opportunity to clarify her relationship with Mark was slim.

Over the next few days, whenever Laura saw Bradford, Saundra was possessively hanging onto his arm, laughing and smiling up at him.

Laura felt sure they must have reconciled. Sad, she tried to distract herself by concentrating on Jenny's birthday celebration, which was only a few days away.

Chapter Twenty-One

The Canoe Race across the Lake

◈

*A*fter breakfast Laura ran back upstairs to change clothes for the canoe race. As she was opening the armoire to choose what to wear that day, her eyes caught sight of her lavender ball gown. As she ran her hand over the silk dress, she thought that this was the most elaborate gown she'd ever owned. She planned to wear the dress at Jenny's party.

When Laura looked at the dress, she was reminded of Mrs. Periwinkle's smile of approval and kind words. "I'm so glad you decided to buy this gown. It was absolutely meant for you. I don't believe I've ever created a more perfect fit," the seamstress had said as she made her final alterations and cut a small thread that hung off the bodice.

Ruth and Laura had left the dress shop with the stunning gown. Laura had carried the package under her arm, dreaming of the day she'd get to wear it. At that time she didn't know when that would be. But now, many months later, that day was almost here. Tomorrow night her dream would be fulfilled.

Boisterous noises from downstairs interrupted Laura's reverie as she carefully hung the gown back in the armoire. The early arrivals for the party were gathering in the grand salon. Some of the guests had traveled from miles away. She decided she had better hurry and dress.

Everyone was getting ready for the canoe race across the lake. The judge had decided it would be fun entertainment the day before Jenny's birthday.

Laura quickly dressed in a casual cotton dress that was both light and cool. She tied a large yellow ribbon in her hair to keep it out of the way while she was paddling.

A few days before, the judge had let her know about the simple rules of the race. Everyone had to paddle, and only two people could be in a canoe.

Late because of her daydreaming, Laura hurried down the stairway. She heard everyone excitedly talking in anticipation of the race. Arriving in the parlor, she realized Judge Taylor was already dividing the guests into teams. He picked Jenny for his partner. Beaming, Jenny stood by him. As he paired everyone off, Laura noticed a tall, nice-looking stranger standing in the corner. She speculated that he must be someone's guest and that they would be introduced later. Startled out of her inattention, she heard the judge say, "Laura, please. For the second time, go stand by Bradford."

Embarrassed, Laura stood beside Bradford, who laughed. "I hope you aren't too disappointed. I'd love to know what you were thinking about when you were chosen to be my partner."

"Well, if you must know, I was wondering about the man who's going to be Saundra's partner," Laura whispered. "Is he someone's guest?"

"Oh, so you're like all the other women who admire him. His name is Sir Douglas Donley. Sir Douglas decorated Saundra's mansion. He's very talented but has a rather bad gambling problem. He's from England, where he's considered one of the most handsome and eligible bachelors. Unfortunately he's also one of the poorest because of his vice. He does, however, have the title of 'Sir,' which impresses a lot of the women," Bradford stated sarcastically.

Before they had a chance to say any more, the contestants headed down to the lake, where several brightly colored canoes awaited them. Laura hurried toward a red one. Bradford steadied the canoe as she carefully climbed in. The boat rocked to and fro, but he held it as still as he could. He then climbed in and sat behind her. Laura knew how to canoe because she had paddled frequently on the lake by Oak Grove. She took up her paddle in order to be ready when the whistle blew.

Before starting the race, Judge Taylor explained that all the teams were to paddle to the far side of the lake. There, on the bank of the lake, they were to take the colored flag that matched their boat. Once they collected their flag, they were to paddle back to the dock. The winning canoe would be the one that arrived first with its matching flag.

Laura glanced at Bradford, hoping he wasn't too upset that Saundra would be with the handsome Sir Douglas and not with him.

When the whistle blew, they were off. Bradford's muscles rippled under his shirt as he powered the boat effortlessly across the lake. Laura's steady paddle dipped smoothly, coinciding perfectly with his. He smiled his approval as they soon passed all the canoes except Mark and Sara's to the left and Saundra and Sir Douglas's to the right. Out of the corner of her eye, Laura noticed Sara make the mistake of standing up and waving cheerfully to them. Before Sara knew what had happened, she was thrown into the lake. Mark immediately joined her in the cold water. Soaking wet, he swam over to her and helped her right the overturned canoe. They were both laughing uncontrollably, so Laura quit worrying about them and continued to paddle with a smooth rhythm that matched Bradford's.

As they neared Saundra's canoe, Laura noticed an intense look on her face. Sir Douglas and Saundra were deep in a discussion as they paddled with all their might. Laura smiled at them, but they only turned away, nodding to each other in a secretive fashion. Wondering what they were whispering about, she studied their faces. Deciding they must simply be very intent on winning the race, she looked away from them. Laura noticed her canoe rapidly approach an island that filled the middle of the lake. Its lush plant growth made the island unattractive as a place to explore. As they got closer, she spotted a small stream that was almost totally concealed by a thicket of cattails.

Bradford spoke as he continued to slide the canoe closer to the reeds, behind which lay an opening to a stream. "We can take a shortcut by using this small stream that runs through the island, or we can go clear around the island. The stream has a few rapids, but taking it could save us almost an hour of traveling time."

Laura was eager to see this wild, natural island up close. She nodded eagerly as Bradford skillfully maneuvered the canoe through the reeds. Their canoe easily slipped into the opening of the stream. She soon saw yellow and red wildflowers blooming all along the banks of the cool stream.

"You can relax now, for we're well ahead of everyone else. Saundra and her partner were in such a deep discussion that they missed seeing us enter. Most of the others know about this shortcut, but I believe they'll take the safer route around the island," Bradford guessed.

Alarmed, Laura exclaimed, "What do you mean by 'safer'?"

Bradford reassured her, "Don't worry. I can handle the rapids. I explored this island thoroughly when I visited Judge Taylor shortly after my father's death."

Laura, reassured by his confidence, lay down her paddle, turned around to face Bradford, and stretched against a cushion. She pointed out a turtle sunning itself on a nearby log and was thrilled when a large bird spread its black wings and flew right over them. In some places she could almost touch the banks of the stream as she let her hand glide in the cool water. "What are those small white flowers by the edge of the bank?" she asked. "Their fragrance makes the stream smell as heavenly as any perfume I could imagine in the finest Parisian salons. I just love being here. I hope this isn't too much of a shortcut," Laura said, intoxicated with the natural beauty surrounding her.

"The fragrance is coming from confederate jasmine. I thought you'd want the shortest possible route, considering the partner you got," Bradford said with a glint of amusement in his eyes.

Laura smiled back, retorting, "I could be here with my worst enemy, and I'd still enjoy this paradise." Then she became aware of the coldness slowly filling his eyes. With a timid laugh, she clarified, "But I'm glad I'm with a good friend and not an enemy. I feel very safe with you."

"That's why I asked the judge to choose me as your partner," Bradford stated as he gazed at her pensively. "I still can't figure out who would want to harm you."

Laura said, "I can't either. I try to think about other, more pleasant things. Tell me about the work that you have coming up in London."

A spark of enthusiasm that she'd never seen in him lit up his eyes as he explained, "The duke wants a new country estate where he can relax. I'm building it along the lines of the cottage I'm rebuilding for you. His manor house will, however, be much larger, since he entertains quite a bit. He seems quite pleased with the initial plans. I think it'll take me six months to finish the project."

"I know you don't feel I care, but I'm very happy you're enjoying your job," Laura said, as she reached out and rested her hand on his arm. She felt his taut muscles ripple under his sleeve as he continued to move the boat smoothly down the secluded stream.

Then he laid the paddle aside and looked at her. Laura was entranced as she locked eyes with his. She seemed to drink in his emotions as the boat gently nudged a rock. The canoe floated aimlessly near the shore. As they sat, momentarily relishing a time when they both were letting their guards down, Laura felt her love for Bradford flow out. As he placed his other hand on hers, she saw his eyes fill with a warmth that reflected his love for her. No longer were they hidden behind a cold mask. Laura wanted to cry out to him and make him know she loved him, but she suddenly heard a gurgling sound in front of her.

Bradford looked up quickly at the rushing water ahead of them. He was startled to see the water cascading down a narrow set of rocks into a stream of white foam. He quickly grabbed the paddle and began to beat the water. His face was tense as he let the canoe follow the rapids. Sitting in the front of the canoe with her back to the rapids, Laura felt the water fly up, soaking her hair and dress. She tied to relax but felt her hands anxiously grip the sides of the canoe. She thought the canoe would roll over at any moment as the water swirled around, seeming to engulf them. Just when she thought the canoe would tip over into the white foam, Bradford skillfully set the canoe straight. Then, without warning, the canoe came to still water again.

"That was fun!" Laura cried as she laughed loudly. Then she became self-conscious as she surveyed how her wet dress clung to her shapely body.

Bradford took the dry blanket he had been sitting on and handed it to her; Laura welcomed its warmth.

As she wrapped the blanket around her, he smiled at her. "Did you really enjoy the rapids?"

"Yes. Will there be any more rapids?" she asked.

"No, we're near the opening on the other side of the island. I think the rapids are a lot larger now than when I was here before because of all the rain we've recently had. Would you like to stop and dry off before we get our flag and return to the dock?"

"Yes, I would," Laura said as Bradford slid the canoe up to the bank.

He helped her onto a deserted beach populated with dazzling wildflowers. Laura removed her soaked shoes and let the soft sand ooze between her toes. The day had begun to get chilly. As the sun disappeared behind a cloud, Laura shivered.

Concerned, Bradford suggested she take off her wet dress behind the screen of bushes and hang it on a limb while he started a fire. Laura went a little way into the thicket and removed her wet gown. Even though her chemise and pantalets were slightly damp, Laura kept them on. Then, wrapped snugly in the blanket, she sat down by the fire.

The feelings they'd both felt were still on the top of their minds as they faced each other. Without thinking Laura blurted, "How does Saundra like your work?"

Completely baffled, Bradford turned to her, saying, "I don't believe Saundra cares what I do as long as I make money." Then he said quietly, "You never told me whether you felt sorry that Mark is engaged."

Now it was Laura's turn to be puzzled. Soon her puzzlement was taken over by anger, as she stated,

"Just because Mark looks like someone I loved doesn't mean I love him too!"

Bradford chuckled. "The lady doth protest too much, methinks."

"Oh, you and your Shakespeare," Laura said as she stood up, letting the blanket slip, revealing too much of her slender leg.

"You'd better be careful, because that blanket isn't very big," Bradford warned with a laugh.

Knowing he spoke the truth, Laura sat back down on the sand by him, carefully tucking in the edges of the blanket around her legs, her embarrassment showing in her scarlet cheeks.

Sensing her unease, Bradford rose. "I'm going to explore the island. Why don't you stay here and rest." He walked off in the direction of the waterfall.

Laura was glad he was gone. She now felt she must have imagined the warm, loving look she had seen in the depths of his eyes while they were in the canoe. She wondered why he kept bringing up Mark. No matter what she said, he seemed to believe she was in love with him. With that thought in mind, she stretched out by the fire to rest and soon drifted off. Sometime later her eyes fluttered open as she gazed up at Bradford, watching him as he added fresh logs to the fire. The sun was now sinking fast behind the trees. She sat up, carefully tucking the blanket in. "How long was I asleep?" she asked.

"Too long for us to win the race. You looked so peaceful, however, that I decided to let you rest while I explored the island. There are quite a few interesting animals living here. I hope you don't mind that we lost the race, though," he added, as he began to douse the fire. "We'd better get back before everyone gets worried and thinks we've drowned."

Laura agreed and went to get her dress, which the afternoon sun had dried. After dressing, she tried to smooth her hair by running her fingers through its soft strands, but her hair still fell wild and free to her shoulders.

As she stepped from behind the bushes, Bradford couldn't help admiring her beauty, which was as natural as the island itself. The sun gave her skin a slight tinge of pinkness that complemented her golden-brown hair. Her dress had shrunk slightly, emphasizing her sensuous curves on a body he longed to hold.

"I hope I can explore this island more thoroughly later," Bradford replied as he helped her into the canoe. Reaching into their lunch basket, he handed her a sandwich. Famished, she happily took it. After a quick lunch, they started paddling.

When they came out on the other side of the island and reached the bank, they saw that their flag was the only one unclaimed. Bradford quickly pulled it out of the soft ground, and they paddled back toward the dock and the villa.

Since they both were well rested, they made good time. Soon they pulled up to the deserted dock, which was lined with all the other colorful canoes.

"Looks like we take last place," Bradford said.

"Well, speaking for myself, I came in first for having had the most fun," Laura replied, smiling easily at him.

Bradford's face relaxed its guard as he smiled back at her.

Just then Saundra appeared at the top of the mosaic-tile stairs, shouting, "Here they are!"

Everyone soon appeared, hurrying down the stairs to greet them. Jenny rushed up to Laura, saying, "Mama, Mama, we won. Grandfather and I passed everyone!" Then she handed Laura the shining silver cup that her small hands had smudged.

Laura hugged Jenny, saying, "Now you have two trophies. You'll have to put this one next to the one you received at the fair."

Saundra glared at Bradford as he came up to hug Jenny. "We would've won if we hadn't spent our time looking for you! Where were you?" she asked as she suspiciously studied Laura's tousled hair and wrinkled dress.

Self-conscious, Laura excused herself and rushed past everyone to go to her room. As Laura was leaving, she heard Bradford bluntly reply to Saundra that they had just done some exploring. Then, out of the corner of her eye, she saw Bradford bend down to Jenny and carefully examine the trophy she proudly held in her small arms.

Everyone had already eaten a light supper by the time Laura had changed and entered the dining room. She sampled a few of the leftovers and then wandered around, wondering where everyone was.

Laughter and music were coming from the ballroom as Laura entered and sat at the back of the room. Out in the center of the waxed floor, Bradford and Saundra were dancing the latest steps of a new dance that was sweeping London. Everyone admired their fluid moments as the pair flew across the glassy floor. Laura's heart sank as she realized what a handsome couple they made as they swirled past her. When the piano player stopped playing, Judge Taylor rose and suggested, "We all need to practice for tomorrow night. Let's dance."

There were a few groans as several guests with aching muscles from too much paddling stood and began to twirl around the floor. Soon everyone—except a few of the older women whose husbands had been thoroughly worn out by the canoe race—was dancing. Laura sat back and relaxed, listening to the music. As the dance ended, she noticed Saundra's friend enter the room. He was quick to reach Laura's side and personally introduce himself. Before she knew it, she was dancing with Sir Douglas.

He turned out to be a good dancer and a pleasant conversationalist, asking politely how she was enjoying herself. As Laura chatted lightly with him, she was quick to catch an intensity in his black eyes as he stared at her. His hand felt like ice through her gown as he led her around the dance floor. Laura felt herself involuntarily shake.

"Here. Let's move closer to the fireplace. Sit here, Laura. I need to talk to Saundra now anyway. You should warm up soon," he directed as he walked off to join Saundra.

The flames sent out such warmth that Laura quickly stopped shivering. Still she couldn't fight the unease that filled her. Puzzled by her reaction to Sir Douglas, she was deep in thought when Bradford approached. Looking at her he asked, "Is anything the matter?"

"I think I just got chilled," Laura replied, trying to appear casual but not really knowing why she had this strange feeling.

Holding out his hand, Bradford asked, "May I have this dance?"

"Yes," Laura replied in almost a whisper. She soon felt his strong, warm arms wrap around her slender frame. As he held her, her fear disappeared, and she eased smoothly into his arms, wanting to move closer than convention would allow. Just then the music picked up, and he swirled her faster and faster. Laura fell easily into the steps of this new dance as she followed him around the floor. Her skirt flared out as he turned her around then pulled her close. They were like a team, moving as one, complementing each other's moves.

Laura had been so busy concentrating on her footwork that she hadn't realized everyone else had stopped dancing to watch them. As the music came to an end, she swirled around one last time. She swung out, letting her skirts flow. Then she felt Bradford's strong arms pull her back to him. He clutched her tightly as the music ended. Everyone in the ballroom applauded loudly as she turned to face them. Bradford reluctantly released her as several of Laura's friends came up to tell her what a marvelous dancer she was. Mrs. Taylor stood and announced they must get to bed early because she would need everyone's help preparing for the ball the next day.

As Laura turned to thank Bradford for the dance, Saundra entwined her arm in his and led him out of the room.

Laura had been in heaven in his arms. She knew she wasn't that good of a dancer; it was just his technique that brought out her graceful movements. She felt her love for him had allowed her to relax and move easily with the music.

She went upstairs to bed, wishing she could tell Bradford her feelings, but Laura thought it would be wrong to tell him how she felt because he was engaged to Saundra. She knew he had ridden with her in the canoe only because he was a good friend who wanted to protect her.

After checking on Jenny, who was already asleep, Laura went to her room. She put on her favorite pale-green nightclothes and brushed her hair, letting it fall in soft curls down her back. As she stood up, she heard a soft tapping at her door. After putting on her matching robe, she cracked the door to see who had knocked. There, in the soft candlelight, stood Bradford.

"I know this isn't the time to be calling on you," he said as he looked away, trying not to stare at her in her beautiful nightclothes. "I just felt sure something was bothering you before we danced. Has there been any trouble?"

Surprised by his concern and intuition, Laura replied, "Nothing I can say for sure. Just an overactive imagination, I suppose," she suggested as she looked into his worried eyes, framed by arched eyebrows.

"Well, I've moved across the hall." Bradford reassured her as he looked directly into her eyes. "Just call if you need me. Oh, I saw you got to dance with the handsome Sir Douglas," he commented with a glint in his eyes.

"It has been a delightful day." Not wanting Bradford to guess how the stranger's touch had sent chills up her spine, Laura exclaimed, "I enjoyed the canoe race so much! Even though we lost I couldn't have had more fun."

"Again, just call and I'll come. Good night," Bradford softly said as he turned on his heels.

Chapter Twenty-two

Celebration and Desperation

❧

L aura shut the door and climbed between the soft cotton sheets that smelled as though they were still hanging in the sun. She slept fitfully but was undisturbed. She awoke early the next morning when she heard a gentle knock on her door. She eagerly flung the door wide-open when she saw Mrs. Taylor standing in the hall. "Come in," Laura invited as she tied her robe.

Mrs. Taylor rubbed her palms together nervously. "I have so much to do for tonight," she uttered. "I also wanted to apologize for letting Saundra invite herself to Jenny's birthday party. I can't believe the gall of that woman after all she's done. But I couldn't turn her down when I realized she really did us all a favor, even though I doubt that was her intention."

Laura wrapped her arms around Mrs. Taylor's shoulders, which drooped as though they were over-burdened with too many tasks. "Don't worry about Saundra," she said. "It's fine. As soon as I dress, I'll be down to help out." Laura offered her a seat on a bench in front of her dresser.

"Thank you, dear, but that isn't what I came to speak to you about," Mrs. Taylor said. She sat down and faced Laura, who sat across from her on the edge of the bed. "I don't want to pry or interfere. I know your mother is just a few rooms down the hall and might resent me for trying to advise you, but I feel like Bradford is my son and you're my daughter."

Laura perked up at the mention of Bradford's name being linked with hers. "Mother would appreciate your helping me in any way you can. Please go ahead."

Mrs. Taylors's eyes stared hard at Laura's face, hoping to catch a full reaction, as she said, "I know you're in love with Bradford." As Laura started to protest, she continued, "When you were dancing last night, I could read it in your eyes." After a brief pause, she saw Laura slowly nod as she added, "Bradford is also deeply in love with you."

Laura sighed at this, saying, "I only wish that were true, but I understand he's engaged to Saundra."

Mrs. Taylor was startled. "Pshaw! Someone has told you an untruth, for I asked him only a few days ago if he cared for Saundra. He laughed, saying she was a friend that he was afraid could easily become an enemy."

Laura was stunned. Mrs. Taylor continued, "I know you loved my son very deeply for many years, even after his death. I imagine you may even feel guilt about your feelings toward Bradford." Laura nodded meekly as she listened. Mrs. Taylor added, "Gerald loved you too, dear, and I know he'd want nothing more than for you to be happy."

Laura spoke quickly. "Why then, if Bradford cares, doesn't he say so? Whenever Gerald's name comes up, he gets very angry. Once he even vowed to leave me alone and didn't even let me explain my feelings."

"Bradford has lived a lonely and, in many ways, sad life," Mrs. Taylor explained. "I don't believe he's ever had warm feelings for anyone except his mother, who died when he was only two. I'm sure it's hard for him to show love particularly to someone he fears might not return it. In many ways his father rejected him. I'm sure he's never overcome that."

Looking up, with tears glistening in her eyes, Laura confessed, "I've been cruel."

"No, you've had your own fears about a new love to conquer," her mother-in-law responded.

"Are you sure he really cares?" Laura asked as tears fell down her cheeks.

"I know the look of love in someone's eyes. When he looks at you, I have no doubt he has feelings for you." Mrs. Taylor continued, "If Bradford can only find it in his heart to forgive his father and trust in the Lord, I know he can find happiness. I think you and he could be very happy together." Mrs. Taylor looked at Laura pensively and added, "This is going to be hard for you to do, but if you don't swallow your pride and tell him how you feel, he may leave and never know the truth. You too must trust in the Lord."

Laura agreed as she got up and wrapped her arms around Mrs. Taylor. "I'll never forget your kindness and advice."

Mrs. Taylor returned her hug. "You and Jenny deserve the best life has to give. Now I must hurry. I'll be counting on that help," she reminded her as she rushed out of the room, almost colliding with Ruth.

"Nanny personally supervised the pressing of your dress," Ruth said, as she saw Laura's red eyes. "Is anything the matter?" her mother asked as she laid the gown on Laura's bed.

"Everything will be fine now, Mother," Laura said happily as she dried her eyes. She reached down to inspect the rich folds of the lavender silk as it fell off her bed. The puffed sleeves were short, emphasizing the scooped neckline. She picked up the dress and held it up.

"I'm so glad you purchased that gown. It's the most stunning one I've ever seen!" Ruth exclaimed.

Laura laid the dress aside and then dressed casually so she could help out before the party. The entire household was already downstairs doing jobs in preparation for the ball. As she went downstairs to help, Laura spotted Saundra. She wanted to say something spiteful since Saundra had told her all those lies. She knew, however, that God wanted her to love her enemies as herself, so Laura focused instead on her own happiness.

Jenny came over and took her mother's hand. "Mama, would you please help me put these cookies on the tray?"

"Of course, Jenny," Laura replied.

She also assisted Sara, who was happily awaiting the public announcement of her engagement. Laura worked so hard all day that she didn't even see

Bradford; she couldn't wait to find him. She didn't know how she was going to get the courage to tell him how she felt, however, since she still had some fear of being rejected.

As the evening drew near, Laura helped Jenny dress. Jenny then followed her into her room, begging to help her mother dress. She enjoyed helping her mother into the lavender gown.

Jenny gasped. "You look so pretty, Mama!"

Nanny came in the room and had the same reaction, asking, "How would you like to wear your hair tonight?"

Laura thought for a moment then suggested, "Maybe we can put the sides of my hair loosely up, on the top of my head, allowing long ringlets to fall down my back."

Nanny agreed and went to work. Finally she stepped back and said, "Now I feel the effect is perfect!"

Laura surveyed herself in the mirror. Her hair shone like newly polished brass. Her eyes appeared a deep violet as they reflected the color of her light-purple gown. Laura stood and took Jenny's hand, as they descended the winding stairs.

Everyone shouted, "Happy birthday!" As they entered the ballroom, Jenny rushed over to her pink cake with its beautiful white swans swimming on a lake of blue icing. After blowing out her candles, she quickly opened her presents.

Laura's eyes eagerly searched the crowd for Bradford, but she was unable to find him at first. Soon, however, she noticed him ease his way through the crowd to present Jenny with a new leather saddle.

Jenny enthusiastically hugged him and thanked him for the perfect gift.

With the presents opened and the cake served to the children, the adults began to dance. As the crowd moved away from Jenny and Bradford, Laura's heart fluttered as she saw Bradford and Jenny move toward her. She knew she loved Bradford now with total commitment. There was no guilt. Gerald would always hold a chamber of her heart meant for the past, but Bradford would fill the rest.

As Bradford and Jenny approached her, Laura said, "I believe you picked out the perfect gift for Jenny."

"Yes. It's just what I wanted," Jenny agreed. "Can I try it now?"

Laura laughed. "Jenny, you'd better stay at the party and not try the saddle until tomorrow. Some of your friends are over there looking at your gifts. Plus your grandmothers have planned some special games for everyone. Why don't you join them?"

"Okay, Mama." Jenny said over her shoulder as she ran toward her friends, "Mama, you can dance with Mr. Bradford, since I'm too little."

Bradford offered his arm as he escorted Laura toward the dancing.

Laura turned to Bradford. She didn't hesitate and moved smoothly into his arms once the music began. When the music slowed, she rested her head against his shoulder. Her mouth almost touched his ear as she whispered, "I love you."

In total disbelief Bradford lifted his chin as he stared into her smiling eyes. Before he could say anything, Sir Douglas and Saundra approached, wedging their way between them and forcing Bradford to be Saundra's partner and Laura to dance with Sir Douglas.

Laura felt as though she were suffocating in Sir Douglas's tight, clinging arms. Longing for any excuse to get away, she asked, "Would you like a piece of cake?"

"Yes, I would," he said, possessively leading her to the table where they were serving the cake.

Laura was served an unusually large piece of cake on a small china plate. After Sir Douglas got his piece, he kept standing by her side. She realized he planned to spend most of the evening with her. Uncomfortable and very warm, Laura inquired, "May we step outside for a minute?"

"Of course," he said in a cool, surly voice.

As they stepped onto the patio, he seemed to cling to her, almost breathing down her neck. She longed to get back to Bradford but saw no polite way to leave. Stepping onto the top of the stairs that led to the reflecting pools, Laura saw the pale light of the full moon reflect on the lake below.

"Would you care to walk to the lake?" Sir Douglas asked.

Laura felt that might satisfy her duty to him and could think of no gracious excuse to leave him. So she agreed. She stepped cautiously down the stairs, carefully holding the china plate with Sir Douglas following closely behind.

As they got farther from the party, Laura knew she had made a grave mistake. Her concern about him grew as she almost tripped on the last step. Sir Douglas lunged at her, saving her from a fall into the cold lake. During her fall, her piece of cake fell into one of the pockets of her dress, and the china plate slid into the water. She leaned over the lake to retrieve her plate, but before she could do so, Sir Douglas grabbed her around the waist and roughly shoved her into one of the canoes tied to the dock. Then he jumped in behind her. Before Laura could scream, he tied a scarf over her mouth and roughly pulled a burlap sack over her head.

As the canoe slid into the water, Laura felt the boat begin to rock. Before long there was a jolt as the canoe bumped land. His cold fingers grabbed her, forcing her out of the boat. As she stumbled on the dock, one of her heels broke off in a gap in the planks. Muttering an obscenity, Sir Douglas jerked her arm and pulled her up the hill. When they reached the top, he finally took off the sack, which had threatened to smother her. Then he untied the scarf, allowing her to breathe deeply again.

As her eyes adjusted to the moonlight, she saw looming ahead the dark cave she and Jenny had visited earlier.

"What's going on?" Laura demanded.

"I want you to get lost in this cave and never return," Sir Douglas threatened, his harsh laugh ringing in the darkness.

"But why?" Laura pleaded.

"Because Saundra is tired of you interfering with her plans for Bradford," he explained.

"What do you mean?" Laura cried.

"We've both seen the way he looks at you, and it won't do if he's to marry Saundra. My manservant has tried several times to get rid of you, but he failed miserably. We even had the telegram destroyed that Bradford sent to let you know he'd found Jenny. We were hoping you'd die in your grief over losing your daughter. My manservant and I had to return to London for a while, but now we're back, and this time we're taking no chances," he muttered, shoving her ahead of him into the dark cave.

Laura limped along in front of him. Her heelless shoe was terribly uncomfortable, and she almost fell several times. Soon the vast blackness completely surrounded them. Turning a corner, they came into the large space she and Jenny had visited. Now it was well lit with a torch. Sir Douglas grabbed the torch. Using it to light a small candle, he thrust a chamberstick at her, saying, "Take this. Don't try anything, or you'll find yourself in total darkness." Boldly turning he led the way in the cave.

His handsome face was contorted in an ugly grin as he guaranteed, "Behave, and you'll have some light. Misbehave, and you'll wish you hadn't."

Laura's throat tightened as she realized he meant to lose her in this maze. Obviously he was going to let her wander through the caves until she died.

Sensing her fear, Sir Douglas sneered, "After Saundra marries Bradford, she'll be very rich. I'll find a way to get rid of him later, and then she'll be able to marry me. We'll live the life I've always wanted."

Laura tried to stall. "You know Saundra loves Bradford. She'll never marry you after she has a taste of his love."

"Be quiet." Obviously disturbed, Sir Douglas screamed, "We have it all worked out! Now follow me."

Laura was desperate as she nervously rubbed her hand on her dress. Her fingers brushed against the cake that was still in her pocket. As she rubbed its crumbly texture, she thought back to the story her father used to tell her of a little boy and girl who had made a trail of crumbs in the woods so they could find their way out of the forest. In the story the birds ate the crumbs so the children remained lost. Maybe this time a trail of crumbs would work, since there were no birds in the cave.

"Quit standing there," Sir Douglas yelled as he started off.

Following him as far behind as possible, Laura let a white crumb with pink icing fall to the floor of the cave. Winding in and out of many passages, all of which seemed to look identical, she kept her distance from him, hoping he wouldn't see her trail. Every few steps, when Sir Douglas was concentrating on the correct path, Laura dropped another crumb. As they twisted and turned through the cave, she feared the cake would run out before their journey ended. Thank goodness they'd given her such a large piece of cake!

Eventually Sir Douglas turned toward her. Laura could see his striking black eyes, now filled with madness. He stared at her through the flickering light. "I wish you luck," he said with a harsh laugh. "You'll have some light—but not for long. Don't try to follow me, or I'll have to resort to graver measures of getting rid of you."

Laura froze, fearing he would return the way they had come and discover her trail of crumbs. Instead he turned on his heels and disappeared around a boulder before moving quickly in a different direction.

Laura's feet were tired from the long walk in her broken shoe. Putting her discomfort aside, she knew she wouldn't have long if she were to make it out of the cave before her small candle burned out.

She turned around and quickly found her first pink crumb. It was, however, a slow process going from crumb to crumb. She gradually followed her trail around seemingly endless curves. Often she had to crouch low to avoid hitting the ceiling. She knew her only hope was to concentrate on her trail of crumbs and not on the flickering shadows that filled the cave. As she went along, she thanked God for all her blessings and prayed reverently that He would lead her to safety. It seemed she had followed the same trail several times as she wove between rough boulders that dripped with water.

Laura was concentrating so hard on the trail that she had failed to notice how low the candle had burned. She started to worry as a puddle of hot melted wax filled the holder. What if her candle burned out before she found her way out? She moved along faster, making every minute count. Sometimes her trail was very visible; other times it was hard to see. Searching for the crumbs slowed her down as she looked frantically ahead for the next bright spot of pink and white on the dark cave floor in the wavering light. Her hope faded as her candle flame flickered and then finally went out.

She despondently sank against a rock, wondering how long she would survive in total darkness. She made one last effort and called out to God. She sat on a cold boulder, gently touching her cross and taking comfort in the biblical verse Joshua 1:9: "Be strong and courageous. Do not be afraid; do not be discouraged, for the Lord your God will be with you wherever you go."

For what seemed like hours, Laura sat on a boulder before she heard a faint voice. Straining, she lifted her head as she heard someone call her name. Recognizing the deep male voice, she called back loudly, "I'm here, Bradford."

Bradford soon rounded the corner. He rushed to her and lifted her tired, shivering body into his arms.

"How'd you ever find me?" Laura cried, tears running down her cheeks.

"After Sir Douglas interrupted our dance, I noticed Saundra seemed exceptionally tense and preoccupied. I became suspicious since she kept trying to keep my total attention." Laura lay cradled in his arms as he comforted her. "Let's get out of this eerie cave, and I'll tell you everything."

Within minutes they were in the cool, fresh air. After the darkness of the cave, the brightness of the full moon made the night appear very light. Gently seating Laura on a boulder, Bradford explained, "When Sir Douglas returned to the ball without you, I became very concerned, even though he made some unbelievable excuse about your going to your room. I quietly followed him and Saundra as he roughly ushered her outside. Without their knowing, I overheard him tell Saundra how he'd dragged you into a cave. He then asked Saundra how quickly she thought she'd be able to marry him after becoming my widow. There was a brief silence, and I heard Saundra scream, so I rushed onto the patio in time to stop him from striking her again, as Sir Douglas yelled, 'You used me!'"

Bradford continued, "As I struggled with Sir Douglas, his manservant rushed at me from out of the darkness. I hit the manservant, knocking him out. In the meantime Sir Douglas tried to escape, running to the front of the villa. He was trying to steal a horse when two strangers stopped him and put him in handcuffs. The men turned out to be inspectors from Scotland Yard. They arrested Sir Douglas for embezzlement and the murder of an elderly countess during his recent trip to England.

"I told the inspectors that Sir Douglas had taken you away this very evening and abandoned you in a cave." Bradford further explained, "The senior inspector suggested that attempted murder and kidnapping of a United States citizen would likely be added to Sir Douglas's charges.

"Upset and startled, Saundra claimed she knew nothing of Sir Douglas's plan to kidnap and eliminate you. She as well as the manservant have been taken into custody for questioning by the authorities."

"How did you know where to find me?" Laura asked.

"Before the inspectors took Sir Douglas, his manservant and Saundra off, I demanded that Sir Douglas tell me where you were," Bradford answered. "He was sullen and refused to talk until the senior inspector reminded him that kidnapping and murder were hanging offenses in the United States. With a sneer,

Sir Douglas confessed, 'She's across the lake in a cave at the top of the hill. She's deep in the cave so I doubt you'll find her.'"

Bradford held Laura as he continued. "I immediately rushed off to find you. I found your broken heel on the dock and climbed the hill toward the cave as quickly as I could. Fearing I might never find you, I entered the cave and immediately noticed the trail of pink and white crumbs. That was very clever of you! They led me right to you."

"Did it ruin Jenny's party?" Laura asked.

Bradford answered, "No. It took place outside without any of the other guests realizing what had happened."

Pausing, he turned her to face him as he sat by her. "Now that you're safe, there's something I want to ask you. While we were dancing, I must have been dreaming. Did I hear words on your lips that I've longed to hear? Were they meant for me?" he questioned as he looked into her smiling face.

"Yes, my love," Laura whispered as she felt his lips on hers. She ran her hands through his thick dark hair as he kissed her lips again and then her cheek and forehead.

Slowly they pulled apart. As she sat by him on the boulder, she slipped the small gold band off her wedding finger. This was the ring she had worn first out of her pledge of love to Gerald and then out of defiance to Gerald's father. She took Bradford's hand and curled his fingers around the ring, saying, "The promise to love, honor, and obey that I made to Gerald died with him. My love for you made me realize this."

Looking at her sparkling eyes in the moonlight, Bradford said, "Gerald gave this ring to you, and I know he'd want you to keep it. He must have been a fine person for you to have loved him so," he admitted, as his jealousy faded forever. Returning her ring, he suggested, "I guess we'd better get back."

Still curious, Laura asked, "What was it that you and Saundra were going to announce? I'm afraid I was eavesdropping in the secret room in the study at Oak Grove several months back. I thought you were discussing your engagement."

"Oh, no!" Bradford told her. "I had just purchased Saundra's mansion because she'd lost her money on spending sprees and speculative land dealings after her father died. She thought we should have a party announcing my purchase as a surprise so no one would suspect she had lost all her money. I also think she was hoping I might propose at the party. Marrying her was never my intention!"

As they moved arm in arm toward the canoe, Bradford softly said, "I love you, Laura." Turning to look deep into her eyes, he confided, "I've loved you since the first day I saw you as I rode up to your home. There you were, standing on the balcony, your long light-brown hair blowing in the breeze. You were absolutely...beautiful. I've since learned that your beauty goes so much deeper. Will you marry me?"

"Yes," Laura said without hesitation.

Chapter Twenty-three

Two Engagements, Two Weddings

❧

*L*aura and Bradford's canoe softly nudged the shore as they returned to the villa. They could hear the lively music from the ballroom since the party was still underway. Apparently no one had noticed their absence.

Bradford lovingly helped Laura out of the canoe and took her arm as they walked up to the villa. She was thankful for his steadying arm. Her missing heel caused her to be off-balance, making it difficult to walk. Sneaking in a side door, they quietly went up the back stairs toward Laura's room so she could change her shoes.

"How does my dress look?" Laura inquired.

"As charming as the lovely lady wearing it," Bradford said. Then he bent down and lightly brushed the dirt off the hem.

"Are you sure?"

"I'm very sure you're the most stunning woman I've ever seen," he said.

He took her into his arms and gave her a long, loving kiss. Wanting the kiss to last forever but knowing they must return to the party, Bradford whispered in her ear, "We must hurry before they miss us."

After Laura changed her shoes, they went down the back stairs and inconspicuously entered the ballroom. Just as they came in, they noticed Mark standing on the stage, loudly announcing, "Ladies and gentlemen, may I have your attention, please?" Everyone watched as he brought Sara onstage. Facing the crowd, he declared, "I would like to announce my engagement to Sara." As he hugged her to his side, he continued. "You're all invited to attend our wedding at the church the day after tomorrow. We'll have the reception here, thanks to my uncle's generosity. Please come and help us celebrate the happy day we've been awaiting for so long."

Making their way through the crowded room, Laura and Bradford went up to the stage to join Mark and Sara. As the applause died down, Bradford announced, "I'd also like to announce my engagement to Laura." As he looked lovingly into her face, he added, "We aren't marrying the day after tomorrow, but we will be marrying in about a month. You're all invited to our wedding as well. We hope you'll be able to make it." A quiet hush filled the room before another round of thunderous applause broke out.

The guests were stunned that two engagements and two weddings had been announced in one evening. Then someone in the crowd yelled, "Let the musicians play a song to celebrate this occasion. We'll all dance to their future happiness!"

As the music started, Laura looked around the room to see Jenny sitting on the landing watching the ball, as she herself had done as a child so many years ago. When Jenny saw Laura, she jumped up and ran down the stairs to give her mother and Bradford a warm hug. Then she hugged Sara and her cousin Mark. Everyone was very pleased that Jenny's birthday party had ended with two wedding announcements. The party was deemed a huge success.

The next morning they all enthusiastically discussed the weddings. Judge Taylor insisted that both weddings would be at his expense. Since Mark and Sara were marrying the following day, everyone was running around trying to get everything prepared.

Laura took Bradford aside so the others couldn't hear and whispered in his ear, "I have so much to be thankful for. Could we marry in the small chapel by Oak Grove? The chapel and Pastor Jenkins are very special to me, and I'd like to make them special to you too."

As Bradford held her close, he readily agreed. "We'll have a great life together, with God's blessing."

Later that morning, as Laura was walking down the hall, she heard Judge Taylor talking to Bradford. "My boy, I couldn't be more pleased to have you for Jenny's father and Laura's husband. Gerald would have wanted this for them. My daughter-in-law has had a hard time, no thanks to me. I only hope that one day she can find it in her heart to fully forgive me." The judge looked up as he heard someone knock softly on a door that was already slightly ajar.

Swiveling in his chair, he encouraged Laura, "Come on in."

Coming up behind his chair, Laura put her arms around the judge's neck and said, "I overheard what you were saying. You have nothing to worry about. I forgive you and always want you to be part of our lives."

She then turned to ask Bradford, "What'll happen to Sir Douglas and Saundra?"

Before Laura had entered, Bradford had told the judge how Sir Douglas had tried to get her lost in the cave. He stood up and walked over to her. When he put his arm around her, he felt her body shudder. He knew she was thinking of the previous evening when the dark cave seemed to close in around her. Smiling, Laura looked up, welcoming his warm embrace.

"I just got word from the sheriff," Bradford told her and the judge. "Sir Douglas is already in trouble for embezzlement and the murder of a wealthy English countess. Last night the inspectors from Scotland Yard caught up with him here. Apparently the countess had hired Sir Douglas to redecorate her castle. He was able to get access to her finances and started redirecting her funds to his private accounts. The inspectors suspect that she caught him embezzling funds and confronted him. When they struggled Sir Douglas pushed her from a parapet and she died instantly. Several people witnessed the murder of the countess, but he was able to escape from England. The inspectors followed him all the way from London and arrested him after Sir Douglas and Saundra stepped away from the party and went outside. I made sure his manservant also had charges listed for attempted murder for his attacks on you. Saundra will be questioned, too, until the authorities discover what she knew and if she was part of the plot against you. She admitted that she wrote the note that Sir Douglas' manservant put on your pillow the night he broke in. I'm not sure what other role she played, but the truth will come out."

"What do you think will happen to Saundra?" Laura asked.

"Well," Bradford replied, "since her father appointed the judge who will hear the case and it's her first offense, I doubt she will go to jail. Apparently she has an aunt in New Orleans who can take care of her since Saundra has lost all of her money. So, you don't have to worry about her bothering you in the future."

Laura good-naturedly replied, "I'm glad she isn't going to jail, because as you've said, Saundra actually did us a favor." Laura looked down as her daughter ran into the room.

Jenny reached up her hands, trying to hug her mother and Bradford at the same time. Once she succeeded in wrapping her small arms around both of them, Jenny asked, "Can I be in your wedding?"

"Of course, Jenny," Laura said.

"The wedding wouldn't be complete without you," Bradford agreed.

"I'm so excited, because now I'll have a grandfather and father who both love horses as much as I do!" Jenny boasted.

They all laughed and joined everyone for lunch.

After lunch Bradford asked Laura, "Would you like to take a stroll in the gardens?"

Laura smiled. "Yes. That would be very pleasant." She placed her small hand in his. As they walked outside, she looked up into his shining eyes and noted, "What a perfectly lovely day. All the spring flowers will be blooming for Mark and Sara's wedding."

Bradford smiled back. "Hopefully tomorrow will be just as clear and sunny. It'll be wonderful to see Mark and Sara marry. They seem so happy together. When do you think you and I can marry?"

Laura paused, looking up at him as he anxiously awaited her answer. "As soon as possible, since we need to get to London so you can finish your project."

Bradford looked startled. "Do you really mean that?"

"Of course. You're very talented, and I'd enjoy seeing your dreams come true. I've always wanted to go to London too," she confided with a twinkle in her eye.

Bradford lifted her off her feet and swung her around before hugging her tightly. Laura laughed out loud.

Holding hands, they returned to the villa. Upon entering the kitchen, they saw Mrs. Taylor organizing everything for the wedding. There was so much to do and so many decisions to make. What kind of cake to bake? Which musicians to hire? Which flowers would the bridal couple like? Then there were decorations to make and display. She looked exhausted as she said, "I don't know if I can get everything ready in time."

Laura moved over to her and gently placed her hand on her back, leading her to a chair in the study. "You sit down, and I'll take over for a while. We want you to enjoy the wedding too." Turning to the judge, she told him to watch his wife and not let her come close to the kitchen or ballroom.

"I'll try my best, but she's a stubborn woman," he said with a chuckle. "Come on upstairs, and take a nap, dear." Reaching for her arm, he advised, "You'll feel much better after you rest."

Bradford was sad that his time was cut short with Laura, but he knew he needed to let her help prepare for Mark and Sara's wedding. He got out of the way so she could get to work.

Laura had many ideas but first thought that she should ask Mark's mother as well as Sara's if they cared to assist in the preparations. After all, they might feel left out if they weren't included, Laura reasoned. She sent someone to get Mrs. Temple and Mrs. Cooper, the mother of the bride.

Mark's mother entered the ballroom as soon as she was sent for. Smiling at Laura, she said, "Thank you so much for including me in the preparations. I owe you so much. Sara is a dear, and I know she and Mark will be very happy." Surprised at her sweetness, Laura returned her smile. Soon Sara's mother arrived to help as well.

It wasn't long, though, before Mark's mother was ordering everyone around. "Now stop your chattering. We don't have long now, and we want this to be the very best wedding we've ever had in these parts." Clapping her hands and pointing at a table, she said, "Move that table over there for the cake and gifts. Right now," she demanded as everyone looked at her.

Neighbors had come to help too. Progress was quickly made as "the general," as Laura secretly nicknamed Mrs. Temple, accomplished far more than she ever could have in a single day. After making fabulous progress with "the general's" help, Laura fell exhausted into bed that evening.

Laura slept late the next morning. She was still a little sore from her ordeal in the cave and drained from the wedding preparations. As she lay in bed listening to a cardinal cheerfully chirp outside her window, she gave thanks for all her blessings. God certainly had shown her the way once she opened her heart to Him.

After finally turning over and getting out of bed, she dressed quickly in a light-blue dress. She knew Mrs. Taylor was probably hoping she could help again today.

Laura wasn't wrong, because her mother-in-law, looking a little more rested, anxiously asked, "Would you mind helping decorate the wedding cake?"

"I'd be glad to help, but let me get my mother," she replied. As she admired the three-tiered cake that Hannah and Nanny had put together, she noted, "Mother is an expert cake decorator. She has a whipped cream icing that would be perfect. From the icing she can make delicate roses that cascade down the side of this fabulous cake."

Turning to face Mrs. Taylor, Laura asked, "Is anyone helping Sara get ready? That would be something I can do," she suggested, reassuringly patting Mrs. Taylor's hand.

"Sara is upstairs, across the hall from your mother's room. I'm sure she'd be happy to have your help. She's very excited, but she's also taken aback since everything has happened so quickly. As a matter of fact, she might even need to borrow one of your gowns. She's about your size, and I haven't heard whether she even has anything to wear for her wedding."

Laura knew she had her work cut out for her as she approached Sara's room. After asking her mother to assist Mrs. Taylor with the cake, she lightly tapped on Sara's door.

Sara flung open her door and greeted her with a warm hug. "Oh, Laura, I don't know how to thank you! If it weren't for you, we never would've had a wedding. Running off would've been very disappointing to me and our families."

Laura blushed as she returned Sara's warm embrace. "I'm so happy for you!" she told her. "Now we have to get you ready for your special day. Do you have a wedding gown? How do you want to fix your hair?"

Concern filled Sara's face. "I do have a lovely gown, but I don't know how to fix my hair." She walked over to the bed, where Laura saw a smooth silk gown on the bed, complete with a large hoop. The sleeves were long and the waist came in tightly, which would show off Sara's hourglass figure. As Sara lifted her gown off the bed and held it up to her body, she noted, "It's one of the few possessions we were able to save during the war. My mother wore it at her wedding, and I've always dreamed of wearing it at mine."

Laura immediately saw how its ivory color accentuated Sara's flawless complexion. "Oh, it's perfect! I guess this is the veil that goes with it?"

"Yes, my mother's veil got lost in the war, so I made this one." After laying the dress on the bed, Sara asked anxiously, "What should we do about my hair?"

"I think flowers would look pretty in a crown on top of your veil," Laura suggested, thinking they would add color and texture to the material.

"Would you help me pick some flowers?" Sara asked.

Laura replied, "Sara, you can't go outside. Mark might see you. I'll get the flowers and be right back. In the meantime think about how you want to wear your hair. I'll be back shortly."

As Laura exited Sara's room, Jenny collided with her. "Wow, young lady, what are you doing running down the hall?"

"Gran told me you were up here with Miss Sara, and I thought I could help too," Jenny enthusiastically said.

Sara came to the door and bent over, asking Jenny, "Would you be my flower girl?"

"I'd love to!" Jenny replied, sounding all grown up. The effect was soon ruined, however, as she excitedly jumped up and down.

Laura took Jenny's hand, and they went outside to pick flowers. Jenny quickly gathered all the colors she could find in the garden.

Strolling between the flowers, Tabby and her three kittens came scurrying up, wanting to be petted. Jenny had named the kittens Wynken, Blynken, and Nod. She had taken their names from one of her favorite childhood nursery rhymes. Nanny and her grandmother had brought the kittens and their mother in a basket from Oak Grove so that Jenny could play with them. Laura couldn't believe how much Tabby's kittens had grown. She hated to do it but tried to shoo them toward the barn so she could work. Thinking she was playing, the three kittens ran around Laura's legs, trying to get her attention. Tabby sat, anxiously watching them, as her tail swished along on the ground.

Jenny knew too that they had to hurry, so she ran back to the kitchen to get a big bowl of milk. After she placed the milk by the back door, the kittens quickly left the garden and ran toward the dish. Soon they were out of the way, busily lapping up the milk.

"Great idea, Jenny," Laura commented as she gathered lots of roses for the crown on the veil. She thought any extra roses would also add color to Sara's bouquet. After Jenny and Laura finished, they had just enough time to go in and help Sara dress. With only two hours to go until the wedding, they didn't know how they'd have time to dress themselves and help Sara. Fortunately Sara's mother intervened. She arranged the flowers and helped Sara dress, leaving Jenny and Laura time to get ready.

The wedding was held in a lovely church where the Coopers, the Temples, and the Taylors were members. The congregation was large, so the Taylors expected lots of neighbors and church members to attend the ceremony. Everyone was overjoyed that the couple was getting married. Even Mark's mother had a huge smile on her face as she entered the church. When the ceremony began, everyone turned as Jenny entered the sanctuary, looking cute while she scattered red rose petals from her flower girl basket. Once the wedding march started, the guests rose to watch Sara, looking like a princess with her crown of flowers, walk up the aisle on her father's arm. After exchanging vows, Mark and Sara, bursting with happiness, ran down the aisle.

The reception that followed the ceremony was lovely. Mrs. Taylor had done such wonders in a short amount of time. When the dancing started, Laura was in heaven because she had Bradford all to herself for the entire evening. They danced and danced until they were breathless.

Jenny eagerly watched from the landing, thinking she couldn't wait for her mother's wedding to Bradford. *Soon we'll be a family*, she thought happily.

The next day Laura, Jenny, Nanny, and Ruth would return to Oak Grove to plan Laura's wedding. Bradford needed to get some work done while they prepared for the ceremony, so he would return to New York.

Hannah fixed a big breakfast to send them on their way. Laura smiled as she watched Bradford eat his grits, with lots of butter. "You know you've really converted me into a Southerner with the county ham with redeye gravy, biscuits with honey, and grits," Bradford admitted as he asked for seconds.

Laura grinned, thinking how fun it would be to try his Northern foods and see the home where he grew up. "And I don't think it'll be long before you convert me to a Northerner," she said.

"That will definitely be a challenge I'll be glad to undertake!" Bradford laughed, finishing his biscuit and reaching for another.

The Taylors looked sad as everyone prepared to leave. Even Tabby and her kittens were leaving. Seeing how sad they were, Jenny reached into her basket and took out Wynken and Blynken. Wynken was the smallest and fluffiest kitten of the litter. She handed him to Gran and Blynken to her grandfather and said, "Please don't be sad. Taking care of these kittens will help you remember us."

Mrs. Taylor bent over and kissed Jenny's cheek before gently lifting the soft, orange kitten from her hands.

The judge proudly took his striped kitten and held him closely to his side, stroking the soft fur. "I'll take care of My Lady and Snowdust too," he said, "so you'll have your horses to ride when you come back."

Hugging the Taylors warmly, Laura said, "It won't be long until we're all together again." Turning to the judge, she asked, "Would you do me the honor of walking me down the aisle?"

A huge grin filled Judge Taylor's face as he readily agreed. "I'd be honored!"

Bradford stood there, saddest of all. He whispered to Laura, "I'll miss you, but get ready for our big day. It won't be long. Once we're married, we'll never have to be apart again, my love." He kissed her lightly on the cheek before assisting her into the carriage.

Before the carriage had time to pull away from the villa, Hannah ran out with a basketful of treats for their lunch. "I didn't want anyone to get hungry on the ride back to Oak Grove."

The carriage slowly pulled away from the villa. Grinning broadly, Nanny held the basket, thinking of all the food they had already eaten but thankful they wouldn't go hungry. They were sad but also happy as they started to make their way back to Oak Grove, which was once again their own home, thanks to the generosity of Judge Taylor.

After returning to Vicksburg the next day, Laura and her family settled in quickly, knowing they would have a lot to do in a short period of time. They were happy to be home, but they weren't able to relax. Even though they had more time than they had before Sara and Mark's wedding, they knew the next four weeks would fly by if they didn't start preparing immediately for the wedding.

Laura had Mrs. Periwinkle create her wedding gown. The seamstress showed her several designs from which Laura chose a dress with a bustle that was the latest rage. The wedding dress, a copy of one from Paris, was very elegant, with a long train. She planned to wear her mother's veil of Belgian lace. When Ruth lovingly showed it to her, Laura immediately and enthusiastically agreed that it would complement her dress. She felt it would be extra special since it had belonged to her mother. Mrs. Periwinkle also created a trousseau that Laura couldn't wait to wear. She especially loved the beribboned negligee.

Jenny couldn't wait to be a flower girl again. "I know exactly what to do because I'm experienced," she proudly announced one evening during dinner. They all agreed, smiling at Jenny.

As busy as she was, Laura missed Bradford dearly. She cherished his long letters that described everything he was doing on his projects. She was pleased to learn that he was busy but fulfilled. It warmed her heart to think that his new job was one that was both lucrative and creative. Laura kept busy preparing for the wedding and also helping at the church with her adult reading classes. Many of her students, especially Lily, had made remarkable progress. Still the days seemed to drag as the time for Bradford to return to Vicksburg drew nearer.

Late one afternoon Laura was outside, strolling through the garden, admiring the pink azaleas that were in full bloom. She heard footsteps rapidly approach her on the brick path. She was safe now, and no more attempts had been made on her life, but she still felt some uneasiness as she turned slowly around. She needn't have worried. There stood Bradford with a huge smile on his face.

Recognizing her future husband, Laura ran quickly to him, throwing her arms around his broad shoulders and confessing, "I've missed you so much!"

Bradford looked into her dazzling eyes. "I couldn't wait to get back to you and Jenny. As soon as I taught my new assistant what to do, I came here as fast as I could." Gently stroking her cheek, he added, "You look even more beautiful than in my dreams."

Laura blushed. "It isn't proper for a lady to dream of a gentleman, but I must admit you look mighty fetching yourself, sir."

"What's this 'sir' business?" Bradford teased. "Didn't you dream of me at all?"

"Oh, I beg your pardon. I guess I should say you look very handsome, especially since you are my fiancé." Then, looking up shyly, she confessed, "Yes,

I am guilty of dreaming about you, but I think that's okay because we're promised to each other."

"That reminds me," Bradford said as he reached into his pocket and pulled out a small box. "This is for you."

Trembling, Laura gently removed the box from his hand, and opened it, remarking, "Oh, Bradford, it's so lovely!" The ring sparkled in the late-afternoon light. The setting was very fashionable for the day, with a large diamond in the center and pearls set on either side.

With her mouth open Laura stood there, gazing at her stunning ring, when Bradford bent down and reached under her chin to tilt her face up to his. "I bought the ring in New York," he explained. "I thought its intricate beauty mirrored your inner and outer beauty." Before he gently kissed her, he whispered, "I love you, Laura."

Smiling, Laura looked up. "I love you too. Thank you so much for my lovely ring."

They turned and walked arm in arm toward the dining room.

Nanny was the first to see the shimmer on Laura's finger and rushed over to see what was sparkling. Laura proudly held out her hand as Nanny exclaimed, "My, Mr. Bradford, you outdid yourself! Come on in, and have dinner with us. Ruth and Jenny will be excited to see you."

The evening was perfect. As they ate dinner, Laura smiled at Bradford. "You *are* turning me into a Northerner. This lobster is delicious!"

Nanny laughed. "No one wanted to tackle cooking that meal you had shipped. I had a time learning how to cook this lobster. It came live from your uncle in Maine. He kept trying to pinch me—your lobster, not your uncle, that is."

"Oh, Nanny! Well, you did a perfect job! I don't believe I've ever had a better butter sauce to go with a lobster," Bradford complimented her.

After the delicious meal, they discussed the details of the wedding. Everyone was in agreement that, after the ceremony in the chapel, the reception would be held in the downstairs ballroom across from the parlor at Oak Grove. Ruth remembered, "Before the war we often held large parties there. When the furniture is pushed back, everyone should have plenty of room to dance."

Bradford stood and politely suggested, "Laura, now that we have our plans for the wedding, would you like to go for a walk?"

Jenny jumped up saying, "That sounds like fun!"

Jenny's grandmother said, "Oh no, dear, it's time for you to go to bed."

"I'm five now," Jenny said, "and I should be able to stay up later."

"You've only been five for about a month, so I think your bedtime should still be the same," Laura said, as she gently took Jenny's hand and placed it in her grandmother's.

Bradford held Laura's hand as they leisurely walked into the early evening air. They stepped onto the veranda and strolled under the large pillars that formed the edge of the porch. He asked, "Would you want to sit on the veranda or take a turn to the river?"

Laura chose to walk because the receding light from the setting sun was still bright enough to see all the way to the water. The sun's rays sent patches of light dancing on the brick path leading to the river. Blooming azaleas created a burst of color that was even richer in the sunset. Crickets were chirping away as they strolled along, hand-in-hand. They heard the deep bass voice of a Mississippi bullfrog down by the water's edge. Large oaks loomed ahead as their graceful limbs lightly touched the ground, the gray moss gently blowing in the breeze. The scene couldn't have been lovelier. "I think the river is calling us," Laura said as she looked up into his eyes. "Tell me, how's your work going?"

Bradford's face lit up. "I enjoy the designing part of my job the most. Everyone seems pleased with my work, which makes it even more rewarding. I found a top-notch assistant to help me manage the business here in the States while we're abroad. He seems very capable and has done fabulous work. I thought you and I could go on a honeymoon then sail to London so you can personally see how we're progressing."

As they stood by the river's edge, they could see a paddle-wheeler slowly coming down the river. Laura and Bradford saw passengers strolling on the promenade deck and heard them laughing and talking. "Jeannie with the Light Brown Hair" filled the air as the steamboat floated by. Laura turned to Bradford, asking softly, "Where's that music coming from?"

"From a calliope. It's like a pipe organ. Its music sounds even better on the river." Turning to her, Bradford took her into his arms and started slowly dancing as he sang to her in his deep baritone voice, "I dream of Laura with her light-brown hair." He gently lifted a few strands of her hair that had blown onto her cheek and started the second verse, the calliope accompanying his singing.

Laura looked up into eyes that were filled with love. Bradford bent down and gave her a passionate kiss as she lovingly melted into his arms.

Bradford sighed. "It won't be long now until we're married." Squeezing her hand, he said, "It's getting chilly out here. We probably should go back inside." As they strolled along the path, he continued, "After our honeymoon we'll come back here and get Jenny, your mother, and Nanny. Then we'll all sail to London, if that agrees with you. I know you said you'd like to tour Europe. We can do that after I finish my work in London."

"That'll be so much fun! For Jenny it'll be educational too. I can't wait!"

Bradford agreed with a smile as they walked into Oak Grove.

The days passed quickly now that Bradford was home. Everyone enjoyed the time they spent preparing for the wedding. The wedding day arrived with perfect weather.

The chapel was decorated beautifully, thanks to Gran, who had come to Oak Grove to help. She did a spectacular job arranging the flowers and getting Jenny ready before the ceremony. She had made a pink dress for Jenny to wear for the ceremony and had even created a basket for her red rose petals.

Judge Taylor hugged Laura before they started down the aisle. "This is one of my proudest moments. I still deeply regret that I wasn't there when you married Gerald," he apologized with sadness in his eyes.

Laura gently kissed his cheek and said, "The past is over. Our future is bright with God in our hearts."

Bradford stood at the front of the chapel as Laura slowly proceeded down the aisle. She took his breath away as she smiled at him. His bride looked captivating in the ivory gown that perfectly fit her slender figure. Judge Taylor proudly led her to Bradford's side. Turning, Bradford gently lifted Laura's veil. Glowing in their love for each other, they faced their friends and family after saying their vows.

Quickly leaving the chapel, the guests rushed to Oak Grove. They wanted to be in position before the newlyweds appeared. The wedding attendees parted as the bride and groom walked to the center of the ballroom. Bradford took his new bride into his arms as the music began. They waltzed, twirling faster and faster around the room. After the dance, Judge Taylor asked the guests to line up for the Virginia reel. He started to call the dance as everyone formed lines, with Bradford and Laura leading the reel. As the newlyweds sashayed down the line, they enjoyed the joyful banter of their guests. The dancing and celebrating continued into the late afternoon.

When the reception was almost over, Laura stepped to the first landing of the staircase and threw her bouquet to the guests. Laura's longtime friend, Charlotte, was overcome with excitement when she caught the bouquet.

Patrick, Bradford's best man, beamed at Charlotte, and confided to Bradford, "We've been corresponding ever since we met at Saundra's ball. It's been an exciting year, and it looks like it's going to get even better."

Laura slipped away to change into her going-away dress. After she left, Bradford announced, "Would everyone please come out on the veranda while we wait for Laura?" It was unusual for the guests to see the bride after she changed, so everyone was anxious to see what the surprise was.

When Laura returned in her lovely going-away dress, Bradford turned to his new bride and grinned. "I have a surprise for you, Laura." He gently took Laura's hand and picked up Jenny as they walked onto the veranda. Laura gasped as she looked at the *Robert E. Lee*, the fastest and grandest paddle-wheeler on the river. It had pulled right up beside their dock. "Are we going to go on the steamboat?" she asked, hope in her voice.

When Bradford nodded, Laura turned to him and exclaimed, "Oh, Bradford, how exciting! I've watched riverboats for years, and I've always wanted to go on a ride. I can't believe this. It'll be a perfect honeymoon!"

Two carriages pulled up to the front steps, each one decorated with large satin bows and covered with flowers. The first carriage was child-size. Scamp proudly pulled it with Aimee at the reins. She patted the seat, calling, "Come get in, Jenny." Then she handed Jenny an elaborately decorated basket with Tabby and Nod curled up in the bottom. Jenny sat down, and they pulled away.

As their carriage left, Aimee's father, Tommy, pulled up in a regal carriage as Bradford helped Laura get seated. "Hear Comes the Bride" was being played on the calliope as Laura and Bradford waved to the guests standing on the veranda. When the newlyweds arrived at the landing, Tommy handed the trunks to the dock workers on the deck. He watched as Bradford gently lifted his bride down from the carriage.

Bradford and Laura walked over to Jenny's carriage. Each gave her a kiss on the cheek and encouraged her, "Be a good girl while we're gone! We'll be back very soon."

Jenny leaned over, whispering to Bradford, "Remember my wish for a baby brother or sister."

Bradford bent down next to Jenny's carriage and whispered back, "I won't forget."

Smiling broadly, Tommy, who was now one of Bradford's best employees, wished them the very best. He signaled to Aimee to start back to Oak Grove. Jenny and Aimee waved as they turned around, watching Bradford help Laura board the *Robert E. Lee.*

As the paddle-wheeler lifted its gangplank, Bradford turned to Laura. "May I have this dance, my beautiful Southern wife?"

"Of course, my handsome Northern husband!"

They fell into each other's arms, dancing on the deck to the music of the calliope as they floated down the Mississippi to their bright future beyond.

CPSIA information can be obtained at www.ICGtesting.com
Printed in the USA
LVOW09s1505291014

411074LV00001B/164/P

9 781495 249266